I0760381

The Dream Guy

Rebecca C. Smith

Published by Red Frog Publishing a division of Red Frog Media

Visit our website at www.redfrogpublishing.com

First published in 2024

ISBN 9781949877656

Printed in the United States of America

A note from Hazel

This is the story of how I met my soulmate, my dream guy.

It wasn't an easy journey. I'm in my late forties, so that gives you some idea of how long it took.

But there's a reason for that.

And that reason is Logan.

Logan was my husband, and it was love at first sight. For me, anyway, and for twenty-two years he led me to believe it was the same for him. And we had such adventures, from laughing until we cried in Venice when we got caught in a rainstorm to getting married by the perfect Elvis impersonator in Vegas to standing on top of the Eiffel Tower sharing a kiss. Yup, I thought I had found "the one."

And I'd had dreams about my soulmate since I was

nineteen. Always a blurred face so I couldn't see who he was, but the connection was electric. I'd always wake up buzzing afterward.

That's why it was a no-brainer when I met Logan that he had to be my dream guy, especially from all the effort my best friend, Cora, and I put into it. It's my fault really, though I do blame Cora entirely. We were in our twenties, it was the nineties, we'd just watched Practical Magic, and she thought I could do a spell to find this man I'd been dreaming about for the last few years. We jumped in the car and drove to Joshua Tree National Park. I wrote down all I wanted in a man and tossed it in the campfire.

A week later, I met Logan.

Destiny, right?

And one giant whirlwind of spending every waking hour with each other for two weeks later, we moved in together.

So what happened?

My story isn't new. It's not even original. Twenty-two years into our marriage and Logan came out to me as gay. I was devastated. Every instinct and intuition I'd ever had in life I doubted completely. Because how could I not know? What was wrong with me? Why did he lie for so long? I loved him, so I should want the best for him, but why did I feel so betrayed? Like I'd been stabbed in the gut by the person I trusted most in this world.

But those feelings began to lessen, and the love I'd had for him for twenty-two years finally overpowered the negative. I'm genuinely happy for him. Because that's how you feel when you truly love someone.

He moved on, and I knew it was time for me to move on too.

And that's when I found him.

That blurred face came back to me in my dreams.

So grab a cup of hot chocolate (with the little marshmallows), bake those gooey chocolate chip cookies, snuggle inside your cozy blanket, and get ready to hear the story of how I met my dream guy.

It all started with (you guessed it) a dream . . .

Chapter 1
Hazel

The dream…

Hazel Dalton stood in an all-white room with no windows or doors. No *anything* actually. She was pretty sure it wasn't even a room, as she couldn't discern any walls either.

A dream, of course. But she hadn't had one like this in a while. She was *aware*, which was always fun. Lucid dreams. She was pretty sure that was the term for it. Normally, she'd be in a field of grass or something, with blue skies she could jump up into and fly.

But no.

Just a bunch of white nothingness.

Looking around, Hazel focused on trying to change the scenery. If this really was lucid, then she should be able to create her own environment.

After a few long minutes of trying, Hazel realized that

she was stuck here until she woke up.

Great.

A figure began to form in front of her.

Hazel perked up, wondering who her subconscious was going to conjure up.

Not Logan. Not Logan. Not Logan.

After a dramatic swish of colors, a man stood in front of her, but his face was blurred out.

"Dream guy," Hazel uttered aloud. "You were the guy I dreamt about before I married Logan."

"That's me," he replied with an adorable upbeat tone.

"It's been a while. In my defense, I thought I married you."

He shrugged. "No. Just been waiting."

Hazel sighed at that. "Me too, I guess."

Reaching up to his blurred head, Dream Guy scratched it aggressively. "This wig is itchy."

"Hazel, dear, come here a moment," a familiar voice called out to her from somewhere outside the white space.

Hazel's heart stopped in her chest. "Grandma?" Hazel yelled, desperate to see her. She'd been gone three years, and there wasn't a day that went by that Hazel didn't miss her.

Dream Guy tilted his blurry head to the side. "You should probably go see what she wants."

Hazel was about to bust a hole in this reality to get even a glimpse of Grams, but before she did, she asked, "Are you going to tell me who you are?"

"Where's the fun in that?"

He disappeared.

Typical.

"Coming, Grams!" Hazel called out into the white nothingness. How she planned to do that was an entirely different question.

As she moved forward, however, a small prick of color appeared on the horizon. When she walked toward it, it grew bigger and bigger until Hazel recognized what it was.

Her grandmother's greenhouse.

Arriving at its front door, Hazel walked inside, eyes wide with wonder. It was like a plant wonderland, every available space taken with large varieties of greenery, some small, some eight feet tall, some with big leaves, some with tiny ones. There were even pops of teal, orange, red, pink, yellow, and gold from the flowers and fruit trees mixed within the jungle of green.

If she had breath in her dream, it would have been taken away.

Her grandmother, Gladys, stepped out from a cluster of potted plants. "There you are. I got worried."

Hazel smelled a rose that grew in a large pot next to her. Even in the dream, it smelled sweet. "I was talking to my soulmate."

Gladys smiled as she began pruning a lemon tree. "Is that so? Who is he?"

Hazel leaned against one of the tables, careful not to knock anything over. "I haven't found him yet. I've only ever talked to him here in my dreams."

Gladys's eyebrows rose in unison. "Sounds pretty special."

Hazel soaked in the greenery surrounding her in awe. "I forgot how beautiful this place was."

Gladys put her sheers down on a table and walked over to Hazel, placing a hand on her granddaughter's cheek.

The touch felt so real, as if her Grams actually stood in front of her. Hazel didn't want the moment to end.

"This greenhouse will be whole again. You were my best student." Gladys's smile beamed from her entire body.

"You want *me* to bring it back?" Hazel asked, suddenly feeling the pressure.

Gladys nodded, taking her hand away. "You spent more time in here than I did. Remember, you called it Ashdonia, after your favorite book."

Hazel stood up and gently took her grandmother's hand, feeling her soft, papery skin as if she were alive and in front of her. Tears streamed down her face. "I remember."

Gladys squeezed Hazel's hand. "You'll make it Ashdonia again. I believe in you."

"I love you, Grandma." Hazel had to say it fast in case she woke up. "I miss you."

Gladys brought Hazel's hand up to her face and kissed the back of it. "I love you too, sweetheart. And no need to miss me. I'm always with you."

Hazel woke with a start, chest aching with an emptiness that only came from the reminder that one of our loved ones was truly gone.

She could still feel her grandmother's touch as her

mind slowly started to wake up.

The ache began to lessen and transform into a beautiful comfort from her dream.

Then her gaze wandered to her bedroom, full of boxes: empty, half-full, and closed, and reality sank in.

The thought of unpacking made her stomach twist. She really hated moving. But it was nice to finally be in a place that felt like home.

And no wonder she'd dreamt about Grams. This had been her home, after all.

Out of one of the empty boxes a cat jumped, landing on the bed and crawling on top of Hazel's chest.

"Hey, Spike. You want to unpack all this for me?"

Spike's only response was an affectionate head bump to her chin.

"All right, all right. I'll get you your treats."

That, of course, required getting out of bed.

Did she have to?

Ashdonia or bust...

Spike nuzzled Hazel's chin one more time before she finally forced herself out of bed, causing Spike to find a place to land on the covers.

"All these boxes are heaven for you, aren't they?" Hazel reached down and gave Spike a little scratch on the cheek. "I wish you could have met Grams. You would have loved her."

Spike purred loudly.

"You think you could show me my dream guy's face?" He was full-on head-bumping Hazel's hand at this point. "Could you do that? No? Okay. I love you anyway."

Hazel maneuvered her way through a pile of boxes to reach the closet, where a few outfits hung on the valet rod. She debated going through the four large boxes that contained the brunt of her clothing but decided she was too lazy and grabbed the hoodie and jeans she'd already worn three times this week, but at least it was a *Battlestar Galactica* hoodie. That somehow made it less mundane. Quickly dressing, she headed toward the kitchen area, still living the high of not only seeing her dream guy but her grandmother as well.

Walking through the hallway that led to the main part of the house, which included the living room, dining room, and kitchen, Hazel remembered how these walls used to be filled with picture collages of every branch of grandma's family. Hazel knew her mother had them now, mostly in storage, but the neutral white walls only reminded Hazel that her grandmother was truly gone. The house didn't even resemble what it used to look like when Grams was alive, but Hazel's mom wanted to keep the house for future generations, so she'd modernized it to rent out.

Blonde wooden floors lay throughout the one-level, two-bedroom house, the size of it giving her plenty of room for just herself. She honestly didn't even know what she wanted to do with the second bedroom, maybe a cat sanctuary for Spike? Or a living wall full of herbs and lettuces? The possibilities were endless.

As of now, though, it was full of boxes that held all of her framed movie posters that she'd lugged around with her to each place. Once she hung them up, she knew the place would feel like home. Movies, books, and television had always been her comfort. As a shy kid, they were her friends, her companions, her fellow adventurers. It was a special time for entertainment in the eighties, and being a kid born in the seventies and living her formative years in the eighties was both magical and extremely dangerous. (For some reason, back then, there was little to zero adult supervision. Thinking of all the bike stunts she'd performed gave her heart palpitations now). Her poster collection was one of her prized possessions, and most of them were all originals, not reprints. Her favorites being *Star Wars*, *The Goonies*, and a rare print of *The Dark Crystal*. Pretty much everyone she knew worked in the entertainment industry, but Hazel had never aspired to make movies or TV shows herself. She was always afraid seeing behind the curtain would ruin the magic for her. And besides, her true passion had always been horticulture. It had been her major in college, and she'd worked in plant nurseries almost her entire adult life, aside from a few office jobs, and she loved every minute of it.

Sadly for her posters, though, her last apartment was a tiny one-bedroom, which was perfect after her separation from Logan, but there was no space to hang any of them, so they'd stayed under the bed the entire time she lived there. But smaller apartment had meant easier to clean, and right after everything happened, she hadn't wanted to think about it. Not that she wanted to think about cleaning now either, but she was in a much better head space either way.

There had only been two tenants in the three years since Grams's passing, and they kept it in great shape.

Hazel's phone buzzed in her pocket. When she pulled it out, the screen flashed *Mom*.

"You heard me thinking about you?" Hazel answered the phone.

"Always." Her mother laughed. "I just wanted to check in and see how you were settling in."

Hazel entered the kitchen and jumped up to sit on the island, swinging her feet off the side. "Still in boxes, but I'm getting there."

"Is it nice being in Mom's house? Or is it sad? Because you know I just wanted to give you what you want, but I also don't want you to get depressed either."

Hazel could hear the deep, worried tone of her mother's voice. Hazel had wanted financial freedom from Logan. She hated relying solely on him. Loathed it, actually.

Being a horticulture major, for a while she had thought she wanted a career in landscaping, but after working with a landscaping company for a couple of years right out of college, she found that she wasn't spending as much time with the plants as she'd wanted to. It felt more like design work than caring for plants like she wanted. Even her four years at Home Depot in her late teens had been mostly a joy. It was still a retail job with low pay, but one of her duties was taking care of the plants, and it felt like her own paradise.

So after exploring landscaping, she knew in her gut that her true love was working in nurseries. One on one, caring for each and every plant, gave Hazel a sense of peace she'd never found anywhere else. After that, she stuck with nursery jobs, usually just a worker, but once she found Mr. Guinness and The Lively Root, she'd stayed there as long as she could before she had to leave with Logan for his work.

That was seven years ago, which left a seven-year gap in Hazel's resume. It had made it almost impossible for her to get a job in the last year. Even Mr. Guinness couldn't help her, though he did give her extra hours when he could afford it. Hazel was sure he was paying out of his own pocket, though, which only added to her guilt.

As a result, it meant that Hazel was completely dependent on Logan, and it made her stomach turn at the thought.

When Hazel found out from her mom that the current tenants of Grams's house were leaving, she'd asked her if she could move in. The house was paid for, and her parents didn't rely on the extra income, so they'd agreed immediately. It wasn't until afterward that her mother expressed any doubts. Knowing how close Hazel had been to Gladys, she worried it would only cause more heartache for her daughter.

"Mom. I'm fine. Really. It's nice being here. I even had a dream about Grams last night. It was like she was visiting me," Hazel shared.

A short choke of breath on the other end of the phone and Hazel knew her mother loved hearing that. "Oh, Hazel, that's wonderful. You two were so close. I know she's there with you. I wish I could help you unpack." Her mother sighed.

"It's fine, Mom. I'm just procrastinating. It could have been done a few days ago. You and Dad enjoy your vacation." Hazel didn't want her mother to feel guilty.

Her parents had planned a month long Airbnb trip to Spain over a year ago, and it wasn't their fault the window to move in was exactly when they left. "How is it, by the way?"

"Oh, Hazel. It's beautiful here. We'll have to take you someday."

And from the way her mother's voice rose a few octaves, Hazel knew that she was having the time of her life.

As it should be.

"I would definitely be up for that," Hazel said. Going to Spain sounded like the perfect retreat. "Hey, Mom? I was just about to make myself some breakfast."

At the mention of breakfast, Spike hurried over and rubbed against Hazel's leg. "And apparently, Spike needs his treats."

"Give my granimal all the treats he wants. I found the most adorable toy for him yesterday."

Hazel's mom referred to Spike as her granimal since she knew she wasn't getting any grandkids of the people kind. It was the one time Hazel wished she had siblings, so they could provide her parents with lineage to spoil.

"Okay, love you, Mom. Tell Dad I love him too."

Her mom chuckled. "I've been on speaker the whole time, so he heard you. Love you, sweetie."

"Love you, kiddo," her dad's baritone voice rumbled from the background.

Forty-nine years old and he still referred to her as *kiddo*. Hazel's heart grew a couple sizes at hearing it, though.

Hazel ended the call with a smile as Spike meowed as if he hadn't been fed in a hundred years.

"Oh my, yes, I will give you your treats." Hazel laughed at Spike's frantic behavior, grabbing the bag of treats from the counter and placing a small pile on the floor for him. He instantly began gobbling them up. "It's like you've never eaten before."

Spike ignored her as he purred and ate.

The kitchen was on the smaller side, one wall with all the white wooden cupboards, black marble counters, stainless steel appliances, and a sink to match. An island with the same black marble top separated the kitchen from the dining area and living space. It hadn't always been open concept. Hazel remembered hiding in the dining room, waiting for her grandmother to find her in their epic games of hide-and-seek. Though thinking back on that now, under the table wasn't exactly a difficult place to find. But Grams had made Hazel feel like she was a super spy, searching every room, acting like the task of finding her was impossible.

Taking the gardening gloves that lay on the counter, Hazel walked to the back door and opened it.

A few feet in front of Hazel was her grandmother's greenhouse.

It stood in the middle of a decent-sized five-hundred-square-foot rectangular backyard, well, decent-sized for Los Angeles. Everywhere else in the country, it would be considered small. Tiny pebbles filled the lawn surrounding the greenhouse like a sea of baby rocks. Against the house was a line of succulents and drought-friendly plants (her mom wanted simple and easy upkeep for the tenants).

This version of the greenhouse didn't look like the Ashdonia version from her dream.

Grams had loved it when Hazel pretended she'd found the door to Ashdonia by stepping into her greenhouse. The land of Ashdonia existed in Hazel's favorite book, *Escape to Ashdonia*. It was a young adult portal fantasy that she became obsessed with as a child. The love story alone between the main character, Olivia Fry, and the Prince of Dreams, Nikolas Dragontine, was probably why Hazel was so obsessed with finding her soulmate through her dreams. The movie version came out in the eighties, when she was thirteen, and Richard Grinthal played Nikolas, which only added to her crush on the character. Olivia and Nikolas's costumes may have been outlandishly fantasy-eighties, but she'd always dreamt of wearing the gold dress from the ballroom scene. Puffed sleeves, corset top, and a giant bell-skirted bottom with layer upon layer of reflective chiffon, and Nikolas was just as outlandishly beautiful, with a matching deep-gold velvet jacket, tight eighties black leather pants, tall riding boots, and a fluffy mullet hairdo that only men in the eighties could pull off. Looking back, they hadn't pulled off a thing, but back then, he was perfect.

One of her favorite parts of both the book and the movie was the way a character could tell they'd made it into the world of Ashdonia: a wrought-iron bench that stood as a sentry to both worlds. Hazel had begged her parents to buy one for her so she could put it in Grams's greenhouse, but over the years, it never happened, and eventually she forgot. But back then, Hazel had been convinced she'd find a way into Ashdonia somehow, and Grandma's greenhouse was as close as it came.

She supposed part of her love of plants came from the fact that she was obsessed with high fantasy books throughout her entire life, not only *Escape to Ashdonia*, but *Lord of the Rings*, the *Chronicles of Narnia*, and *Riftwar Saga* as well. There was always an elf or a tracker of some kind that could become one with the forest. The way the authors described the trees, the herbs, and the plants created such a perfect fantasy in Hazel's brain, she wanted to recreate it in real life. Or at least be as knowledgeable as all of her favorite characters. And with Grandma's greenhouse, it made it easy to pretend.

The greenhouse now was a bit on the older side, though still in good shape, but the glass walls and gabled roof were speckled with dirt, and the wrought-iron framing was dented and peeling. But the bones were there, and they gave Hazel hope.

"Okay, Grams. I got this."

With determination, Hazel opened the greenhouse door. And just before she stepped in, Spike beat her to the punch and strolled inside.

The space itself was large, at least ten feet by ten feet if Hazel were to guess, but the contents inside were in rougher shape than the outside. No broken glass, at least. The sun took Hazel's breath away as it filtered through the glass roof in long beams of morning light. Of course, the brightness also highlighted all the dirty shelves that were attached to the iron framing on every wall, and the plastic tables weren't exactly the cleanest either, but everything was solid. Nothing a little elbow grease couldn't fix.

A few dead plants adorned one shelf, but there was a stack of empty plastic pots in the corner, at least ten. The last tenants even left a few bags of soil leaned up against the wall next to the hose.

Spike rolled on the dirty floor happily.

Hazel shook her head in amusement. He'd be bathing himself for a week.

But looking around at the empty canvas in front of her, Hazel's chest lifted with hope. "Don't worry, Grams. I'll make this into Ashdonia before the month is out."

"In a month? Even your grandma wouldn't expect those kind of results." Cora's voice sounded from the kitchen.

Hazel turned to see her best friend standing in the doorframe of the kitchen with a bag of groceries.

Even Cora didn't think Hazel could take care of herself. Though to be fair, her fridge *was* empty.

"Oh good, you're here. I have to tell you about my dream last night."

"Should I be worried?" Cora eyed her skeptically.

"No, it's a good one," Hazel reassured her.

Hazel left the greenhouse and entered the kitchen with Cora, Spike right behind.

Plopping the grocery bag on the island, Cora opened the fridge. "You've been here a week, and there's still nothing in here?"

"That's why you brought me food, because you know me so well." Hazel batted her eyes.

"That's a lot of GrubHub." Before Hazel could defend herself, Cora continued, "Don't deny it. I saw the receipts poking out of your recycling."

Damn.

Not that Hazel would lie, but she'd fully planned on bending the truth. The last thing she wanted to think about was food, and GrubHub was just . . . well, it was easy.

"You'll be broke if you keep it up." Cora gave her the disapproving-but-I'm-really-not-disapproving glare.

"I *am* broke, hence why I moved here." Hazel knew Cora was trying to get her back on track, and she fully appreciated it. She really did need to get her life together.

"You know Logan is financially obligated to give you alimony. You quit your job for him and his travels for work. It's going to take a while to get you on your feet again," Cora reminded Hazel for the umpteenth time.

Hazel groaned, tired of hearing it. "I don't want his money. It's been a year, and I hate that I'm still relying on him. I know he's happy to do it, and yes, I know legally after twenty-two years of marriage I'm *supposed* to think of it as our money, not his money, but my brain doesn't work that way. So just leave it alone, please?"

"Hazel. Tell me, who got Logan his first job as a producer?"

Hazel knew where she was going with this, but she answered, "Me."

"You. And who had to help him write apology email after apology email after he'd throw one of his many fits on set or on phone calls?" Cora tilted her head, waiting for the answer.

"Me."

"And actually, who was the one who convinced him to work with the most promising fellow film student, as opposed to what he wanted to do and work with someone who wasn't as talented and easy to get along with?"

"Me."

"And that promising fellow film student did what?"

"Got him on the TV show he's been working on for the last seven years." Hazel sighed.

"Exactly. He wouldn't have any work or any career without you. It's your money too," she huffed. "Okay, I'm done."

Hazel opened her mouth to speak, but she closed it, and her expression softened. "Thanks, Cora."

"Just talking facts." Taking the bag of groceries off the counter, she shoved the entire thing into the fridge. "You can sort it out later." Turning to her, she continued, "I'm just glad you didn't take his last name. That would have been a pain to get everything changed back."

"To be fair, his last name is Zeman. I can't imagine having a *Z* last name."

"No, Dalton has always suited you. I mean, I kept Blum. I never understood the concept behind changing a name because you get married." Cora shrugged.

"But it is cute that Maisie took both your names, and she already sounds like a famous director: Maisie Blum-Covitz. Speaking of which, where are Jack and Maisie?" Hazel sat down on a stool behind the island. She had thought the fam would have showed up together. Jack had been a close friend to both of them in the early nineties, but his eyes were only for Cora. She played hard to get for a couple of years, maintaining their friendship, but Hazel had always seen how her eyes sparkled when they were together. Maisie was their daughter and had turned nineteen a few months ago. She was in her second year of film school at USC. Hazel didn't see her as much as she'd like, but Maisie always found time for her auntie Hazel.

"He finally got the word that he's directing another *Law and Justice* episode in New York. He found out yesterday and flew out this morning with Maisie, so I'm all yours for two weeks." Cora said with a raise of her eyebrows.

"Oooo, so all your summoning stuff worked?" Hazel nodded, impressed. Jack had directed at least one episode every season for the last decade, and it was becoming one of his and Cora's superstitious lucky charms. Cora had done at least three tarot readings about it, started wearing attraction oil (which she then forced Jack to douse on himself as well), and she'd had Hazel bring out the pendulum to ask if it was going to happen or not. For the record, the pendulum had said yes, but it had also said she was going to have two children back in the day, so it was always a crapshoot.

"Right? And production agreed to let Maisie shadow him."

Hazel clutched her chest. "Awwww. Father-daughter directing duo. I really love that she wants to follow in his footsteps."

Cora's eyes sparkled as she obviously thought of her husband and daughter together in New York.

"Okay, you said you had a dream. Tell me."

Hazel opened her mouth to begin telling Cora everything, when Cora's phone buzzed.

"Hang on." Looking down at her phone, Cora rolled her eyes. "I'm supposed to be on hiatus for the next month, but this costume ball coming up in a few weeks is killing me. Everyone keeps coming to me for a hookup."

"To be fair, you are a big deal." Hazel beamed with pride when thinking of how Cora went from sewing cute baby doll dresses for them in the nineties to becoming one of the top costume designers in the entertainment industry. She'd even been nominated for an Oscar a couple of years back and managed to snag an extra ticket for Hazel. It had been one of the most exciting nights of her life. She'd pretty much just hung out with Maisie since Cora and Jack did all the schmoozing shenanigans they were required to do. The best part of the night was when Cora won the Academy Award! Hazel had bawled her eyes out when they announced Cora's name. So much so, the cameras assumed she was Cora's partner and kept cutting back to her the entire speech, until Cora thanked her husband, and it was a quick swish of the camera angle over one chair to Jack. He still laughed about that.

The entire evening had been pure magic.

Aside from her passion for plants, movies and TV shows were a close second for Hazel. She loved them obsessively and wasn't ashamed to admit it. Logan had never shared her full-immersion love for movies and television even though he, too, worked in the industry as a producer. He liked movies enough to choose it as a profession, but he didn't *love* movies. Hazel had overlooked it because she was in love, but she vowed for the next relationship, he'd have to share her passion for cinematic storytelling. The one time she'd taken him to Comic-Con in the twenty years that she'd been going, he complained about the crowds the entire time and said he'd only come back if he was on a panel. Still waiting on that one.

Cora smiled at Hazel. "I am kind of a big deal, aren't I?"

"Heck yeah." Hazel eyed Cora's phone. "Do you need any help? I can pin like no one's business."

"I might take you up on that." She placed her phone down on the island. "You sure you don't want to come to the ball? It could be really fun. Eighties themed and all?"

It sounded beyond amazing, but Hazel wasn't ready to be out in public yet. Yes, it had been over a year and the divorce papers were final, but she still needed her hermitage for the time being. "I'm sure."

"Well, if you change your mind, you know I have access to all the good stuff." Cora had an I'm-not-going-to-give-up-on-this face. And really, Hazel *could* change her mind, but for now she just wanted to focus on her grandmother's message.

As if reading her mind, Cora said, "Now tell me about this dream."

Cora leaned in across from Hazel, eyes open and waiting for her to share.

"Grams was part of it. She told me to build my own Ashdonia like her greenhouse used to be," Hazel began.

"*If you build it, he will come.* You think she was giving you a message?" Cora clutched her heart and bit her lower lip in appreciation. "That's so magical. Was it a dream, or do you think it was really Gladys?"

Though she couldn't fully admit it to herself or her mother earlier, talking to her best friend, Hazel knew in the depths of her soul that her grandma's spirit had visited her last night. "I know it was her."

"Oh, I love that." Cora hurried to her purse and pulled out several packets of plant seeds. "How perfect is this, then? I bought these seeds for you on my way over here. I researched all of them on my phone, and every single one of these plants is pet friendly." Cora handed them to Hazel.

"Hibiscus, prayer plant, ooooo rattlesnake plant, those are gorgeous, and peperomia ginny! Thank you so much, Cora!" Hazel leaped out of her seat and pulled Cora in for a tight hug. Cora had always had a streak of the sixth sense, and these seeds proved it yet again.

"Let's plant them!" Cora said as they pulled out of the embrace.

"Yessss! Also, I'm not finished telling you about the dream yet."

"There's more than being visited by Gladys?"

They walked out of the kitchen and to the backyard.

Eyeing the outside of the greenhouse, Cora said, "I'll help you clean this place up too. Where's the hose?"

"Not now, we'll be soaked. Let's just get some of these planted," Hazel argued.

"Wouldn't it be better to have it nice and clean, *then*

plant the seeds. Kind of cathartic, don't you think?"

Cora gave Hazel the you-know-I'm-right stare. "Hose?"

"There's one inside in the corner and one right there." Hazel pointed to another coiled hose attached to the side of the house.

"Where's the greenhouse one attached to?" Cora asked, curious.

"Grams had a pipe laid directly to the corner," Hazel answered. "You know we're going to get fully soaked here?"

Cora laughed. "It'll be worth it, trust me."

"I'll do the inside, you do the outside?" Hazel offered, knowing full well she'd end up the most drenched.

"Let's do it," Cora said with an evil grin.

Hazel knew that smile. Things were about to be fun.

Dodging into the greenhouse, Hazel yanked the hose out from the corner and turned on the water full blast. Sticking her finger in the top of the hose to force the water to travel farther, she hit Cora square in the chest.

"Oh, you're so dead!" Cora squealed and hurried to the hose outside, cranking on the water.

But Hazel hadn't accounted for the fact that Cora's hose had a garden hose nozzle attached to its top, which basically made it a high-powered water gun.

Flipping a plastic table over and using it as cover, Cora sprayed the surface, missing Hazel entirely. But hey, it was cleaning the table of dirt.

Hazel blindly lifted the hose above her head and tried to aim the stream of water toward Cora but hit the front wall of the greenhouse instead.

When she slowly peeked her head above the turned-over table to locate Cora, a gentle shower spray of water hit her face.

Hazel stood to avoid drowning, but Cora just kept watering Hazel like she was a newbie plant. "I put it on the soft rain setting at least," she said, laughing.

"It actually feels good," Hazel responded, amused.

With one last spray at Cora's leg, Hazel motioned to the greenhouse. "Let's get this done."

Chapter 3
Hazel

Are these seriously the best these apps have to offer?

The greenhouse, both inside and out, was drenched from the thorough wash Hazel and Cora had given it. But the sun, even more vibrant now that it didn't have to filter through layers of dust and dirt, was making quick work of drying all the surfaces.

Cora dragged the last bag of soil back into the greenhouse. They'd had to pull all three bags out when they'd finally gotten serious about hosing down the space. No sense in making piles of mud, and they needed it to plant the new seeds.

Soaked to the bone, Hazel stood in front of one of the plastic tables and took in her surroundings with a fresh eye. It may not have been spotless, but it was clean. A blast of new beginnings tingled all the way down to her toes. Or maybe that was the slight wind making her teeth chatter.

"Are you seriously cold? We're in Los Angeles. It's seventy-five degrees outside and about eighty degrees in here with a growing humidity despite having the door open, and your teeth are chattering." Cora snorted in laughter as she surveyed her best friend.

"I'm not cold, really. I think I'm just . . . excited?" Hazel tried to find the words to express how she was feeling. Because she wasn't cold (which was a rarity for her). She was . . . What was she? Something felt different. A good different, though, not like the bad different she'd been experiencing in the last year. Like she'd finally made it around a bend she'd been racing toward ever since Logan had set her down and told her he was gay. Was this how he had felt? Excited by the new possibilities?

"Oooo, I like *excited*. This makes me happy. But I also know you, and a part of it is that you're cold, so hang on." Cora dropped the last bag of soil, leaning it against the glass wall, then hurried inside the kitchen.

Hazel didn't want to think about the muddy footprints Cora was undoubtedly leaving in her house, along with the puddles of water anytime she'd stop for more than three seconds. But the house was already in flux anyway, so what was dirt when you had the memories of having a water battle with your best friend? No comparison really.

While Hazel waited for Cora to return, she counted five of the plastic pots that were stacked together and yanked them loose. One by one, she placed each pot in row on the table in front of her.

Cora came back wearing Hazel's penguin fleece onesie, holding a towel and a Chewbacca fleece onesie. Hazel's favorite. Cora was also barefoot, Hazel just noticed, and she'd left her muddy shoes by the kitchen door. Oh, Cora. Always being the sweetest. "Everything is in boxes, so all I could find was the onesie collection. Plus, your onesies are the only thing that will fit me." Cora handed Hazel the onesie and a towel.

"I love you." Hazel laughed as she moved outside of the greenhouse to get dressed in a semi-dry area.

Cora and Hazel had known each other for thirty years, since they were nineteen. They'd been roommates several times over those years, and they'd been in countless dressing rooms together, so there was no shame in stripping naked, drying herself off and putting on the Chewbacca onesie. The fabric's buttery-soft texture was like heaven on her skin. Only her feet were bare on the smooth tiny pebbles.

Laying the towel down on the floor of the greenhouse, Cora nodded Hazel in. "Better?"

"Much."

Joining Cora's side, Hazel lugged up a bag of soil and began filling each pot about three-quarters of the way up.

Cora began opening the seed packets. "Tell me about the rest of this dream."

Hazel took one of the opened packets and placed seeds about four inches away from each other in the pot in front of her. "I dreamt about *him* again."

Cora stopped mid seed placement to make eye contact with Hazel. "You mean *Dream Guy*? Are you serious? It's been what? Over twenty years?"

"Since before Logan, yeah."

Cora resumed positioning seeds in the pot as Hazel poured soil on top of the seeds she'd just laid down.

"What happened? Was it part of the dream with your Grams? Or was it its own dream? Or was it just a dream dream?" Cora flooded Hazel with questions.

"I don't know what that means." Hazel tried to dissect each question one at a time.

But Cora clarified, "Do you think it was your subconscious telling you it's time to date again, or do you think you were actually talking to *him*, a real person?" She evenly placed new seeds in the next pot.

Hazel patted down the soil. "It felt really real. But he did say 'this wig is itchy,' so the jury is still out."

"Or he wears a toupee?" Cora offered.

"I hope not." Hazel walked to the corner and grabbed the hose, filling up a watering can. As she walked back and gently watered the pot, she sighed heavily. "I still blame the spell we did."

Cora groaned, but her voice also had a defensive ring to it. "We were both convinced, and let's face it, Logan hit every single thing you put on that list. It was the things you *didn't* put on it that were the problem." Cora patted down the topsoil of the planter in front of her.

Hazel watered it. "I don't know. Now that I'm awake, I'm doubting. Maybe he's in my imagination, an illusion. He doesn't exist."

"Do you believe that?" Cora raised an eyebrow as she took the watering can and watered the other pots closest to her.

Fidgeting, Hazel answered, "I don't know."

"And you still can't see him?"

"No, just a blurred face."

"Kind of creepy."

"Yeah," Hazel agreed.

Hazel's phone blipped from outside. Walking out of the greenhouse, Hazel pulled the phone out of her pants pocket on the ground. Her gut twisted.

"What is it?" Cora asked, obviously seeing Hazel's reaction.

Hazel didn't want to say it out loud, so she simply showed Cora the phone.

A picture of Logan on social media being kissed on the cheek by a very handsome man.

"Okay, your phone beeped. Do you have an alert set for Logan posts?" Cora crossed her arms.

"Don't be judgy. He sends me cute kitty reels. We're still good friends, you know." Hazel defended her now-obvious poor "alerting" choices.

Cora's shoulders dipped. "Oh, Hazel. You knew this was coming. It really has been over a year."

"I know. It's still weird, though. Very weird." Hazel didn't know how she felt in that moment. Her stomach was still doing flip-flops, but she was also numb? Or at peace? She couldn't pinpoint it.

Cora hugged Hazel tight, and she fully needed it.

Hazel's phone rang, and the two jumped away from the sound.

Looking at her phone, Hazel cringed. "It's Logan."

"He always did know whenever you were talking about him. Are you going to answer?"

"Yeah?" But she paused as it kept ringing. "What is wrong with me? He was my best friend for twenty-two years. I talked to him every day of that, endless texts. Why am I so nervous to answer?"

"Don't beat yourself up. You don't have to answer. Let it go to voicemail if you want." Cora squeezed Hazel's arm supportively.

"Screw it." Hazel swiped to answer. "Hello?"

Cora mouthed, "Put it on speaker."

Hazel hit the speaker button.

"Hazel. Hi. I . . ."

Mouthing again, Cora said, "He sounds nervous."

Hazel covered the mouthpiece and whispered, "Probably realized I saw his post."

Cora nodded emphatically.

"You calling about your post?" Even as the words exited her mouth, her stomach flip-flopped thinking of his pic. She knew it was irrational, but sometimes feelings were irrational.

"Yeah. I took it down. I'm so sorry. I should have cleared it with you first. I don't know what I was thinking." His voice was distraught, worried, but most of all sincere.

Hazel mouthed to Cora, "He's sounds sorry."

"He should be." Cora mouthed, crossing her arms.

Going back to Logan, Hazel said, "It definitely took me by surprise. I knew it would happen someday, but I guess I'm just more hurt that you didn't tell me you were dating someone. The post reiterated how much we aren't in each other's lives anymore." Hazel tried to verbalize what she was feeling.

"I get that. I figured you didn't want to hear about it at all, so I never brought it up."

"And then suddenly it's public knowledge," Hazel said softly.

"Good one," Cora whispered from the side, in full bestie mode.

"I know." Logan's voice was just as quiet. "I won't post for a while. I'm really sorry."

"No." The word came out like a visceral gut punch. "Logan, as much as it hurts, I genuinely want you to post about your new boyfriend. I want you to scream it from the rooftops if you want to. The pain comes from letting go of the past and all the dreams and expectations I had that are gone now, but that's my own journey. It's not yours." It may have been a ramble, but it was true. Hazel didn't want to take Logan's joy and excitement of finding someone new from him. Someone right for him. Because it wasn't her anymore.

Cora pulled Hazel into an embrace, holding her, supporting her as she finished the call.

"It's just social media. I really don't have to." Logan still sounded unsure.

"No, Logan, I want you to. I mean it. I'm happy for you." And from the core of her being, she knew it was the truth.

Cora kissed the top of her head.

"What about you? You getting back into the dating pool?" he asked.

"Nothing to age you like calling it the 'dating pool.'"

They both laughed. Even Cora joined in, though she

stayed quiet so Logan wouldn't hear.

And it felt good. It felt right.

"Cora's been trying to talk me into going on some apps," Hazel shared.

Cora nodded emphatically.

"Well, any guy would be lucky to date you."

"Thanks."

"You're not ready for those kind of accolades from me yet, are you?"

"The automatic eyeroll kicked in. I had no control over it."

Laughing, Logan said, "How about: I wish you the best of luck?"

"That works." Hazel's smile stayed on her face, which gave her a sense of peace.

"Talk to you soon?"

"Absolutely. Bye, Logan."

"Bye."

Hazel ended the call, and sudden tears flowed down her cheeks as she leaned into Cora's hug. She hadn't been lying; she was happy for Logan. The tears were more from raw emotion that had no specificity.

But one thing she was sure of.

She was ready to move on.

Pulling away, Cora brushed the hair from Hazel's face. "It's time. Let's get you on those apps."

Hazel wiped her eyes and groaned, but she didn't argue.

It *was* time. Hazel felt it when she had that dream last night. She didn't like the idea of dating apps, but she was willing to give it a try.

"Well, what are you waiting for?" Cora seemed way more enthusiastic about this idea than Hazel.

"Now?"

"Yes, now. Let's go." Cora ushered Hazel into the house and to the kitchen island.

Once they were inside, Cora was all business. "Get your phone. Let's do this."

"You sound like we're applying for jobs." Hazel took out her phone and slid onto a stool behind the island.

Cora sat next to her, and Hazel placed the phone between them.

"Shouldn't we do this on my laptop?" Hazel asked, thinking how the only things she ever used her phone for were texting and checking Instagram.

"Maisie says we have to do it on the phone."

"Maisie uses dating apps?" Hazel gulped.

"I know, right? But she's an adult. At least that's what I keep telling myself."

"Does it help?"

"No." Cora groaned, then navigated to the app section of Hazel's phone. "She says the best apps are One Heart Beat and Love to Match."

"And we're taking dating advice from Maisie now?" Hazel raised an eyebrow.

"As opposed to . . . ?"

"Solid point. Okay, download them." A nervous wave rushed through Hazel.

Cora opened up the first app, Love to Match. "It says to add pictures. Do you have pictures on your phone?"

"Maybe? But mostly pics of Spike."

"Let's look."

Cora scrolled through Hazel's library of pictures, and among the hundreds of Spike pics, Cora finally found a snapshot of Hazel.

It was a selfie from right after she had moved in. Originally, she'd planned on posting it to Instagram, but the slight blur and the dark circles under her eyes made her look like a "found photo" of Nosferatu. No filter could fix ancient vampire.

"Um." Cora squinted at the photo.

"Yeah," Hazel finished her friend's thought.

They both stared at the screen a moment longer, then turned to each other at the same time and said, "Laptop," in unison.

Sliding over her laptop, Hazel quickly navigated to the websites for each dating app.

"Websites are so much easier. We just won't tell Maisie," Cora said.

"Or wait until she gets back in town, and she can give us a tutorial." Hazel chuckled.

"Oh, we're never going to admit to this. She'll just roll her eyes and say we're old." Cora took over the typing as she created a new profile for Hazel. "All right, what kind of pics do we have on here?"

Reaching over, Hazel popped up her photo library, and yet again it was filled with pics of Spike. But scrolling down, she found one that she liked.

"Oooo, that one is nice. Where was that?" Cora asked.

"It was when Logan and I went to Vegas for our

anniversary. He took that at a restaurant who's balcony overlooks the Bellagio fountain show." Hazel looked so happy . . .

"Turn it into a new memory?" Cora's entire demeanor shifted into mama-bear mode, and Hazel knew if she asked to stop, Cora would shut the laptop and make some popcorn so they could watch one of their favorite movies. *Only You* sounded like a good one right about now.

"Yeah. I got the whole magic hour lighting going for me. Let's use it." Hazel breathed in deep. She could do this. She *wanted* to do this.

Cora uploaded the picture and set it as Hazel's profile pic. "We'll take some new ones later, but this one is good enough to start."

"Maybe we should put a picture of Spike up there too. I don't want any cat haters." Hazel never understood the whole "dog person" versus "cat person." You were either an "animal person" or not. You could have a preference, of course, but some of these "dog" people could be downright mean when it came to cats. And pretty much every single person she knew who had a cat loved all animals. Cat haters was a giant red flag and a deal breaker for Hazel.

"Good idea. But there are way too many here for me to pick from. You pick."

Hazel scrolled through the library again and found one of her favorites: Spike reaching out his paw to the camera with his giant luminous green eyes.

Cora bit her lower lip. "He is seriously the cutest. Someday I'll win him over."

"He gave your hand a head-bump once," Hazel offered.

Spike was only affectionate toward Hazel. He tolerated everyone else and even "allowed" a few scratchies from the people close to her, like her family and Cora's clan, but not even Logan could get Spike to cuddle with him. Spike was a one-person cat, and Hazel was his person.

Uploading the Spike photo, Cora moved on to the written part of the profile. "Okay, here's where we need to be specific yet adorable."

"Specific as in how we forgot to put 'straight male' into our spell twenty-two years ago?" Hazel was having flashbacks to that fateful night by the bonfire at Joshua Tree forest.

"Yeah, like that. Although, that's something we click right here." Cora moved the mouse to the "sexual preferences" section and clicked accordingly.

"Wow. If only the spell had had clear options like that."

"We're choosing science over magic this time around."

Hazel wasn't sure she liked the sound of that, but being practical over being heartbroken sounded really good right now.

"Describe yourself and what you're looking for." Cora's hands stayed on the keyboard to type, but her eyes swung to Hazel's, expectant.

On the spot, Hazel cringed. "I don't know what to say. What should I say? I like *Star Wars*."

"Yeah, we'll make that your entire bio. *Star Wars* fan, must like *Star Wars*. Deal breaker." Cora laughed.

Hazel playfully hit Cora's arm. "Shut it. But seriously, I do want to put that in there. Logan couldn't care less about *Star Wars*. I gotta tell you, it was kind of a bummer." *Star Wars* had changed Hazel's life back in 1977 when her parents and her had stood in line through two showings at the Grauman's Chinese Theatre to see it. She'd been Princess Leia three years in a row for Halloween after that. Plus, she'd been positive the Rebel Alliance would show up at her doorstep to invite her to be an X-wing pilot for the rebellion. Logan had at least attempted to be supportive of her fandom-love, but she could always tell it was more of a toleration. He loved her enough to fake it, she guessed. In more ways than one.

"There's a likes and dislikes here. We'll put it in the likes. Any other movies and TV shows you want to put in there?" Cora asked.

"I mean, yeah, but is that too weird? It's so much easier to talk about entertainment than plants."

"But you should put plants in there too. That's so much of who you are."

"Maybe we should Google it."

"Google plants?" Cora's face crinkled in confusion.

"No, what to write. I need an example." Hazel always did better when she could see a version of something first.

"Oh, good plan." Cora typed "top dating profile examples for women" into Google, then skimmed all the findings. "They say short and sweet." She scrolled down the result page. "Here's a top-ten list." She clicked on the link. "Oh, this is funny: 'My TV crush is Chandler from *Friends*. I love a guy with a sense of humor. I'm driven. I love pizza (who doesn't), and I make fun of people who do CrossFit.'"

"Can I date *her*?" Hazel said, half-kidding. "All right, what about something like this: I'm into movies and television, but *Star Wars*, *Ashdonia*, and *Battlestar Galactica* (both versions) are a must. I'm into horticulture and creating my own Ashdonia in my backyard." Hazel's stomach instantly twisted in self-doubt. "Is that stupid?"

Cora shook her head. "No, it's perfect, but we need to add the cat thing, so I'd finish it with: I'm an animal person, cat haters are a deal breaker." Cora finished typing. "How's that?"

"I mean . . ." Hazel wanted to delete it immediately. "Good?"

"Don't be nervous. We can always tweak and change it later. The important thing is that you're doing it." Cora pulled her hands from the laptop's keyboard to wrap her arm around Hazel and side-hug her. "You want to do the honors? Just hit Publish."

Hazel's heart pounded in her chest, but she shakily reached forward and clicked the button on the site.

It was done.

"Now, to cut and paste all this to the next site," Cora said cheerfully.

Hazel groaned.

Date #1

Why did I decide to give this a try again? Hazel thought as she sat at a table for two alone.

She was at one of her favorite restaurants, Forester's, not too casual, not too fancy, and it was packed, every table filled. And from the looks of it, all of them were couples.

But Hazel sat alone.

Her date was already forty minutes late.

Hazel really hated it when people were late. Not five or ten minutes, that was totally understandable, life happens. Even thirty minutes isn't so bad with a text or call giving her a heads-up. But forty minutes? Without any communication whatsoever?

Huge red flag.

Hazel pulled out her phone and texted Cora: *He's 40 minutes late. Should I leave? I kind of want to leave.*

Cora texted back: *Ugh. I hate late people. Give him 5, then take off.*

One of the many things Cora and Hazel had in common.

Hazel: *It's a sign. I'm not ready.*

Cora: *Don't shut down all dating based on one date.*

Hazel: *What date?*

Cora: *Ugh.*

"Hazel?" a man's voice sounded from behind her.

Hazel turned to see . . .

John.

The guy from the app.

Surprisingly, he looked like his pictures. Hazel had been prepared for any kind of catfish situation.

"That's me. John?" Hazel placed her hand out.

John took it and shook it like a floppy fish.

Weak handshake.

Noted.

At least it wasn't sweaty.

He sat down across from her. "I hear this place is good."

Hazel was a bit taken aback by John completely breezing by the fact that he was so late. If he had a good excuse, she'd think about giving him a shot.

But nope.

Acting like it didn't even happen.

"It was. I ate while I waited," Hazel joked to break the ice. Also annoyed.

But John didn't pick up on her passive-aggressive sarcasm and took it seriously. He reared back his head slightly. "You did?"

"No, I'm kidding." But she kind of wished she had.

John smirked in a condescending way. "Oh, a joke to try and make me feel bad about being late."

Yeah, pretty much. "You'd have to care that you were late to feel bad." She might as well come out swinging at this point.

"Yeah, and I don't," John said defiantly.

Aaaaaannnnnd scene.

***

"It's been a week since that loser. You should try again," Cora suggested as she pushed the cart down the jasmine section of The Lively Root nursery.

The owner, and Hazel's ex-boss, Mr. Guinness, had called her in to give her a few hours of work, and Hazel had enjoyed every minute of it. It was closing time now, though, and Hazel wanted to buy some plants for the greenhouse. The seeds she'd planted were already starting to germinate, but she wanted to have a few starter plants, maybe even a couple full-growns.

"God, that smells good. I could stay in this section forever." Cora closed her eyes in delight.

The beautiful aroma of the night-blooming jasmine reached Hazel as well. "If it wasn't poisonous to cats, I'd buy some. I'd love to smell that every day. You should get one for your upstairs balcony, though. Your animals don't go out there." Cora's fam had two dogs, three cats, and a tank full of fish. To say they loved animals was an understatement.

"Nah, knowing my luck, Fizzgig would get out there and devour the whole thing," Cora predicted.

"True."

Fizzgig, like his namesake from *The Dark Crystal*, was a fluffball of teeth and claws, always getting into things he shouldn't, but he was also the biggest cuddle-muffin of all of their cats.

Turning the corner, they arrived at Hazel's destination. There was an array of pet-friendly plants in front of her, from rattlesnake plants to prayer plants to a beautiful full-grown Scarlet Star bromeliad. Hazel took all three and placed them into the cart.

"Hazel, I've got your pay," Mr. Guinness's gravelly voice sounded from behind them.

He walked over to her and Cora, handing Hazel a wad of cash.

"Oh, thank you, Mr. Guinness."

"We've worked together on and off for a decade. When are you going to call me Frank?" He laughed. Frank was well into his sixties, with deep laugh lines and eyes that crinkled and sparkled. Gray-speckled hair and a thick mustache since she'd met him, Hazel always thought he looked like a cross between Albert Einstein and the actor who played Mr. Coreander from *The Neverending Story*.

"For some reason, Mr. Guinness sounds more magical, and since this place is like a second home to me, it always felt fitting, but thank you, *Frank*, I really appreciate the work," Hazel conveyed sincerely.

"Magical, huh? You know I love that." He nodded toward her cart. "On the house."

"Oh no, Mr. Guinness, please let me pay. Look, I have cash." Hazel smiled.

"You're the one person I could probably pay in plants and you'd be happy. But I insist. You've been through it, and you deserve it." Frank squeezed Hazel's arm supportively.

"Thank you, Frank." It was difficult for Hazel to accept gifts. Easy to give them, but difficult to accept them. But she could see in Frank's expression that he genuinely wanted to do this and that paying him would disappoint him.

"My absolute pleasure," he said.

"We need a group hug." Cora opened her arms, and both Hazel and Frank leaned in.

Pulling away, Frank tipped an imaginary hat. "I'll leave you two to it. I'll call if I have any work for you. Thanks for today. Your work with the perennials was perfection as usual."

"Thanks, Frank. I'll come by to visit soon."

With that, he went back to his office, and Hazel and Cora pushed the cart out of the nursery and toward Hazel's car to load it up.

"You know, Mr. Guinness is the only nursery in town that actually puts the pet-friendly plants in one place," Hazel observed as she opened the hatchback.

Cora placed the rattlesnake into the back. "I wish they had a chart or list or something. I bet you a lot of people don't even think about the fact that some of these plants might be poisonous. They just think . . . ooo pretty, and buy it."

"Right? It would be great to have a plant store that only sold pet-friendly plants." Hazel sighed.

Cora raised her eyebrow. "Something to think about."

"You mean me?"

"Why not?"

"I don't know. I've never been a 'boss' before, only an employee. You think I could start my own business?" Hazel's imposter syndrome kicked in hard.

"Um, of course I do. Not only do you have a horticulture degree, but you've worked in nurseries almost your whole life—actually, yeah, your whole life including Gladys's greenhouse. I'm a hundred percent behind this." Cora closed the hatchback after Hazel placed the last plant inside.

A growing warmth radiated throughout Hazel's body.

Yes.

She *could* do it.

The only question was how?

"But seriously, give the dating apps one more try?

Don't let a jerk ruin it for you," Cora said as they both slid into the car.

Hazel started up the engine, and it gave a little shudder and a wheeze.

"That does not sound good, Hazel."

"I know. I'm going to take it in. I keep forgetting."

"How can you forget when it sounds like that?"

"Well, not forgetting, more like ignoring," Hazel admitted. "But I'll take it in, I promise."

"You better." Cora switched into protective mode.

With one last squeak, the car switched to a nice and normal purr of the engine. "See? It's just when I start it." Before Cora could argue with her about how that didn't actually mean anything, Hazel changed the subject back to dating. "All right. I'll give it another go. There's a guy named Alex that looked interesting."

Distraction successful. Cora turned to her, excited. "Text me as soon as you set it up."

"Yes, Mom."

Date #2

Hazel couldn't believe she'd let Cora talk her into another date.

As she sat across from Alex, she couldn't keep up with what he was saying. Eventually all it started to sound like was me, me, me, me, me, me, me, me, me. He wouldn't stop talking about how great he was. This guy needed a giant main course of humble.

Why am I here again?

Hazel had actually chosen to do this *on purpose.*

There was no way she was going to let Cora talk her

into another one of these.

No way.

Date #3

"I went to UCLA. I really loved it," Hazel told Bob, her date.

"Oh, nice. I went to Harvard. My parents wouldn't tolerate me going to a state school."

Yeah.

"Well, they must be proud."

Cora, I swear. Never again.

***

"I've been on three dates already, and all three were disasters." Hazel moaned as she placed another pin on the hem of an enormous 1800s bell dress. The woman inside said dress was a TV executive named Roberta Coolidge who had asked Cora to help her tailor the stunning monstrosity to fit. Considering Roberta was five-foot-two and the dress was made for a woman five-foot-six, Hazel was using a lot of pins. It was all for this eighties ball coming up in a couple of weeks that the industry was going crazy for. The deep-green satin was slippery in Hazel's fingers, but she remembered this dress well. It was worn by the character Constance Flynn in the eighties miniseries *North & South*, and Hazel had wanted to wear it herself back when she first saw it as a kid, with its Celtic embroidery on the skirt and bodice, and the fluffy, off-the-shoulder puff sleeves that were more eighties than 1860s. At least Roberta had the decency to pick a character from the North, though.

Roberta chimed in, "Are you app dating?"

Placing another pin in the hem, she said, "*She* talked me into it."

Cora stood behind Roberta, pinning the more complicated part of the dress, the bodice. "How else are you going to meet anyone?"

"You work at home?" Roberta asked.

A flush of embarrassment filled Hazel. Admitting she didn't have a job to a woman who ran a television show felt humiliating. She knew she shouldn't feel that way, her therapist had reiterated this several times, but it twisted her stomach all the same.

Before she could answer and be judged, Cora said, "Hazel is starting a new business. She's a horticulture expert and decided to finally open her own pet-friendly plant store. But it's online, so she has no way of meeting anyone dateable."

Hazel smiled up at her best friend. Cora was Hazel's biggest hype woman, always making her feel like she could do anything. Hazel had already started percolating about her new venture, but she hadn't launched anything yet.

Roberta's eyes lit up. "Entrepreneur. We love to see it. Let me know when you're up and running. I have a ton of friends who have pets that would be very into this."

"I will, thank you." Hazel concentrated on the pinning because her head spun with excitement.

"And I can let you know as well." Cora winked at Hazel. What that really translated to was: *I'll make sure Roberta remembers, in case Hazel has a panic attack and freaks out about calling.*

This was going to work.

Hazel could feel it.

Roberta gazed down at Hazel with a mischievous smile. "I say try one more of these app dates. Fourth time's a charm?"

With an exasperated sigh, Hazel nodded. "Fine."

Date #4

Hazel waited for her date on the used bookstore side of her favorite restaurant slash café, Nookish Corner. She normally wouldn't meet someone in a place so special to her, not on a first date anyway, but she was really craving their roasted chicken, brie, green apple, and arugula sandwich. And the fact that not only did they have the most amazing coffee, but there was a used bookstore attached? Heaven.

The bookstore side was two levels, every wall lined with bookshelves and a row of five more freestanding bookshelves that filled the bottom floor. A small counter on the far wall served as the cash register station made of oak, stained a deep brown with stacks of books adorning its surface along with a lone cash register. A round mahogany table stood at the front of the store acting as the divider for the restaurant, filled with books, some lying flat in stacks, and some on display racks.

That was where she currently stood, staring at the book she'd planned on buying for weeks but kept talking herself out of for some reason. Displayed front and center on the table was a used paperback of *Escape to Ashdonia*, weirdly signed by a guy named John Larry with the inscription "I miss you," and not by the true author, Freya

Fairweather, which she found hilarious. The price wasn't the trouble; it was the fact that Hazel already had quite a collection of her favorite book at home. Seven copies to be exact, and for some reason she found it difficult to justify buying another. Plus, she kind of loved visiting it here at the store. It weirdly felt like *her* book.

Picking it up, she flipped to the front to laugh at John Larry's signature. He signed it as if he had written the book itself, which was so odd. And who did he miss? Was he giving this copy to someone?

Maybe she should buy it.

In case the date went horribly wrong like the others?

Hazel was about to hop over to the cashier when a tap on her shoulder startled her. Placing the book back on its display rack, Hazel turned.

"You my swipe-right?" The man that she'd agreed to go on a date with gave Hazel the finger point.

The finger point!

Hazel shook her head and walked toward the door.

Nope.

Practically running to her car, Hazel slid in and started the engine like she was running from a murderer. Of course, it didn't help that it sounded like her engine was dying with a couple of squeaks and pops, but eventually it evened out and she was on the road, calling Cora.

"Oh no. How bad this time?" Cora's voice filled the car through the side speakers.

"I just can't, Cora. Not with apps. Not with bars." Hazel was at her wit's end at this point.

"Not with any known way to meet anyone." Hazel could hear the sarcasm dripping from Cora's every word.

She chose to ignore it. "I've always met guys through work or through a friend. That way I can get to know them *before* I decide I want to date them."

Cora's tone perked up. "You wouldn't be opposed to me setting you up?"

Hazel wanted to throttle her friend through the phone. "No. I'm opposed to that too. Just let me do things my way."

"So you're not going to date?" The judgment was real.

But also not wrong. "No, probably not."

Cora sighed, and Hazel could hear the resignation in her voice. "Honestly, I'm not going to push."

Hazel laughed. "Yeah, right."

Pulling up in her driveway, Hazel reached for the End Call button. "Okay, I'm home. Call you tomorrow."

"Love you."

"Love you."

Hazel ended the call.

She exited the car and walked toward her front door.

The flash of another vehicle from the corner of her eye unexplainably demanded her attention. She glanced curiously at her neighbor's house across the street, where the car came to a stop in the driveway. A man, who looked to be around Hazel's age, exited the driver's side.

His eyes met Hazel's.

She gave him a friendly wave, still staring.

Why am I staring?

But he smiled and waved back, which actually made Hazel's fingers tingle.

Shaking her head, Hazel turned and unlocked her front door.

He's cute.

Chapter 4

Ethan

My soulmate, Spike

W*ho is that?*

Ethan Rhodes watched the woman across the street enter her house. From that little wave, she was already ten times nicer than the couple who used to live there. Seeing their moving trucks a couple of weeks back was like a little prayer being answered. Not that they were *horrible* per se, they just didn't like other humans was the only way Ethan could describe it. He'd always try to say hello or give them a friendly nod, but neither the man nor the woman would ever respond. If anything, they seemed offended that he'd even tried to enter their social space.

But they'd been quiet, which was always a perk.

The neighbors before them were a family who seemed lovely but mainly kept to themselves as well.

No.

The best neighbor that ever lived in that house was the original owner: Gladys.

Ethan's chest squeezed at the thought that she'd been gone for three years now. Gladys wasn't just the greatest neighbor to ever live in that house, she was the greatest neighbor to ever live. He'd place money on that. But even more, she ended up being a friend. He'd moved into his house fifteen years ago, when houses were still kind of affordable in Los Angeles, at least *this* part of Los Angeles. And Gladys had been at his door the very day he moved in with a giant plate of the most amazing chocolate chip cookies he'd ever eaten. Gladys had supplied him with those cookies every month (sometimes weekly) for the next twelve years.

Gladys wasn't just the sweet grandma type either. She was a genuine badass. Ethan remembered the time he'd been dating a married woman (he didn't know she was married) and her raging jealous husband showed up at Ethan's door and busted it down with his ginormous frame. Ethan had been sure he was about to die, but in walked Gladys with a garden hoe, holding it up like she was about to decapitate the guy, threatening to slice his nuts off. Needless to say, the guy ran, and Gladys brought Ethan over to make him some cookies, and also to lecture him on dating married women.

He missed those lectures.

Not having the best relationship with his parents, Gladys made Ethan feel like someone actually cared.

He smiled at the sudden memories flooding in. What was it about the new neighbor that made him walk down memory lane with Gladys?

And why was he still standing like an idiot in his front yard, staring at said new neighbor's door like a creep?

"Ethan!"

Ethan jumped from the sound.

A shadowy figure climbed out of his front shrubbery.

"Gretchen?" Ethan asked incredulously. "Didn't I just drop you off at your house? I thought the date was over?"

Fully extracting herself from the bush, Gretchen wore a short blue cocktail dress, had leaves stuck in her hair, and her mascara smudged under her eyes. "It's just, you left, and it was only seven o'clock. I thought you were mad at me."

Fair. Seven o'clock was a bit on the early side, but Ethan had wanted to go home and read, so he'd dropped Gretchen off right after dinner.

Also, she'd climbed out of his shrubbery . . . Ethan slowly started to back up. "It was our first date. I didn't want to keep you late. And besides, I don't know you enough to be mad." All true, but also, really good book.

Gretchen cried in relief, walking toward him.

"You seem very unstable." Ethan knew those probably weren't the best words to use, but all his life he attracted women and was attracted to women who were either physically unavailable or emotionally unavailable or women like Gretchen, who needed help that he couldn't provide.

It was difficult for him to admit that he always seemed to ignore all of these traits when he first met someone. He didn't know why, and frankly, he was tired of it. He was a romantic at heart, so he tended to confuse obsessive behavior with passion. But he was trying to fix it, trying to change.

But Gretchen wasn't helping.

Then a thought suddenly hit him. "How did you even beat me here?"

"You're a very slow driver. I've been hiding here for at least ten minutes."

Okay, a little offended. "I'm not slow. I just hit every red light."

Gretchen stepped up to Ethan and brushed her hand against his cheek. "You want to invite me inside?"

Ethan wanted to slap himself, because on some level, yeah, he kind of did.

Shaking himself out of even the slightest temptation, Ethan responded as kindly as possible, "Old me would say yes, but new me is trying to make healthier choices in life, and *this* doesn't scream healthy." Those hundred self-help books had to be good for something.

Gretchen's face fell, genuinely disappointed. "But I came all this way."

A tug of guilt yanked at Ethan's chest, and he paused, uncertain. "You're right, you did."

Taking this as a possible yes, Gretchen reached up and kissed his cheek. "Come on. Let's go inside."

Her words began to make sense to him. She must really like him for her to come all the way to his house after their date. "Yeah, maybe you're right. We had a really good time tonight."

Taking Ethan's hand, Gretchen led him to the front door.

Ethan's feet stopped as another thought flashed through his mind. "Wait. How did you know where I live since tonight was our first date?"

Gretchen sighed, shaking her head as if Ethan didn't understand common sense. "This was our first *live* date."

Uh-oh.

"*Live*? We've had other dates before that didn't include me participating?" This didn't seem good at all.

"Is that a problem?" Gretchen asked. Her big eyes looked up at him seductively.

Was he seriously falling for that?

Gah! Part of him was! They really did have a nice dinner.

No.

Ethan closed his eyes for a moment of zen, then opened them, steering Gretchen toward his car. "Old me would have probably been into this, but new me is taking you home, or possibly the police station."

Gretchen blew air out of her nose like a bull, frustrated. "Your loss." She walked away and down the street to where Ethan could only assume was her car. Neither one of them had had any alcohol, and she hadn't appeared intoxicated in any way, so he decided to let her go on her own.

He waved at her departing figure. "I had a lovely evening. I hope you get the help you need." Taking a deep, calming breath, he said aloud, "It was a good decision."

"Meow."

Ethan's focus moved down to his feet to find an adorable black-and-white cat staring up at him. As if their eye contact started his motors, the cat rubbed his face against Ethan's leg affectionately, purring loudly. "Hey, little guy. You lost?"

Kneeling down, he carefully reached under the cat's chin and read the collar. "Spike, huh? I like it." Glancing at the address beneath Spike's name, he looked up to see that it was the new neighbor's. Gladys's house.

He quickly looked at his phone: 7:30 p.m. "It's early enough. I don't want her to be worried about you all night." Or, he instantly thought, there might be a "mister" living there as well. "Or *they* might be worried. I'm just going to take you over."

Spike placed his front paws on Ethan's knee, then reached up to head-butt his chin.

"You are the cutest creature I've ever seen."

Understanding him completely, Spike jumped onto Ethan's squatted legs, then stretched his front paws up to his shoulder.

"Pick you up?" Ethan asked incredulously.

Spike answered by nosing Ethan's chin again.

Ethan picked up Spike easily, and he settled into Ethan's arms as if they were his cat bed. "I'm seriously debating stealing you," Ethan confessed, and he kind of meant it.

But a part of him felt a flush of anticipation at meeting the mystery woman who lived in Gladys's house.

Walking across the street, Ethan took a deep breath before he knocked on the door, trying to balance Spike with one arm. In response, Spike snuggled closer to Ethan's chest. He felt like his heart would burst. "You'll be the death of me." Can someone die of cuteness overload? Ethan may be the first.

After a few moments and no answer, Ethan tried the doorbell. "You think she's asleep at seven thirty?" Spike looked at him blankly. "I don't judge. I just don't want to wake her up."

Again, he assumed it was only the woman living there. "*Them.* I don't want to wake *them* up. If there are two of them. Or more. There could be kids. Do you have a big family?" Ethan had slipped into baby-talk mode with Spike, especially when Spike played along and touched his paw to Ethan's cheek. Ethan bit down on his lower lip to keep his head from exploding.

Still no one answered the door.

The sound of clunking and clattering from the backyard.

Ethan remembered Gladys had a greenhouse back there, but he was pretty sure someone was at least in the backyard.

"Hopefully we won't scare her and get smacked by a garden hoe."

Spike meowed back.

"Even your meow is adorable. I just can't with you." Ethan never wanted to let him go.

Moving to the side of the house, Ethan cautiously walked the length of the wall until he saw the back porch light, fully illuminating Gladys's greenhouse. For reasons he couldn't explain, an overwhelming sense of happiness overcame Ethan at seeing the greenhouse not only intact but in beautiful shape.

His heart leaped into his throat when he saw his new neighbor filling planters with soil.

She was beautiful.

He had seen how beautiful she was when he saw her earlier, but being this close, he knew he was in trouble.

Big trouble.

Knowing his luck, she would most definitely be married.

"Hello?" Ethan called out.

Her eyes met his.

Oh, man.

He was a goner.

My first customer!

The man's voice startled Hazel, her concentration focused solely on planting the next set of pots.

Turning, ready to use her trowel as a weapon, she was even more surprised to see the cute neighbor guy holding Spike in his arms.

In his arms!

Spike never let anyone hold him besides Hazel. He had loved Logan, but not enough to let him hold him . . . *like that.*

It left Hazel a little speechless.

"You didn't answer, but I heard noises back here and took a shot. This little guy wandered over to my house. I live across the street," he explained as if she hadn't just seen him exit his car earlier.

Hazel finally found her voice. "I remember. I saw you

earlier." She found she was a little nervous around him, not in a bad way, more like the *good* way, which made her even more nervous.

Hazel, finally coming to her senses, rushed over to the man and gently took Spike into her own arms. "He normally doesn't like anyone. I can't believe he went up to your house and let you hold him. I'm so sorry." The fact that Spike hadn't taken a swipe at this man's face when he picked him up astonished her.

"Don't be sorry. I love animals. And Spike is a little cuddle muffin, despite his name." He laughed, then continued. "Which I love, by the way."

Hazel found herself laughing too and placed Spike on the ground when he started to squirm. Speaking of swiping and claws, she didn't really feel like having Spike use her forearm as a diving board.

"I found him the day after my grandma died. We used to have *Buffy the Vampire Slayer* nights, and Grams's favorite character was Spike. He helped me through it. This house was hers."

"Wait. Gladys was your grandmother?" The man seemed positively stunned.

And him knowing Grams's name stunned Hazel right back. "You knew her?"

He nodded enthusiastically. "I'd say on a scale of one to ten for neighbors, Gladys was a million. She treated this whole block like we were family. After she passed, it hasn't been the same. She was kind of like the glue."

This made Hazel's heart sing. "That sounds like Grams."

"And she was my friend," he added quietly, as if unsure whether to share.

The sweetness of it gave her a compelling urge to hug him.

As if Spike heard her inner thoughts (and she was still not convinced that he couldn't), he rubbed his nose on the man's leg.

"My god, he likes you." Hazel shook her head, dumbfounded. What? Was this guy made of catnip?

His smile was soft, and he looked at Spike with adoring eyes.

She decided to officially introduce herself. "I'm Hazel."

"Ethan. Nice to meet you." He ducked his head.

Another pang in her chest.

Okay, this guy was really getting to her.

"You too." She smiled.

They both kept making eye contact, then looking away, like they were in junior high.

Ethan glanced at the greenhouse behind her. "Whatcha got going on here?" he asked.

"I had a dream my grandmother wanted me to bring her greenhouse back to life, but I'm going to start my own plant business. But only pet-friendly ones. I don't know, just playing around." Hazel's neck tingled at admitting her ambitions. He'd probably find the idea weird or stupid.

But Ethan's face lit up. "That's amazing. I've killed every plant I've ever owned. I even killed a cactus. I hear that's difficult to do, but I gotta say, it was pretty easy."

Hazel laughed, and she found she wanted to giggle.

Giggle? How old was she again? Right, forty-nine. *Forty-nine*! But she couldn't deny the utter giddiness she felt with Ethan. "You just haven't found the right kind of plant."

"You think you could help me? I could be your first customer. Start this new venture right now?" His eyebrows lifted enthusiastically.

Hazel's entire chest lightened to the point she thought she'd start floating like a balloon. Was this really happening? A customer? And an adorably sweet one at that? Should she hire Spike as her marketing director? Pulling customers in one person at a time? "I would love that," she answered.

Ethan and Hazel entered the greenhouse as he took it all in.

The place was starting to fill out. Each shelf had at least one or two full-grown plants resting on its surface. With the added new plants from Mr. Guiness's and the sprouts already growing from the ones she'd been planting, the greenhouse was well on its way to becoming Ashdonia.

"So which plant would you recommend for someone like me?" Ethan asked with a goofy grin.

"You mean a plant killer? Let me think," she joked.

Ethan laughed. "Ooo, a plant killer, I kind of like that. Makes me sound like I'm in a biker gang or something."

"A biker gang member that's so tough he kills plants for the fun of it."

They both laughed.

"Okay, when you say it like that, it sounds pretty lame."

Hazel's face flushed, as their proximity was only inches away from each other. Though part of her hoped this wasn't some kind of hot flash. Leave it to her to finally meet someone she may even have an inkling of liking, and her body confused it with menopause.

"I have the perfect one." Hazel brought them back on topic, mainly to calm herself down.

Walking over to one of the partially grown nursery plants, Hazel took down a rattlesnake plant. Its leaves were thick and wide with light green on the top and dark green accents, but underneath a deep maroon. "It's still pretty new, so I might have to come over to your place to find the perfect spot for it."

Oh god.

Did she just invite herself over to his house?

She could already feel her neck burning. "I mean, you could pick it up later maybe, after it's fully grown." Terrible recovery.

"You can come over." Ethan smiled at her, and he moved his hand as if he wanted to reach out to touch her, but he pulled it back quickly, as if also realizing how *that* looked *and* sounded. "Unless you don't feel comfortable. I can absolutely wait. Whatever you want."

And Hazel laughed. They were two grown adults that were acting like they were at a high school dance. And she loved every second of it. "No. I'd like to. I mean, I'd like to find the perfect place for the plant. Besides, if you were a serial killer, Spike wouldn't like you this much."

Spike rubbed against Ethan's leg as if answering.

"To be fair, though, you did name him after a

homicidal vampire. His judgment might not be sound." Ethan's smile made Hazel's toes curl. Plus, he knew *Buffy*, also brownie points.

Hazel laughed.

Again.

So much laughing.

Her cheeks began to ache from it, showing her just how long it had been. Her face was out of practice.

"Fair, but Grams liked you. That's all the confirmation I need." Saying that out loud hit Hazel hard, but she realized it was true. This stranger wasn't actually a stranger at all. He'd known her grandmother, even if it was just as a friendly neighbor, and it made her feel a kind of bond with him.

Plus, he was *really* cute.

"It's called the rattlesnake plant," Hazel informed him as she placed the pot on the table in front of them.

He raised an eyebrow. "Oooo, I like it already."

At this point, they were arm to arm, looking at the handful of thick, rigid leaves. When did that happen? Hazel felt the heat of Ethan's arm against hers, and she was finding it difficult to concentrate. "Also known as Calathea lancifolia." *Great. Hit him with nerd talk.*

Ethan's face moved even closer to hers as he leaned down toward the leaves. "Does it make a noise like a rattlesnake?"

He turned to make eye contact with her, waiting for an answer.

Hazel had to fight the urge to lean in and kiss him.

Kiss him!

Calm yourself, woman! she scolded herself. "You'd think so, but no, completely silent. It's also almost impossible to kill."

They were so close.

The heat palpable between them.

Was he going to kiss *her*?

Hazel laughed to break the tension. "But I believe in you."

They both laughed and separated enough for Hazel to gain her bearings back.

"Well, I will try my best to keep it alive. You busy now?" Ethan's expression was a mixture of hope and uncertainty.

Hazel picked up the plant and nodded toward the exit. "I'm all yours." *Did I really say that? Focus!* "When it gets bigger, we'll have to put it in a better pot. This was just from the nursery." Plus, that would give her an excuse to see him again.

Ethan took the plant from Hazel to carry. "I don't know. I kind of like it. Less pressure."

They both laughed again. Okay, her cheeks were really hurting at this point, but she wouldn't have it any other way.

Walking to the front yard, they headed toward Ethan's house.

"Your grandma used to make the most delicious chocolate chip cookies I've ever eaten," Ethan confessed.

Nostalgia flushed through Hazel at the thought of her grandmother's special recipe. "Right? You know, I have the recipe. I can make some, though they never seem to come out as perfect as hers."

Crossing the street, they reached Ethan's yard, and Hazel's stomach growled. "Okay, now I'm craving her cookies."

"They're not the glorious cookies from Gladys, but I do have some Oreos." Ethan lifted both his eyebrows in invitation as they walked up to the front door.

"That actually sounds good," Hazel said.

"It's great that you're reviving Gladys's greenhouse. From what I could see, it's been kind of abandoned after she passed," Ethan said quietly.

"I actually had a dream about Grams the other night, and she told me to rebuild her garden. She taught me so much about plants. I never thought I could make a business out of it. Still don't." Hazel wasn't sure why she was being so open with Ethan. She hadn't wanted to be vulnerable with anyone ever again after Logan if she was truly being honest with herself. But there was something about Ethan that brought out the truth. Like she wasn't afraid. She felt strangely safe with him.

Ethan held the plant in one hand and pulled out his keys to unlock the front door with the other. "Look how fast you made your first customer, though. You got this."

"I just need Spike to lure people in."

Ethan opened the door as Spike came out of nowhere and strolled in next to them.

"Spike? What the heck?" Again? Spike obviously felt the same amount of comfort around Ethan as she did. Should she take it as a sign?

"He's just following up with customer satisfaction.

There's a reason he's your top salesman." Ethan chuckled. "My house is his house." Ethan waved his hand at his open-concept living space, kitchen on the left, dining room in the center, and living room on the right. "Welcome to the abode. I'm sorry, I don't know why I said 'abode.' That was weird."

But Hazel laughed, or giggled, or laughed, ugh! What was she doing?

Enjoying herself, that's what.

His house was clean and well organized, which was already a good sign. With new appliances and quartz counters and island, the kitchen had obviously had an upgrade somewhat recently. The deep-green cupboards with the stark-white quartz was a beautiful touch. A dark round wooden table stood before them with only a stack of mail resting on top, the flooring a blonde oak. And the living room's gray plushy couch and matching recliner framed an entertainment center with a good-sized TV (always a plus).

Then she saw it.

The perfect spot for the rattlesnake plant. She walked over toward the living room, motioning for him to follow with the plant.

"Right here is perfect. No direct sunlight but near the sunlight from that window. Plus, it's east facing." Like it was meant to be.

Ethan placed the plant down on the side table Hazel referred to, their arms touching. Turning to her, gently he asked, "How much do I owe you?"

Money? Why did Hazel hate taking money? This was

supposed to be a business, but after the array of happiness she'd felt since Ethan's first hello, the last thing Hazel wanted from Ethan was money. She waved the offer off with the arm that wasn't still leaned against Ethan. "We'll call you bringing this guy back safely as payment."

Spike jumped up on the side table, rubbing his face on the rattlesnake plant.

"So if I'd kept him, I wouldn't be getting a free plant?" He laughed at her, the heat of his arm melting her brain.

"Were you going to keep him?" she asked softly, but still laughed at him.

"He's pretty damn cute."

Yes, he is. "Irresistible."

They stared at each other, arms still touching, each second growing more and more intense. Even Spike had lost interest in the plant and watched them.

"Let me give you something at least." Ethan broke away first.

Hazel needed a second to gain her bearings, her mind reeling with feelings she hadn't felt in . . . years. "No really. It's fine."

"Stay here." Ethan looked at her as if he was afraid she would bolt. "Or not *here,* on the couch, or the chair, just don't leave."

With one last smile, like he was up to something, Ethan headed to the kitchen.

Suddenly realizing her knees were a bit shaky, Hazel walked over to the couch and plopped down.

What a freaking night.

Can I walk you home?

Hazel leaned back on the plushy gray couch and at that moment noticed some wonderfully nerdy framed posters on the wall of some of her favorite movies, *Army of Darkness, Brazil*, and the piece de la resistance, *Star Wars*. Same taste in movies, *really* good sign. The couch was to die for, definitely went for comfort over style, which was exactly what Hazel liked as well.

So far, Ethan was looking like an excellent prospect for her dream guy.

Spike jumped up on the couch next to her and rubbed his face on her arm. She scratched him affectionately. "What do you think, Spike? You think he could be the guy I've been dreaming about?"

Spike head-bumped her hand for more scratches.

"I think so too." Then Spike turned his head toward

the side wall, as if he'd noticed a fly or moth. He even did that hunter chitter that cats love to do, thinking they're fierce but are actually adorable. "What do you see, Spike?"

The wall had a frame on it, but from Hazel's angle, the standing lamp blocked her view. It looked like some kind of collage.

Standing, Hazel walked over to the hanging frame, and her mouth dropped. Underneath the glass were at least a hundred movie tickets displayed in ten even rows.

"Oh my god," she whispered under her breath. The tickets dated back to the eighties but were mostly from the nineties and 2000s. But what made her heart jump into her throat was the fact that she'd been to over a dozen of these exact showings. Same theater, same time, same date, *she'd* been there. "Ethan!" she yelled out.

Ethan walked back in from the kitchen, holding a wooden tray with a plate in the center, Double Stuf Oreos stacked in a beautiful spiral, with two giant mugs of hot chocolate filled to the brim with mini marshmallows next to it.

"Um, that looks delicious." Hazel almost wanted to squeal from the oh-my-gawd adorableness, but she was too excited about the movie tickets.

Ethan placed the tray down on the rustic wood coffee table, then joined her at the framed collage. "I saved all my favorites."

"Ethan, I went to a lot of these showings. We were at the same movies at the same time." Hazel was breathless from the implications. Most of the overlap happened before she had even met Logan. That meant she and

Ethan had sat and watched movies together *a lot.*

Ethan's eyes widened. "What? That's crazy."

"Right?" Hazel couldn't hold back her shocked excitement. She pointed her finger at a ticket. "*Jurassic Park* midnight show at the Avco."

"And Spielberg went to the ten p.m. showing . . ."

". . . so we were waiting in line until one a.m. when they finally let us in," Hazel finished excitedly.

Ethan's face lit up. "I fell asleep twice even though I'd drank three cups of coffee."

"My friends and I were so mad we didn't get to watch it with him." Hazel shook her head.

Going back to the collage, Hazel pointed at *Star Wars*. "The re-release with the new added scenes at the Chinese ten p.m. showing."

"Where when Obi-Wan said that Darth Vader betrayed and murdered Luke's father . . ." Ethan began.

Hazel finished, "A guy in the audience yelled . . ."

"Liar!" they both said in unison, laughing.

Ethan shook his head. "This is amazing."

Hazel pointed at another she recognized. "*Iron Will* at the El Capitan, seven p.m. They put snow on Hollywood Blvd. in front of the theater . . ."

"And had dog sled racing. That was incredible! I remember looking over across the street at the Chinese and thinking LA was the most magical place," Ethan reminisced.

"Same," Hazel said, awed.

She motioned to the rest of the tickets she recognized. "Cinerama Dome, *Fight Club*, ten p.m. showing. *Galaxy*

Quest, Cinerama Dome opening, ten fifteen p.m. showing. Midnight showing of *Big Trouble in Little China*, Vista. *Phantom Menace*, ten p.m. showing, Village . . ."

"The roar of that audience when 'A long time ago, in a galaxy far, far away' popped up . . ." Ethan tilted his head at the memory.

Hazel raised her arm to show him her goosebumps. "Right?"

Then her eyes found a very old and worn ticket from the eighties: *Escape to Ashdonia*. It was a theater in Chicago. She pointed to it.

"No," he said incredulously.

Hazel laughed. "No, I didn't go to this showing, but *Escape to Ashdonia* is my favorite book, and I loved the movie so much."

"I loved those books, and the movie was perfection. I wanted to be Nikolas Dragontine, hair and all."

"You'd look good in an eighties mullet," Hazel teased.

"I think they're actually coming back in style," Ethan said with a grin.

"Hey, if I was into them back then, I could be into them again." She raised an eyebrow. "But Olivia's golden dress at that ballroom scene. I mean . . ."

Ethan nodded emphatically. "It was like *Dallas* meets *Labyrinth*."

"Right? I definitely got Sarah-Labyrinth vibes." Hazel tried to control her rush of giddiness at Ethan loving both her favorite book and the movie it was based on.

They stared at each other, eyes still wide at the coincidences.

"Amazing." Hazel sighed happily.

"Truly." Ethan grinned, then motioned to the couch with his head. "We can sit and eat while we figure out how else our paths have crossed over the years. And then later you can tell me how to take care of the rattlesnake plant."

Hazel and Ethan sat down on the couch, Hazel still buzzing about the serendipity. She focused on the display in front of them. "Yum."

Ethan beamed as he handed Hazel her mug of hot chocolate. "Probably a little late for this much sugar, but screw it."

"Yeah, screw it." Her stomach would pay for this later, but after realizing how many times she'd crossed paths with Ethan, she was pretty sure her adrenaline would burn it off. She sipped from the piping-hot mug, and her eyes rolled back from the rich chocolatey deliciousness.

Dunking an Oreo into his mug, Ethan took a bite and closed his eyes in bliss. "Oh yeah, that's the stuff. Not close to Gladys level, but hitting the spot."

Another reference to her grandmother touched Hazel. He really did know her grandma. Not that she had doubted it, but only a true fan of her grandma's cooking would still remember it three years later.

After a few cookies were in them both, Ethan leaned back, relaxed. "So why the move?" he asked.

Hazel sighed heavily before she could stop herself, and Spike jumped in her lap, curling into a ball, as if sensing her discomfort.

"Uh-oh. None of my business?" Ethan obviously

picked up on Hazel's shift in mood.

"No. It's fine. I should be used to telling people by now. My husband of twenty-two years came out to me over a year ago." Rip the Band-Aid.

"Whoa. Like came out, came out?"

"Yeah. He's already dating and posting it on social media." Hazel didn't know why that mattered, but it somehow felt relevant to the conversation.

"What about you? You start dating again?" Ethan looked at her thoughtfully, but there was something else . . .

The pull Hazel felt between them was undeniable.

"Just the app kind," she answered, trying to hold back her feelings of disgust.

Ethan laughed. "And by the grimace on your face, I take it the apps are not for you?"

"Are they really for anyone?" She genuinely wondered.

"Fair." Ethan shifted on the couch to where their legs touched.

A sudden thrill raced through her at his touch.

Spike unfurled from Hazel's lap and strolled over to Ethan's.

Ethan's mouth instantly dropped, and he sat very still, as if any move would scare Spike away. After making a few biscuits on Ethan's leg, Spike curled into a ball and closed his eyes.

Mouthing to Hazel, Ethan seemed beyond excited. "Oh. My. God." Then he whispered, "I'm never moving."

Hazel shook her head. "He literally only cuddles with me." Their eyes met. "He really likes you."

Ethan's stare sent more shivers down Hazel's spine. Then he said, "I really like him."

Hazel didn't think they were talking about the cat at this point, but to ease her pounding heart, she asked, "So, what do you do?"

"Can you hand me an Oreo and my cocoa? I don't want to move," Ethan pleaded.

Laughing, Hazel handed him an Oreo and his mug. "Your *cocoa*? How very Hallmark movie of you."

"First *abode* now *cocoa*, what am I, ninety?"

They both laughed.

"To be fair, both are perfectly legit words, far underused in my opinion." Hazel took a sip of her hot chocolate.

"I aim to please." Ethan laughed. "To answer your question, I'm a graphic designer. I'm lucky, though. I have a set of clients that I've worked freelance for, for years, so I don't have to panic like most graphic designers I know."

"Do you like it?" Hazel asked.

"I love it. I love being able to see something in my head, then create it on the screen." Ethan's entire demeanor became animated as he talked.

It was such a pleasure meeting someone who actually loved their job.

"That's how I feel about gardening and planting. And finding the perfect plant for someone? It's magic." She'd always been afraid to admit that something that was a hobby for most was her passion in life. But it was true. Growing and nurturing plants brought her true peace.

Hazel suddenly noticed Ethan staring at her, eyes sparkling.

"I'm sorry about what happened with you and your ex," he finally said.

Taking another sip from her mug, she admitted, "Part of me wishes it never happened and I was still with him, but part of me is weirdly . . . happy? Relieved? I don't know. Either way, it feels messed up."

Her staring into Ethan's eyes intensified, like a kiss was imminent.

Was she ready for that?

Turning away shyly, Hazel nodded over to the rattlesnake plant. "So the plant. They're pretty tough."

"With a name like rattlesnake, I would think so," he said with a laugh.

"All you have to do is water it every two weeks or so. Basically, just keep the soil wet but not soaked. Here's a good trick." Hazel stood and walked over, grabbing the plant and bringing it back to them. Carefully taking Ethan's mug and placing it on the coffee table so as not to disturb Spike, she then just as carefully handed him the plant. "Feel that weight?"

"Yeah, it's a little heavy," Ethan observed.

"That's how it feels after it's been watered. So in a couple of weeks, lift it again, and if it's really light, you know it's time to water. Or stick your finger a couple inches down, and if it's dry, you'll know it's time." Hazel shared the first tips her grandmother had taught her as a child.

Ethan tilted his head in appreciation. "I might actually be able to do this."

"I'll remind you." *So I can see you again.*

"Probably a good plan." Ethan's eyes flashed . . . joy?

Was she reading into this?

Hazel took the plant and placed it back in its spot, then sat back down on the couch.

Spike stretched lazily out of the donut position and jumped off Ethan's lap, sauntering toward the front door.

Hazel said the words she wasn't feeling, "I guess it's time to go."

"Yeah, of course. Thank you so much for the plant." Ethan stood with Hazel.

Standing so that they were facing each other, Hazel said, "Thank you for bringing back Spike and the cookies and the *cocoa*." She laughed at that.

"I'm never going to live that down, am I?" Ethan laughed back, and the urge to kiss him was almost impossible to resist.

"And it was nice seeing your *abode*." Hazel tried to relieve the tension with a bit of teasing.

Ethan groaned, then laughed. "Can I walk you home?"

They both cracked up, considering how close Hazel's house was, but she didn't want to say goodbye yet either. "Sure," she agreed.

Heading for the door, Spike pranced next to them like he was their leader.

As they walked outside in the fresh night air, Hazel suddenly realized how silly this was. "I really can walk the rest of the way."

But Ethan wasn't having it. "I wouldn't want anything to happen to you. It's a long way across the street."

They both suppressed a chuckle as Ethan walked Hazel across the street and to her front door.

"Well, thank you for walking me home." Hazel gazed up at Ethan.

This would be the moment.

The good-night kiss.

Was she ready?

Spike sped off toward a tree, completely distracting them both.

"There he goes." Ethan shook his head, then stared at Hazel intensely. "And it was my pleasure." His voice was heavy.

This was it.

Hazel both wanted him to kiss her and was also terrified of it.

Ethan began to lean in . . .

"Can I walk you home?" Hazel asked with a breathless laugh.

Laughing back, Ethan touched her cheek gently, sending shivers through her entire body. "I would love that."

Pulling his hand away, in what appeared to be self-consciousness, he waved for her to lead.

The pair strolled across the street and up to Ethan's front door.

Hazel didn't think the tension could get any thicker, but it was like a whole other person between them at this point. Yet at the same time, Hazel felt pulled toward Ethan as if they were both magnetized.

She hadn't wanted to be kissed in years.

Not even from Logan.

But this stranger showed up in her backyard, holding Spike, reminiscing about Grams, finding out they'd been at the exact same events since the nineties? Plus, being adorable in every way, all she wanted to do was lean in and feel his lips on hers. It was so overpowering she found herself shifting forward.

Ethan's eyes screamed volumes as he seemed to stare into Hazel's entire soul.

He felt the same, right?

She wasn't imagining this?

As Hazel took the lead this time, leaning in, Ethan stumbled backward slightly. Then he laughed and asked, "Can I walk you home?"

Giggles.

Sheer giggles.

From *both* of them.

It hit them both so hard they were practically on the ground laughing.

"It would be an honor, sir," Hazel announced as if she were in a Jane Austen book.

Ethan took her cue and held out his arm for her to take. "M'lady."

Happily, she slid her arm through his, and they walked toward her house.

Here they were again.

As Hazel was about to try to say something witty, Ethan apparently had dropped all pretenses and kissed her.

Really kissed her.

Her mind nearly exploded from the touch of his soft lips on hers, and she found she needed more. Pressing in deeper, Ethan responded in kind, the intensity reaching a breaking point in her self-control.

Hazel pulled away, and they both stared at each other, stunned.

"Whoa," they both said at the same time.

A new light grew inside of Hazel. This felt so very right. Ethan felt right. She'd never felt like this before, not even with Logan.

But panic filled Hazel when she saw Ethan's eyes bug out.

"We should probably just be friends, though, right?" Ethan asked, wiping sweat from his brow.

"Um, what?" Hazel couldn't believe what she was hearing after a kiss like that.

"It just feels fast?" He said it as if he was asking a question.

Did he really want her to answer?

But like all good things, this one was apparently too good to be true. She slumped her shoulders in disappointment. "Of course," she replied, chest aching. Opening her door, she turned to Ethan before she closed it. "It was nice meeting you, Ethan."

Hazel shut the door.

She wanted to cry.

But weirdly, she also wanted to celebrate.

That kiss was amazing.

Did he panic?

Or did he find the kiss repulsive?

But he'd said "whoa." That was a good indicator that he'd liked it. Right?

Hazel needed to talk with Cora immediately.

Walking to the kitchen, she pulled out her cell phone and called her best friend.

"Hazel? You okay?" Cora's tone sounded worried.

"Get over here and bring your tarot cards." Hazel got right to the point.

"It's ten o'clock, and I'm forty-nine. Can't it wait until tomorrow?"

True.

"First thing, though."

"I'll be there at dawn. Not really, but early," Cora said with a yawn.

"See you tomorrow." Hazel ended the call and took in the entire evening. "What the heck just happened?"

Chapter 7
Ethan

I'm an idiot

W*hat did I do?*

Ethan stared at Hazel's closed front door in shock.

That was the best kiss of my life, and I friend-zoned her?

Rooted in utter disbelief, Ethan tried to force himself to turn around and go back home, where he could ponder his idiocy in private.

Maybe I should knock? Tell her I was stupid and ask her out on a proper date?

Why can't I move?

Ethan realized he couldn't *move* because he didn't want to believe he'd actually did what he did. He could make it right, though. He had to make it right.

Spike wandered up, looking at Ethan with his big green eyes.

"I was a total idiot right there, wasn't I?" he asked the cat.

Spike's response was a disappointed glare, then a full walk off.

"Yup."

Great, now Spike hates me. I *hate me.*

Ethan rubbed his chest from the deep-seated pain he felt. "Why do I feel like my heart just fell out?"

His foot finally budged, and he was able to pull himself away from Hazel's house.

As he walked across the street and toward his place, he was hit with an overwhelming sensation of loss. It was so powerful it nearly stopped him from moving again. But at this point, his home was his sanctuary, and in some crazy way, he thought he could ground himself once he stepped inside. It rarely worked, but for some reason his brain kept telling him it would. The door was unlocked, and he pushed his way inside, closing it behind him.

His eyes wandered toward the living room and his new plant, plus the remains of their cocoa date and his framed collage of movie tickets. He needed to be somewhere else. It was like a slap in his face. It was a slap in *her* face.

Why do I do these things?

Hurrying to his bedroom, Ethan sat down on the edge of his California king and pulled out his cell.

He needed to talk to his best friend, Mateo.

"Hello? Ethan? What are you doing up?" Mateo sounded amused.

"It's only ten." Ethan defended himself.

"Like I said, what are you doing up?" Mateo repeated confidently.

"Fair," Ethan conceded. "Mateo. I need you, man. I messed up."

Mateo groaned. "If it's about that girl you went out with tonight, I swear . . ." he began.

"No. I did the right thing and sent her away. No, it's the opposite. I think I found *the one*." The words came out of Ethan's mouth before he could stop them.

Did he really mean them?

Was Hazel *the one*?

As soon as the thought entered his mind, he knew with certainty: absolutely.

When he thought about it, they'd practically been in each other's whole adult lives considering how many movies they'd gone to at the same time.

"Are you being serious right now?" Mateo asked, doubt lacing his tone.

"Yes, and I ruined it." Ethan felt the pain of each word.

Mateo's voice softened. "Calm down. I'm sure it's fixable. Austin and I will swing by tomorrow. We'll come up with a plan."

Ethan groaned. "Tomorrow?"

"We're on set until midnight, but we'll be there first thing," Mateo promised.

"With Krispy Kreme?" Ethan felt like a toddler at this point.

"Yes, with Krispy Kreme," Mateo said.

"See you tomorrow." Ethan hung up the phone, then fell back on his bed, groaning.

After a few moments of self-loathing, Ethan mustered up the energy to pull off all his clothes down to his boxers and T-shirt. Might as well go to bed. There was nothing he could do about Hazel right then. He had been all intent on reading his book when he'd been on the date with Gretchen, but with everything that happened with Hazel, he didn't feel like reading anymore. He was too upset with himself to concentrate.

Crawling under the fluffy comforter and settling into his memory foam pillow, Ethan attempted to close his eyes to try to sleep.

Too bad he left the lights on.

He wondered if he could sleep with them on. The effort it would take to turn the lights off felt like way more energy than he had in him. But after at least five minutes of trying to sleep, he threw back the sheets and comforter angrily and practically smacked the wall switch, turning off the lights.

Settling back into his bed, he took a few deep breaths to try to relax.

Did I lock the front door?

Yes, I did.

Did you, though? Because you were kind of out of it.

No. I did.

I really don't think you did.

With an almost roar that shocked himself, Ethan pulled back the covers yet again and stormed out to his front door.

Not locked.

His anger lessened, as this journey wasn't a total waste.

As he shuffled his way back to the bedroom, Ethan couldn't help but see the rattlesnake plant out of the corner of his eye.

Stop.

But Ethan *couldn't* stop. His head kept spinning.

He sent Gretchen home because he was trying to stop his toxic behaviors, but then he pushed away quite possibly the most perfect woman for him he'd ever met? Unfortunately, it tracked with him. He grew up in a household where feelings weren't exactly discussed. They were kind of ignored. No hugging, no affection, no "I love yous," just discipline and rule following.

Luckily, Ethan's older sister had become a doctor, because Ethan knew he was a monumental failure to his parents being a graphic designer no matter how much proof of success he had. But Ethan didn't rebel until after he left the house and was paying his own bills. His parents had wanted him to go to college near them in Chicago, but he moved to Los Angeles and worked at a CD store instead, until he could figure things out. It took him a while, but when he switched jobs and started working at a video rental store, he always had an interest in the posters of the movies. He had taken a basic computer design course, which, being that it was in the late nineties, was pretty rudimentary. It was enough of a seed to lead him on his path, though, and he'd never regretted a single day since.

He'd been pushing away healthy relationships his entire adult life. Fear, he assumed, but maybe it was something deeper.

But no one like Hazel.

Maybe that was because of their age? When you get to your forties, you stop caring about what people think. Of course, there are exceptions, but overall, it was a much nicer way to view the world. Ethan had only been in love once in his life, but it was when he was young, twenty-two, and thinking he'd conquer the world. Kelly Churlington. They'd met working at said video rental store. That was back when Ethan wrote screenplays (well, *a* screenplay; turned out he didn't really like writing, and according to everyone who read it, he wasn't very good at writing either, it had no plot, or character arcs, or anything interesting about it) *but* at the time he thought he could be the next Quentin Tarantino. In fact, the knowledge that Tarantino was a video store clerk was the *only* reason he applied for the job. Ethan didn't have many original thoughts back then. He blamed his hormones, and that weird fact that brains didn't fully form until twenty-five. So at twenty-two he was a half-formed human as far as he was concerned. He chuckled at the memory of when he told his parents he wanted to be a screenwriter back in his twenties. The vein on his dad's forehead had almost burst.

But Kelly? She had seemed so perfect. Kind, beautiful, funny, into the same movies and things Ethan was into, which was basically just movies at the time. They'd dated a year, and Ethan had seriously considered proposing. (Yes, proposing before his brain was fully formed.) Alas,

Kelly decided she wanted to play the field a bit more, without actually telling Ethan about it. He'd walked in on her making out with their coworker, Gary, in the supply closet. It had pretty much crushed his soul, though looking back, he couldn't really blame her. They were so young. She'd even Facebook friended him eight years ago, and they'd commented on each other's pics now and again. Kelly was happily married with three kids in Montana, or at least "social media happy." Who knew what life was really like behind closed doors?

Ethan suspected all his trust issues with women began with Kelly. His emotionless parents might have had something to do with it as well. But didn't recognizing these facts make it all go away? Being aware of it should cure it, right? Somehow on a deep cellular level he knew that wasn't accurate, but living in delusion was a valuable skill he'd honed over the years.

Finally, diving back into his bed, he truly snuggled in and allowed his body to relax.

Taking a few deep, calming breaths, he closed his eyes.

Did I lock the back *door?*

Boone
(Don't @ me about his douchey name)

Lying in bed, staring at the ceiling, Hazel's mind was on overload. She couldn't get Ethan's kiss out of her head. It had been utterly magnificent. Never experiencing a kiss that explosive, she could still feel his lips on hers.

Stop!

But had it only been *her* that felt it? She didn't want to overanalyze, but that was how her brain functioned. Turning over on her side, Hazel aggressively pushed thoughts of Ethan aside. She had to. She needed to accept it was a lost cause and not turn it into an endless obsession like she normally would.

He didn't want her.

He didn't like the kiss.

He liked her enough to be friends.

Probably because of their love of movies and the fact

that they'd literally been sitting in the same theater with each other dating back thirty years. The coincidence was insane! Too much to just discard and ignore.

So friends they would be.

End of story.

Hazel's stomach sank at these thoughts (though she was sure some of that was from all the sugar she'd ingested), but she had to accept what happened. She couldn't go down that path again, creating excuses as to why men she liked behaved a certain way. Doing that with Logan was how she ended up marrying him, overlooking red flags that didn't feel like red flags because she'd rationalize why they weren't red flags.

No.

Ethan was clear.

He wasn't interested.

And Hazel needed to accept that, no matter how much it made her chest hurt.

Flipping back over to lie on her back, Hazel breathed in deep, calming herself. "Okay, Grams. Give me a dream tonight. Let me dream of my dream guy. And maybe give him a face? That would be helpful. Okay, good night. I love you. And thank you for this place."

A calm settled in Hazel's chest and mind.

Yes.

Grams wouldn't let her down.

Closing her eyes, she fell instantly asleep.

***

Another lucid dream. That was a good sign.

Before her was a beautiful field of grass with

wildflowers sprouting up in colorful bouquets all around. Looking down, she saw that she was in a flowing pink dress that blew perfectly with the wind. The sun was out with lazy, puffed white clouds.

Twirling as if she were Julie Andrews in *The Sound of Music*, Hazel closed her eyes, enjoying the moment. When she stopped, she opened them.

Dream Guy stood in front of her, wearing a T-shirt and jeans, blurry face and all.

"Hey," he said.

"Hey," Hazel answered. "Who are you?"

"You know who I am," he said confidently.

"I know you already?"

But he didn't answer; instead, he began to walk away.

"Wait! Don't leave," Hazel called after him, then decided to follow as his figure grew farther and farther away.

The scenery shifted before her eyes in a swirl of colors and shapes until Hazel stood in an office setting amongst a sea of cubicles.

Dream Guy was still walking ahead of her, but his back was to her, and apparently, he'd changed outfits, now wearing a dress shirt and slacks from what she could tell.

Following him through the twists and turns of the cubicles, she finally caught up to him and grabbed his shoulder, then spun him around.

"Boone?" Hazel's eyes widened as his face came fully into view.

Boone had been a coworker from back in her temp days between plant nursery jobs. She'd definitely felt an attraction for him, but she was married, so she never let herself go there.

But the Boone in front of her didn't see her; in fact, he was still in his early thirties, and considering Hazel worked at iTech fifteen years ago, she knew it was because that was how she remembered him.

As if watching a play, Boone walked into a cubicle where Hazel could now see her younger thirty-something self sitting at her desk, gathering her things in a box. Boone walked over and sat across from the Hazel of the past.

"I remember this. This was my last day of work," she said aloud, but neither person heard her. Hazel was watching a memory.

Focusing on the two of them, Hazel listened.

Boone stared at younger Hazel with an expression that was pretty obvious that he had feelings for her. "I wish you didn't have to leave."

But what surprised Hazel more was the fact that her younger self mirrored the same expression. "Me too. Blame the company, not me. I'd stay if I could."

Boone and younger Hazel stood up and faced each other, and there was a moment where Hazel racked her brain wondering if she'd actually kissed Boone. Because it really looked like they were about to make out in the middle of that cubicle.

"Logan is one lucky man." Boone's voice was quietly intense.

Younger Hazel blushed and tilted her head down.

"Oh my god, I was so into him," she observed in

shock. Hazel knew she'd fought feelings for Boone, but seeing it like this in front of her made it real.

Her younger self turned abruptly and reached down to pick up the box on the desk. "See you around?"

Before she could take hold of the box, Boone pulled her into a tight hug.

It was intense.

"Holy." Hazel shook her head, watching the scene like it was a movie.

Both Boone and her younger self had expressions of pain. *Pain!*

"What the heck?" Hazel couldn't peel her eyes away.

"Yeah, see you around." Boone turned away.

Were those tears?

***

Hazel woke up from her dream, eyes still wide.

Then slowly she began to smile, and smile big.

"Boone." Hazel said his name as if she were conjuring him to her.

Yes.

She'd never explored anything with Boone because she was married, but maybe now was the perfect time?

Maybe Ethan running away was destiny so that she could be clear-minded with Boone.

Flinging the sheets and quilt off her, Hazel rummaged through a box of clothes and picked out a fun *Doctor Who* dress she hadn't worn in a while. She was feeling a bit nostalgic for some time traveling at this point, so it seemed appropriate for her mood.

Leaving her bedroom and walking to the kitchen,

Hazel opened up the fridge and pulled out a yogurt. “Boone,” she said again, rolling his name off her tongue just to hear the sound of it. “I haven’t thought of him in years.”

Spike bumped his head through the kitty door and wandered up to Hazel, rubbing his nose on her leg, then walked to the human door, meowing. “You literally just walked through the cat door.”

But Spike stared up at her as if he were frustrated she couldn’t understand his language and meowed again.

“Fine. I need to check the plants anyway.” Hazel opened the door, and the two of them walked into the greenhouse together.

Hazel reared her head back in surprise, as the sprouts that were tiny last night had grown almost a full inch by morning. “Talk about signs.” Glancing up at the sky through the glass ceiling, she said, “Thanks, Grams.”

Through the open kitchen door, Hazel heard the doorbell ring, followed by a buzz from her cell phone.

From Cora: *I’m here. Let me in. I forgot my key.*

With a jump to her step, Hazel rushed back into the house and to her front door, swinging it wide.

Cora stood there, looking tired and disheveled but wearing a grin as she motioned to her large tote bag on her shoulder. “I brought every deck I’ve ever owned, runes, I-ching, and a Ouija board. Though Maisie tells me that kids these days highly don’t recommend it.”

“Come in, come in. I have so much to tell you.” Hazel found that seeing her best friend only ignited the giant burst of excitement inside her.

"I need your help first." Arriving in the kitchen, Cora plopped on a stool behind the island, laying the bag on top while Hazel stood across from her.

Cora rarely asked for anything. It was usually Hazel who'd have to pry whatever she needed out of her so she could help, so the fact that she was asking? Putting her love life aside was easy when it came to her best friend. "Of course. What is it?"

"Maisie is refusing to go on set. She says her dad is being condescending."

"He can be a little condescending." Hazel threw that out there. Jack was a great guy, but when he was over-focused, his "tone" leaned toward the arrogant.

"Hazel!" Cora feigned offense, then she shrugged. "Yeah, he can be." With an exasperated sigh, she said, "She won't listen to me either. Do you think you could talk to her? She always listens to you. I just don't want her to miss this opportunity because she's annoyed with her father."

"Of course, although she's going to know you put me up to it." Maisie always did.

"Yeah, I know, but I think she'll listen anyway. You have some kind of magic language with her. Help me, Hazel Dalton. You're my only hope."

Hazel shook her head. "'*Do not cite the deep magic to me, witch.*'"

"You trump my *Star Wars* quote with a *Narnia* quote? Well played. And I am a witch, thank you very much."

"True. All right, hang on." Hazel pulled out her phone and hit the FaceTime button for Maisie. After one ring, her beautiful face filled the tiny screen.

"Did she put you up to this?" Maisie raised her eyebrow, already on the defense.

"You know she did." Hazel smiled in what she hoped would soften Maisie's mood.

Cora bit down on her lip to stop herself from interrupting.

Maisie groaned. "He's criticizing everything I say or do, and I'm not even supposed to *say* or *do* anything. I'm just there to observe. But how can I *observe* when he's constantly bombarding me with questions like I'm in some kind of pop-quiz nightmare. I don't think he understands the meaning of 'shadowing.' *I'm* the one who's supposed to be asking questions so I *can learn*." She ended her rant with a frustrated grunt.

Hazel knew instantly that Jack was excited his daughter not only was on set but was interested in following in his footsteps, but being overzealous was always part of his personality, in both good and bad ways.

"And if you say it's just because he's happy I'm on set, Mom already tried that. It's no excuse." Maisie eyed the screen as if she were daring Hazel to say it.

"Okay, your mom said that because it's true. Your dad has zero clue of how he comes across sometimes. When we first met, I told him I loved *Star Wars*, and he proceeded to ask me a bunch of trivia questions about it. He thought he was connecting with me, but I thought he was an arrogant jerk who was trying to make me prove I was an actual fan. It wasn't until I told him one of my favorite characters was Wedge Antilles that his whole face lit up and I knew he really was just excited to be talking to another *Star Wars* geek. The point is, when your mother and I say your dad is just excited, it's a million percent true." Hazel had wanted to punch the guy a handful of times in her life, but she'd stand in front of a train for him any day of the week.

Maisie let out another groan. "Can you get him to stop with the questions at least?"

"The easiest way to turn things around with your dad is to answer a question with a question. So if he asks what kind of light would you use in this scene . . ."

"Oh my gawd, he *did* ask that!" Maisie interrupted.

Hazel smiled. "So instead of answering, ask him, 'What kind of lighting do you think they used in *Taxi Driver*? That was really moody.' Or something like that. Watch how his whole demeanor will change, I'm telling you. Actually, any Scorsese film or any Spike Lee film. You may have to hear a twenty-minute gush fest, but it's better than what he's doing now. Also, if he won't let it go, quote *Speed*, 'pop-quiz, hot shot,' and he'll probably laugh and realize how he's acting. Talking about his favorite movies and quoting them is the easiest way to distract him."

Cora nodded vehemently since she knew she couldn't speak.

Maisie upgraded her groan to a sigh. "He does love it when I quote movies. It was always our little thing."

"See? And, Maisie, I'm telling you, the guy is over the moon about you being there. I know it's hard to see because he's your dad, but he's been talking about doing this ever since you went to film school and said you wanted to be a director. He just wants to show you his world."

"Great, now I have 'A Whole New World' stuck in my head. Thanks for that." With a lifting of her shoulders, Maisie smiled. "All right. I'm in his trailer now. I'm going back out."

A relieved yelp exited Cora's mouth.

Rolling her eyes, Maisie shook her head. "Of course she was there the whole time. Hi, Mom."

"Hi, sweetie." Cora made an "oopsie" face.

"Wish me luck." Maisie raised her eyebrows.

"Good luck, you got this," Hazel said, then Maisie ended the call.

Cora walked over and kissed Hazel's cheek. "God, I love you."

Laughing, Hazel responded, "I love you too."

Cora's whole demeanor then perked up when truly observing Hazel. "What happened in the time you hung up with me in the car after your crappy date and bedtime? Did you meet someone?" Cora asked as she began to pull out her tarot decks from the bag.

"Yes and no. Or yes and yes. Okay, let me explain. First, don't get too excited, but I met my neighbor last night."

But Cora didn't listen to her, she leaned forward, smiling from ear to ear. "Okaaaay. Is he cute?"

"I told you not to get excited, but yes, ridiculously cute. And we actually had an amazing talk, and he had this framed collage of movie tickets he's saved over the years and, Cora, we went to so many of the same movies at the same freaking time!"

"What? Um, that sounds like destiny."

"And he kissed me."

Cora put her hand to her mouth. "Hazel! Why shouldn't I be excited about this? Was he a terrible kisser?"

"I'm getting to it, but no, it was the best kiss I've ever had," Hazel confessed.

"Hazel!" Cora was beside herself. "Where's the shoe? What happened?"

"Right after, he said he just wants to be friends. So it obviously wasn't as earth-shattering for him." Hazel wanted to throw up at having to say that out loud.

Cora's shoulders slumped in answer. "Oh, Hazel."

"I know. That's when I originally called you. But . . ." Hazel gave her friend a sneaky smile.

"There's a but? He came to his senses and John-Cusack-boom-boxed you?" Cora raised her eyebrows in hope.

"Better."

"Better than *Say Anything*?"

"I asked my grandma to help me dream of my dream guy, and she did!" Hazel's voice rose a few octaves from her elation.

"And it was your neighbor? What's his name anyway?" Cora wasn't letting go of Ethan.

"His name is Ethan, but no. It wasn't him. I think it was fate that he friend-zoned me, because I dreamt about *Boone*." Hazel said his name like revealing a twist that she felt Cora should have known.

But Cora scrunched her face. "Boone? Who's Boone?"

Hazel groaned, irritated. Of course Cora wouldn't remember. "Remember fifteen years ago when I worked at iTech? The guy that everyone called my 'work husband' because of how well we got along? But I shot that down because I thought it was inappropriate because I was married?"

"His name was Boone? That's such a douchey name."

"Cora!" Not what she wanted to hear at the moment, even if she'd felt that way herself back in the day.

"Sorry. I'm focused. Boone. Okay, Boone. And you had a connection with him?" Cora had skeptical face.

"Big-time," Hazel reassured her. "We never did anything about it because of Logan."

"Wow. That's truly messed up knowing what we now know of Logan, but moving on. Do you want to do a reading, or do you want to track Boone down?" Cora was in romance mode, to Hazel's delight.

"Both?"

"Just what I was thinking. But tarot first. Also . . ." Cora pulled a bottle of red wine out of her bag and placed it on the island with a large grin. "I brought wine."

"Um, Cora, we don't drink wine. It gives me heartburn, and it gives you migraines."

"Someone sent it to me for helping her with her costume, and it seemed so perfect, tarot and wine," Cora said dreamily.

"It does sound perfect." Hazel had to agree.

"But we're not drinking it, are we?"

"Absolutely not."

Cora sighed, nodding in agreement, placing it back

in her bag. "Jack'll drink it. That man can still digest anything, the lucky bastard." Motioning back to the tarot decks, she said, "Pick a deck."

Hazel examined each and every deck, most of which were oracle cards that had some kind of Celtic theme to them, but finally she picked her favorite. It was a classic tarot deck that used to always work for her back in their twenties. One reading in particular she remembered that told her Logan might not be the right person for her. But she'd ignored that completely. The artwork of each card were photos of beautiful quilts that the creator had made herself. Grams used to sew quilts, so Hazel felt a special bond with the cards. And the reason she didn't have a deck of her own was because this one actually used to be her deck. When the cards had given her what she construed as a "faulty" reading about Logan, she'd given them to Cora since they still seemed to be "working" for her.

Time to reconnect with the deck.

Cora nodded in approval. "Good choice. You want to shuffle?"

Hazel shuffled the cards thoroughly, then spread them out on the island, swirling them around until she felt a connection to a card, then picked it up. When she'd chosen three, she handed them to Cora and gathered the leftover cards in a stack, placing them to the side.

Cora spread the three cards facedown in front of her, then flipped over the first one. "Eight of wands. That's the 'signals' card." Picking up the compendium book, Cora read aloud, "Take action and do it now. Initiate contact. Time to respond."

Hazel's whole body surged with an electric charge. "Um, hello?"

Smiling, Cora tilted her head, thoughtful. "Yes, but this could still be about neighbor guy."

Ugh. Would she let it go already? "Cora. He literally rejected me. After *kissing*! It was a little humiliating. Which is why Grams sent that dream last night. Next card." She needed to shut down any romantic Ethan talk. Friends. They were just going to be friends.

By the slight frown on Cora's face, Hazel could see she didn't look convinced, but she lifted the next card without bringing Ethan up again.

Nine of pentacles.

Hazel knew that card well, and she couldn't help but smile. "Ooo, a money card. I definitely could use that."

"Nine of pentacles. Yeah. That's a good one." She flipped to the page. "Financial independence, self-reliance, abundance, unexpected source of income."

"You think that could be about my plant shop? Technically, Ethan was my first customer last night. He paid me in Oreos and hot chocolate, but still." Hazel hoped the card was a sign she was on the right path for financial freedom.

"Are you kidding me with the Oreos and hot chocolate? That's adorable." Cora sighed as if she wanted to live the date herself.

Not helping.

"Cora."

"Sorry, we'll focus on the plant shop. Yes, makes

sense. With Ethan as your first customer and Roberta waiting in the wings with all her studio exec pet-owning friends, I think it's a good sign. It's also a new venture as well, which could go back to the eight of wands. I'm liking this reading for you. Last card." Cora flipped it over.

Ace of hearts.

Hazel's hand flew to her mouth. "That's the 'new love' card." She had wanted that card with Logan when she'd first asked about him.

Nodding, Cora read from the book, "New beginnings, new love, birth of new feelings. You are open on a new level." She smiled at Hazel. "You couldn't get a more perfect card."

Hazel grabbed her laptop and opened it, typing in Boone's full name. "Okay, Boone. Where are you?"

Cora walked around to see the screen herself.

On screen was Hazel's Google search of "Boone Franklin."

"That's seriously a hideous name." Cora shook her head.

"Stop."

Pages of Boone Franklins.

"Apparently, there are a lot of them," Cora observed.

"Let's look at images and go that way," Hazel suggested.

As she clicked on images, a flood of pictures of Boones young and old filled the screen. Scrolling down, Hazel stopped when she saw him.

Older than her dream, but definitely her Boone.

"There he is."

"He's cute," Cora conceded.

"Right?" Hazel's stomach fluttered.

She clicked on the image, which took her to his Facebook page.

"You want to message him?" Cora raised her eyebrows conspiratorially.

It suddenly hit Hazel that this was real and happening. "Is this dumb?"

Cora turned Hazel to face her by placing her hands on her upper arms. "No. You never got to see what could have happened. This is your chance."

Looking in her best friend's eyes, Hazel knew that she was right.

Okay, Boone. Let's see what you're up to.

Chapter 9
Ethan

I don't need a therapist. Okay, I need a therapist.

Ethan sat on his couch in full coma mode waiting for Mateo and Austin to arrive. He hadn't had any energy to dress himself, so he was still in his boxers and T-shirt, but for the sake of company he tossed on his Obi-Wan Kenobi terry cloth robe. He figured he needed some Jedi mojo after the disaster he created last night.

Having the sudden urge for sugar, Ethan leaned forward and grabbed a leftover Oreo from the abandoned tray.

Before he could have another spiral of self-loathing, the doorbell rang.

Jumping to his feet, Ethan hurried to the door and opened it.

Mateo and Austin stood in the doorway, Austin holding a box of Krispy Kreme.

"My saviors." Ethan only had eyes for the donuts, but he meant it for Mateo and Austin too.

Knowing his friend well, Austin handed over the box, which Ethan took gratefully.

"Come on in. You want some Oreos with your donuts?" Ethan waved them inside.

Shaking his head, Mateo walked into the house followed closely by Austin. "Oreos? This must be bad."

Ethan had met Mateo over twenty-five years ago, back when Ethan thought he'd like working on a movie set (he needed to know what set was like if he planned on becoming the next Tarantino, after all). Mateo was a line producer and hired Ethan as a production assistant, and pretty much regretted it immediately. Though Ethan's ineptitude made for enough laughs that the two became inseparable as friends, Mateo never hired him again.

He couldn't really blame Mateo. Back then, GPS didn't exist for an everyday consumer. Cell phones weren't even common. Everyone had a pager. The only way to get around Los Angeles was through something called a Thomas Guide, which was basically a map in book form, which made it easier to track streets and plan out routes. Easy for people who weren't geographically challenged like Ethan. He never could figure out the Thomas Guide, and on his first day as a production assistant he was tasked to make a quick errand to a vendor in Hollywood to pick up a few items. Two hours later, he was in freeway traffic almost to Long Beach, thirty miles away from Hollywood. Needless to say, Mateo fired him as soon as he got back, but he felt so bad for him, he took him out for drinks.

And the rest was history.

Mateo moved up the ranks to hot shot executive producer, and that was when he met Austin, a set designer for a TV show pilot Mateo was producing. That was ten years ago, and they moved in together almost immediately. Love at first sight, Mateo always said dreamily, and it must have been true because the couple had been inseparable from their first date. Thankfully, Austin and Ethan hit it off on their first meeting.

Opening up the box of donuts next to the tray of Oreos, Ethan grabbed one and sat back on the couch, biting into its deliciousness. Normally, he'd do the seven seconds in the microwave to make the Krispy Kreme the perfect ooey-gooey perfection, but he didn't have it in him today. The room-temperature crispy glaze satisfied his sweet tooth nicely at the moment. His bowels would pay for it later, but he didn't care. One thing that no one told him about aging: you can no longer digest anything properly, or at least not the good stuff.

Austin grabbed both a donut and a couple of Oreos and sat back in the recliner next to the couch. He received a side-eye from Mateo.

"What?" Austin seemed affronted. "He offered."

Mateo let it go, not partaking in any sweets, and focused on Ethan, sitting down next to him. "So what's going on?"

With his mouth full of donut, Ethan cried out, "I met *the one*!"

Mateo and Austin shared a look of exasperation, as if they'd dealt with "this version" of Ethan before, but it was

Mateo who spoke. "Yes, you said that on the phone last night. But is this *the one* like the other *the ones*? Because you have a pattern of picking women who are emotionally unavailable or unavailable unavailable."

"What are you, my therapist?" Ethan asked, feeling a little triggered.

Under Austin's breath, he said, "You need one."

"I heard that," Ethan grumbled.

"You were meant to." Austin smiled back. Can smiles be sarcastic?

Mateo continued, "Or you run away from the healthy ones."

"Yeah, he's done that too," Austin echoed. "Remember Jackie?"

Mateo laughed. "She was the one that Ethan thought was cursed?"

Ethan interrupted defensively, "From the day I met her, I got a flat tire, then the next day I lost a gig, then after our first date, I slammed my finger into the car door. I *had* to break up with her."

Rolling his eyes, Mateo said, "And what happened the day *after* you broke up?"

"I don't know." But he did.

"Your roof caved in."

"It was residual. The universe didn't get the message that I broke up with her yet." Ethan crossed his arms.

"You keep telling yourself that." Austin gave his uh-huh-right face.

"You're not helping." Ethan directed his glare at Austin. Standing up, Ethan ran his hands over his head anxiously. "But that's exactly what I did. We had a perfect moment, and I immediately friend-zoned her and ran. Or she shut the door in my face, and I stood there, but metaphorically I ran."

Mateo sighed but still had the shrewd look of an investigator. "And this woman isn't a murderer, thief, mentally unstable, stalker . . ."

He listed off pretty much all of Ethan's exes, except maybe the murderer one, but honestly, Ethan couldn't rule it out. "No," Ethan interrupted him. "She's none of those things."

"We're not going to be dealing with another Trixi-pocalypse?" Mateo prodded.

"Her name is Hazel, so no." Ethan didn't want to think about Trixie. She had put a key logger on his phone to access all his logins and passwords, then proceeded to take over his social media accounts and post pictures of herself. In the descriptions, she'd pretended to be Ethan gushing about how she was the most perfect girlfriend and how much he loved her. He had initially thought it was kind of sweet, until she used the same key logger to hack into his bank accounts and drain him dry.

But Hazel was the opposite of Trixie. "Hazel moved in across the street. She's Gladys's granddaughter."

Austin tilted his head to the side and raised his eyebrows in memory. "Oh, I miss Gladys. She had the best cookies."

"Right?" Ethan exclaimed. "That's why I have the Oreos!"

Mateo and Austin shared a confused look at that last

statement, but Mateo moved on. "Why can't you just 'un-friend-zone' her?"

"I can't go over there!" Ethan yelled. What was this? Logic? That was insane.

Austin rolled his eyes and took another bite of his donut. "Seriously, you need a therapist. I have a good one."

"No. I don't need therapy. I can do this on my own." Ethan didn't need a shrink. He just needed Hazel.

"Though I agree with Austin about you needing a therapist, you can do *this* on your own, if you go over there and tell her you like her," Mateo encouraged.

"I really can't do that." Ethan's terror reached an all-time high, and he was pretty sure a panic attack was soon to follow.

Under his breath again, Austin said, "I have the number right here on my phone."

Mateo stood with Ethan, holding his arms, looking him in the eye. "I don't know if this woman is *the one*. You have questionable taste. But knowing she's Gladys's granddaughter is a point in her favor. Now get your butt over there and tell her you want to take her out for coffee."

Coffee. Ethan could do coffee. Somehow, giving him a specific mission made Ethan start to relax a bit. "Yeah. Yeah. You're right. Coffee," he repeated. "No big deal. We had Oreos and cocoa last night. Coffee is even better."

Austin snagged another Oreo. "Oreos and hot chocolate? Too cute."

Convincing himself, Ethan waved at the rattlesnake plant. "She gave me that plant too. And when she saw my ticket collage, we discovered we've seen a dozen movies together since the nineties. I walked her home. She walked me home. I walked her home again. We kissed . . ." Ethan suddenly felt the need to give them all the details. It helped to pump him up for what he knew he needed to do.

Mateo's sighed dreamily. "I'm kind of dying right now. What are you waiting for? Go!"

"And you don't think I need therapy?"

Austin nodded a big yes as he ate his Oreo.

Mateo tilted his head and scrunched his eyes as if he were about to agree with Austin, but then he shook his head. "Not for this. Now go over there!"

Ethan clapped his hands like he was breaking away from a football huddle. "Here I go."

"You should probably change out of your Obi-Wan Kenobi robe and underwear first, though," Austin noted.

"Right."

Changing quickly, and before he could talk himself out of it, Ethan marched over to Hazel's house and knocked on the front door.

I can do this.

I can do this.

I can do this.

The door opened and there she was.

Hazel.

"Oh! Hi, Ethan. Did I forget something at your place?" Hazel asked with a friendly smile.

Say Something.

What did she just ask me?

Words were definitely spoken, but I didn't hear any of them.

Wait. She asked if she forgot something.

"Uh, no. I just wanted . . . I didn't like . . . I . . . I'm sorry . . ."

Words.

It would be helpful to speak ones that made any coherent sense.

Hazel shook her head with another dazzling smile. She was so beautiful.

"Don't even worry about it. I'm actually taking it as a sign," she said cheerfully.

"A sign?" Ethan gulped. He wasn't liking the sound of this.

But Hazel's being suddenly looked like it had been imbued by some kind of magical force. "Yes! I had a dream last night about a guy I worked with fifteen years ago when I was married. I'm going to see if there's anything still there, if you know what I mean," she said playfully.

Ethan's chest tightened. "Oh, that's great." He wasn't prepared for how painful that was to hear.

"So, if we had . . . you know . . . I probably never would have remembered him." Hazel said this in an obvious attempt to make Ethan feel better, but it only nailed him tighter into his coffin.

"Well, I'm glad I could help," he tried to joke, but he was sure his whole demeanor screamed defeat.

But Hazel was apparently too happy in the high of her dream to notice. "We can still be friends though, right? Like you said last night?"

"Absolutely. That's why I came over. To make sure we were good." Lies. But Ethan had to save face.

A woman's voice called from inside of Hazel's house. "Hazel! He messaged you back!"

Hazel gave a small yelp. "I should go. Oreos later?"

"I'd love that." Was it possible for one's chest to collapse in on itself?

Spike ran over from the side yard and head-bumped Ethan's leg. Reaching down, Ethan scratched him affectionately and desperately wanted to hug him to help with his misery. "Hey, buddy."

When Ethan looked back up at Hazel, he could see she still appeared amazed at how much Spike liked him. Then he swore he saw a flash of disappointment.

The woman from inside yelled again, "Hazel!"

Ethan gave Spike one last scratch, then stood back up. "Destiny calls."

Hazel called back to her friend. "Coming!" Then she turned to Ethan. "Yeah."

Spike pranced inside the house as Hazel brought up her hand for a small wave. "See you around." She shut the door.

For the second time in twenty-four hours, Ethan stared at Hazel's closed door.

He had been right.

He'd messed up.

Ruined his only chance with Hazel.

Shuffling away from her house like a zombie, Ethan somehow made it back to his own place. Once inside, he stood in front of his closed front door and groaned.

"How did it go?" Mateo asked, though Ethan could tell from his expression that the two of them could already tell how it went.

Turning to Austin, Ethan said, "I need the name of that therapist."

Pacoima? How far out does he live?

Hazel exited the freeway after passing the "Welcome to Pacoima" sign trying not to think about how far it took them to drive there. Over an hour, and that wasn't even with traffic. Hazel imagined it would be twice that long, maybe even more, during rush hour.

Sitting in the passenger seat, Cora stared out the window. Nothing but strip malls and dead grass on hills. "You really think your soulmate is in Pacoima?"

"Okay, Miss Judgy. There's nothing wrong with Pacoima," Hazel said, but as the GPS led them farther and farther away from civilization, she was soon realizing Boone lived *outside* of Pacoima and not in the city proper.

As if Cora had the power to prove her point, a small fire popped up on a distant hill. "It's like Phoenix lite. And I can say that because I lived in Phoenix. Twice."

"Well, then you of all people should know, sometimes we have to move to a place we don't necessarily want to." Hazel smothered her with logic.

Cora groaned. "His address looks like it's in the middle of nowhere." She looked more carefully at the GPS.

Hazel had to agree. The destination on the map was a dot in a sea of green nothing. "It's fine," Hazel placated, and suddenly realized she was trying to convince herself as well. "Thanks for being my backup." Having Cora there definitely took the edge off of her growing doubts.

"Are you kidding? There's no way I'd let you see this guy alone, especially anyone named Boone."

"You liked Boone on *Lost*," Hazel countered.

"That's only because it was Ian Somerhalder. But his character *Boone* was trying to sleep with his sister. I rest my case," Cora said with finality.

"Well, this Boone is much less incesty. And besides, they were stepsiblings on the show." Hazel couldn't let Cora get the last word in.

Cora made a face in response.

As Hazel drove forward, the scenery grew much more sparse and the road seemed to be getting smaller.

"And you're sure he's not a serial killer?" Cora joked, but Hazel could tell there was a slight twinge of worry there.

"Grams wouldn't have sent me that dream if he was dangerous." *Right?*

"*If* she sent it," Cora argued.

"*And* the reading?" Hazel countered.

"Okay, okay. But I've got my taser in my purse, and I

plan on staying behind him at all times."

"Please don't taser my ex-work husband."

They both laughed.

"I'm not making any promises." Cora tapped her purse for emphasis.

"It says it's right up here." Hazel glanced at the GPS while trying to keep her eyes on the tiny road.

A shipping container sat on the flat of a hill, with an old beat-up Toyota Corolla next to it.

"He still has the same car." Hazel felt a pang of nostalgia.

Then it finally sank in that there was no house, only a shipping container and nothing around as far as the eye could see.

Making eye contact with Cora, she saw that her best friend couldn't hide the horrified expression on her face. "Oh god, we're going to die."

"'Goonies never say die.'"

Cora sighed heavily, then repeated, "'Goonies never say die.'"

"We'll be fine. I messaged him through Facebook, and he's expecting us." Hazel knew she had to at least *look* as confident as possible for Cora to actually exit the car, but inside she was starting to have her doubts.

"Oh, goodie," Cora mumbled under her breath as she opened her passenger door.

They both exited the car and took a moment to stare at the shipping container.

Cora crossed her arms. "Does he seriously live in a shipping container?"

"You saw from his profile. He's really into the environment. That's a good thing."

"You don't have to live in a metal box to save the environment," Cora argued.

"Cora." Hazel had no rebuttal to that, and she kind of wanted to get this over with at this point.

But then he walked out of the shipping container.

Boone.

And Hazel's stomach fluttered in response.

Though he looked a lot different from fifteen years ago, even from his profile of clean-shaven and short hair, it was still the same Boone. Though this Boone had a thick beard, maybe three inches long, curly hair, jeans with a few holes and a plain white T-shirt. He stood at the front door of his shipping container and waved enthusiastically with his signature sweet smile.

Cora softened. "Aside from looking like Charles Manson, he's being really cute."

"See? Grams wouldn't steer me wrong." Hazel waved back to Boone and hurried toward him.

Like a romance novel, Boone ran toward her as well, and when they met in the middle, he lifted her into his arms and spun her around happily.

"It's so good to see you!" Hazel said through the second spin.

"I've missed you," Boone said with an almost choke to his voice as he set her down on her feet, but he was smiling ear to ear.

"I've missed you too." Hazel made their eyes meet.

Cora arrived at their sides, and Hazel stepped aside

for her. "Boone, this is Cora."

Reaching down, Boone squeezed Cora in a bear hug as if he knew her too.

"Oh, uh, hello. Nice to meet you," Cora huffed out from the tight embrace.

Boone pulled away still smiling, then stared at Hazel with sparkling affectionate eyes.

Hazel noticed Cora's eyebrow rise in appreciation. Okay, maybe she was coming around.

Waving toward the front door, Boone led the way toward the shipping container. "Come on in."

Cora's expression of appreciation soon turned to dread as they walked toward the container, and true to her word, she trailed behind Hazel and Boone.

Opening the metal door, Boone stood to the side for both of them to enter, which Hazel did immediately, but Cora stopped in the doorway, motioning for Boone to go first. "After you," she said strongly.

Boone gave her a friendly smile. "I assure you, I'm not a serial killer."

"Would you really admit it if you were?"

"Fair point. I'll leave the door open, and I'll go in first. Better?" Boone kicked a door stopper under the door.

"Better." Cora nodded, then followed Boone inside.

Hazel had been so focused on the two of them, she hadn't noticed the interior of the shipping container.

It almost took her breath away.

Like an Instagram post for tiny homes, it had all new furnishings and beautifully painted walls with giant abstract art pieces. The entire opposite wall from the door was a folding glass door that led to a stained wooden deck. There was a small kitchenette to the left, a round dining table to the right, and an antique room divider separating the queen-sized bed also on the right.

Cora's eyes widened. "Wow. This place is actually nice."

Boone laughed. "Thank you. I did all the work myself."

Hazel reared her head back slightly. "That's amazing, Boone. I had no idea you were so handy."

"I wasn't back when we knew each other. I learned as I went, so there's a lot of 'oopsies' that I made along the way." His chin dipped.

"Well, it looks incredible," Hazel gushed.

"Can I get you guys anything to drink?" Boone offered.

"Sure. Water if you have it." Hazel was suddenly parched.

"Nothing for me, thanks," Cora said, and Hazel knew it was because she was making sure Hazel didn't get poisoned because that was how Cora's brain worked.

Boone poured Hazel a glass of water from a contraption on the counter clearly labeled reverse osmosis and gave it to Hazel.

Their hands touched, and Hazel's shy smile matched Boone's.

"Thanks," she said as her fingers still lingered on his.

"You're welcome." His eyes danced as he stared at her.

Pulling his hand away, he smiled. "So what brings

you here after all these years?"

Hazel tucked her hair behind her ear. "I just thought we left things unfinished. And I had a dream about you last night. So I figured I'd reach out."

Translation of Cora's face: *Don't overshare*.

Boone stepped closer to Hazel, as if he wanted to take her in his arms, but he kept his distance. "We did kind of leave things unfinished. And you said in your message you're divorced now?"

Cora mouthed, "You told him that?"

Hazel answered both of them at once. "Yeah."

"I'd like to take you to dinner sometime," Boone asked quietly.

Nodding slightly, even Cora seemed pleased by that.

"That sounds nice," Hazel responded and meant it. Through the thick beard and wild hair was the guy she never let herself consider because she'd been with Logan. Though she could admit now that there had been a few times where she'd let her mind wander back then.

Hazel and Boone couldn't keep their eyes off each other, and Hazel wondered if her eyes were twinkling as much as his were.

Cora cleared her throat. "No TV? Or does one of these paintings turn into one?"

Hazel pried her eyes away from Boone, and he did the same, answering Cora, "No TV. I got tired of all the lies. Figured I'd get my news from the source instead. Stay a lot saner that way."

"Yeah, seriously. Fake news is the worst," Hazel agreed, and tried to ignore the word *source* as a red flag.

"Exactly." Boone nodded emphatically.

"What's the source that you get your information from?" Cora obviously didn't have the same motivations for ignoring red flags.

And part of Hazel wanted to change the subject. She was enjoying seeing Boone so much.

But Boone seemed excited to share. He nodded toward the folding glass doors. "Out here."

Hazel and Cora walked over to the glass doors and looked out.

A hundred feet away was a ten-foot-diameter satellite dish slowly rotating in different positions.

"Whoa," Hazel and Cora said at the same time.

It reminded Hazel of the old dishes rich people used to use for cable back in the eighties. Her neighbor had one, and she'd been so jealous, until she realized he couldn't get MTV. Then she was perfectly happy with her parents' cable package.

Boone stared at the dish proudly. "And I receive all the information it gives me here." He stepped over to the room divider and folded it to the wall.

Next to the bed was a small desk with a computer tower underneath and two monitors on the desk's surface, all displaying running text and open chat boxes.

"Is that legal?" Cora eyed the monitors suspiciously.

"Information is free, but the billionaires would like you to hear their own agenda. They're the real leaders of the world, and it only benefits them to keep the masses uninformed and divided. My work here will stop them. One way or another." Boone leaned down to check something on the screen, typing in a chat box.

Cora and Hazel proceeded to have an entire conversation on facial expressions alone.

Cora: *We need to leave.*

Hazel: *He's not exactly wrong.*

Cora: *One way or another? What the hell does that mean?*

Hazel: *It could mean anything.*

Cora: *Are you kidding me? We're in a shipping container in the middle of nowhere!*

Hazel: *Fine.*

Hazel cursed to herself. She'd said she wouldn't ignore red flags; it was why she had quickly snapped things shut with Ethan, so why was she already making excuses for a guy she hadn't seen in fifteen years that, sure, she had chemistry with, but he was obviously going through some phase in life.

Boone finished typing, chuckled, then stood up straight.

Cora placed her hand on her mouth as if she'd remembered something. "Hazel!"

Jumping slightly, Boone turned to Cora.

"I just remembered. We have that art opening for Roger tonight."

With Boone's eyes on Cora, Hazel raised her eyebrows, mouthing, "Roger?"

Motioning toward the door, Cora shrugged apologetically. "And being in Pacoima with traffic? We might not even make it if we leave now."

"Oh, shoot," Hazel played along. "We don't want to

disappoint Roger. He's been preparing for this show all year."

"And he's such a good guy. And a great artist." Cora dug in deeper.

Hazel feigned disappointment to Boone. "So sorry to cut it short."

Boone touched Hazel's arm. "No worries. We can still do dinner this week."

"You know where to message me." Hazel was already composing the polite rejection message in her head. *Grams? Why did you send me that dream?*

With a quick hug, or quick because Hazel pulled away fast—Boone had wanted to linger—they walked out of the shipping container and directly into the car.

As Hazel started up the engine, Boone waved from his doorway.

She waved back, then backed out on the road and started putting some distance between them.

"Please tell me you're not seriously going to date him." Cora obviously needed verbal confirmation that Hazel was officially uninterested.

Which made Hazel think more carefully about the dream she thought her grandmother sent her. "Now that I think about it, technically my dream started out with blurred-face Dream Guy, then switched locations to the old office and Boone."

Cora swung her head to Hazel, appalled. "You're saying blurred guy didn't actually turn into Boone?"

"Not technically, no. I was talking to Dream Guy, then suddenly I was watching the day I left the company and my goodbye with Boone." Why had she ignored that fact before?

"Hazel!" Cora's nostrils flared. "Now you've got a conspiracy-theorist-potential-billionaire-terrorist in your life!"

"I'll be fine. I'll message him that I'm freaked out and not ready to date yet." Hazel tried to calm her friend down.

Cora crossed her arms. "Next dream, you're telling me every detail before we do *anything*."

Hazel perked up at that. "You think there will be another dream?"

Cora shook her head, smiling at Hazel. "Yes, my hopeless romantic friend, I do."

Chapter 11
Ethan

Where has therapy been all my life?

Ethan sat in his car, staring at the building of his new therapist.

Jane Jerome. What kind of name was that? It sounded like a comic book character. Which, now that he thought about it, sounded kind of cool.

Cool name or not, Ethan may have thought he needed therapy, but now that he was here, he definitely did not.

But he needed validation if he was going to drive off, so he called Mateo.

"I thought you were in therapy." Mateo's voice sounded confused.

"I was about to, but I don't really need it, right? I'm okay without it." Yeah. What had he been thinking? Why waste this woman's time, when she could help someone who actually needed her.

"You do need it. You've needed it for years. You've finally made the step. I'm proud of you. Now, get your butt in her office."

Ethan's internal groaning almost made it to the surface, but he managed to hold it back. "But . . ."

"No buts." Mateo stopped him.

"I . . ." Ethan began.

"No I's." Mateo cut him off again. "Ethan. You need this. Deep down you know you do. It's not just about your neighbor, it's about you. It's time."

Each word was like a punch.

"All right," he finally uttered.

"You're just scared." Mateo's tone had softened.

"I don't know about that . . ." Ethan started.

"Ethan."

Ethan stopped. "Yeah, I'm scared."

"I was scared the first time I went to therapy too, but when I tell you it changed my life, I'm not exaggerating."

Mateo's words settled into Ethan's brain. "And that's when you met Austin?"

Ethan could imagine Mateo nodding as he said, "That's when I met Austin."

"And therapy helped you with that?"

"Yes, it did. Whether it's your neighbor . . ."

"Hazel."

". . . Hazel, or someone in your future, this will help you be your best you."

Looking at the clock, Ethan had two minutes until his appointment. "Okay, I'm going to do it. I got this." Ethan pumped himself up.

"You *do* got this. Call me after."

"Will do." Ethan hung up the phone and exited the car before he could chicken out.

Because Mateo had been right, his entire denial about needing therapy stemmed from fear.

And he was tired of it.

It was exhausting being afraid all the time.

And if this could help him? How could he say no?

Walking directly into the building, he headed for Jane Jerome's first-level suite.

He got there a lot faster than he expected.

Now that he stood in front of the door, he found he was having trouble reaching for the doorknob.

I got this. He repeated in his head. *I got this.*

Grabbing the knob, he twisted and pushed the door open.

A waiting room.

Ethan didn't know why he expected to immediately be walking inside a room with a couch he'd lie down on and Jane Jerome sitting in a leather recliner, with pad and pencil, ready to take notes.

Nope.

Four empty chairs, a TV playing a babbling brook, a door that led to what Ethan could only assume were the actual offices, and yoga music in the speakers.

He should be outraged by the obvious manipulation, but he felt too soothed and calm to do anything about it.

Stupid babbling brook.

Sitting down in one of the chairs, Ethan noticed a square panel on the wall next to the door. Staring at it closer, it was a list of therapists with a button next to each, and a sign above indicated to press the respective therapist's button.

Never one to turn down a good button press, Ethan hit Jane Jerome's button, then sat back down.

Only seconds had passed when the door opened to reveal a woman in her thirties, with her hair tied back in a ponytail, wearing jeans and a blouse with flowers on it. A lot more casual than Ethan expected, but also made the situation feel a lot less pressurey.

"Ethan Rhodes?"

"Yeah, that's me," Ethan muttered nervously. Why did he feel like he was about to see the principal?

"Hi. I'm Jane Jerome, pleasure to meet you." She smiled warmly and placed her hand out.

Ethan shook it probably a little too vigorously, though Jane didn't react either way.

He followed her through a hallway and back to an office with two plushy chairs facing each other. There was a five-foot standing plant in the corner, a coffee table between the chairs, and little side tables next to each chair with coasters for drinks.

"Please, sit." Jane motioned to the chair on the left.

Ethan did as he was told, and she sat across from him.

"So what brings you here, Ethan?" Jane asked politely.

Shifting in his seat, Ethan tried to speak his thoughts. "I dunno. My friends said I should come here . . . Girls." Eloquent.

Jane nodded, giving Ethan a reassuring expression. "*Women*, not *girls*."

Oh, right. That may have sounded bad. "Yes, women," he clarified.

"Tell me what you'd like to work on? Is it with a current relationship? Or do you want to work on your past behaviors?"

"Both?" Ethan answered honestly, then panic shot through him like a lightning bolt. He almost stood up and ran but instead said, "I think this was a mistake. I should go."

Jane made sure she maintained eye contact with Ethan, which was both comforting and a little unsettling. *Stop looking at me!*

"You came here for a reason. That means somewhere inside you, you know you need help, or at least someone to talk to and work things through. I can help you. Let me at least try. If after this session you still feel the same, we can part ways and never see each other again," Jane told him calmly.

"That's dramatic." Ethan squirmed.

"It was meant to put you at ease." Jane smiled reassuringly. "Why do you think you interpreted it as dramatic?"

Oh boy.

Therapy was starting. She was asking questions. And Ethan didn't know how to answer.

After an excruciatingly long pause, Jane finally spoke again. "Ethan. I only want to help you sort some things out. This isn't an interrogation. I don't want you to feel threatened in any way. I also don't want you to feel defensive."

"*You're* defensive." What was he? Five? Taking a deep, calming breath, Ethan said, "I'm sorry. The unknown scares me, I guess." That was about as honest as he could muster at the moment.

Jane's shoulders relaxed. "It scares most people. Do relationships scare you?"

"Good ones do. Yes," he admitted.

"What do you mean by *good*? You mean healthy?" Jane clarified.

"Yeah. When I can see a future with someone, I run. And now I've met someone . . . Hazel . . . that I think is really special, and I panicked."

"Okay, let's try to break it down even further. In this new situation, what happened that triggered your panic?"

"I kissed her. And it was the most mind-blowing kiss I've ever experienced, and before I could stop myself, I told her I wanted to be friends."

Did Jane just flinch?

I'm pretty sure she flinched.

"But what made you want to push her away?" Jane prodded.

What *did* make him want to push her away? "I don't know."

"That's okay. You're not going to figure everything out in one therapy session. But maybe we can uncover a bit of why you felt like you needed to distance yourself from someone you obviously like."

"My first girlfriend cheated on me?" Ethan had always suspected this was where all his relationship trauma had started.

"You said it like a question," Jane observed. "Do you think that's why you push away healthy relationships? Fear of being cheated on again?"

"Maybe?" He phrased it like a question again. He needed to stop doing that. "I mean. I think I pick unhealthy relationships, usually obsessive ones, because it's like a meter for me, of knowing for sure that they like me. Like if they can be that possessive, then they *must* like me."

"But on that logic, Hazel kissed you, and you said it was great, so isn't that an indication that she likes you back?"

Why did everyone insist on using logic? Didn't they know Ethan ran on irrational fears?

And it hit him in that moment.

"What are you thinking? Your whole body shifted." Jane eyed him curiously.

"I was thinking how my entire way of thinking always runs on fear. My family is a goal driven family. They're not affectionate in any way. We don't even hug. I think I'm always searching for the affection I wanted as a kid . . . heck, as an adult, that they aren't capable of giving me," Ethan sputtered.

"Ethan. That's pretty profound." Jane sat back in her chair. "It sounds like you've been doing a lot of self-work on your own to recognize something like that."

"Just self-help books," he mumbled. Ethan had thought the countless self-help books he'd read in the last couple of years could be a substitute for therapy, but now that he was here, he realized it was like reading a textbook without a teacher. And he needed a teacher.

He knew in that instant it would be Jane.

"They've obviously helped you. I think your family dynamic is something we should explore more." She shifted forward. "I'm going to give you some exercises that might help you overcome these deep-rooted fears of rejection you have."

"Rejection?"

Jane nodded. "You're a sensitive person, Ethan, and that's a great thing. But to grow up with a family that doesn't show or tell you how they feel about you, you processed it as rejection. And because you see so much potential with Hazel, your fear triggered you to reject her first before she could do it to you."

So many thoughts began clicking in Ethan's brain to the point where he couldn't move.

Jane handed him a box of tissue.

Was his nose running?

Then he felt a drip of water on his jeans.

A tear.

His eyes were leaking.

Taking the tissues, he wiped his cheeks.

"Next time you talk to your parents, I want you to think of their emotional unavailability as a phobia. Like you wouldn't be upset or angry if they were scared of spiders, right? Sometimes, just reframing how we see people can help us to see them in a new light."

"We have our scheduled weekly call tonight, so I can try it then."

"Good. Remember, if you want to tell them how

you feel about something, go for it. All cards on the table. Then when they react, or more likely, don't react, remember that this is their phobia."

Feelings? His dad probably won't know what to say, and his mom will assume he needs money. Even though he had never asked them for money in his entire adult life.

"And for Hazel, even though it may feel uncomfortable for you, I want you to tell her two things about yourself that you'd be scared to otherwise. You're trying to strive for emotional vulnerability here, so make them personal."

Gulp. "Okay."

After that, the rest of the hour went faster than Ethan could have ever expected, and before he knew it, Jane said, "That's our time. But I think we made good progress." She stood up and placed her hand out for Ethan to shake.

But he hugged her instead, which he realized in the moment was highly inappropriate.

Jane seemed to understand, though, as she gently pulled out of the hug. "See you next week?"

Ethan wiped his cheeks clean. "Wait. I have to wait a whole week?"

Chapter 12
Hazel
Surprise visit

Hazel had yet to tackle the second bedroom, but she was determined to put in a new showerhead today.

By herself.

No help.

No Logan.

No Cora.

Just Hazel.

The old one was fine, but at her age, water pressure was a cheap form of back therapy. It was why she had heated car seats as well. Her last back pull (from the dangerous act of picking up one of Spike's toys off the floor) had put her out for a week, but an hour drive each day with the heat cranked on the seat always seemed to help. For a little while anyway. At this point, she'd take what she could get, and this showerhead sounded like a back massaging dream. And with the amount of time she'd be spending in the greenhouse, her neck was going to need it as well.

With a bag of tools at her feet, full of every tool her and Logan had purchased over the years, she had literally no idea which one to use.

Time for a YouTube video.

Pulling the site up on her phone, she typed into the search engine: *how to install showerhead.*

Over a hundred options popped up, which made her feel not so alone in this world.

She picked the most watched video and hit play.

First, she paused on the "tools you'll need" frame and dug into the tool bag, trying to find anything that looked somewhat similar. After pulling out a couple of different types of wrenches, Hazel was sure she could make one of them work.

Here went nothing.

Reaching up to the showerhead, Hazel fastened the wrench around the base and turned counterclockwise just like the man in the video said to.

With a creak and a pop, the showerhead came loose, followed by a small spill of water.

"'I will triumph!'" Hazel quoted from the rom-com she and Cora had watched endless amounts of times in the nineties, *French Kiss*. "Okay, next." She placed the old showerhead on the floor and yanked up the new one. "Now, I have to screw this one on. Easy."

After a few turns and a good tighten with the wrench, Hazel stepped back to admire her work.

Spike wandered in with curious eyes.

"You here for the test?"

Spike snorted, then walked out the door.

"No faith."

Hazel reached for the water lever and turned on the water.

A whole lot of glugging followed by a loud hiss. "That doesn't sound good."

Boom!

The showerhead popped off the pipe and slammed to the bottom of the tub.

Her phone buzzed in her jeans pocket.

Pulling it out, it was a text from Logan: *I'm out front. Rang the doorbell, but no answer. You home?*

Hazel groaned. Part of her wanted to see him, and part of her wanted to pretend she wasn't home. But she texted: *be there in a sec.*

Deep breath.

Hazel left the bathroom and walked to the front door, opening it.

Logan.

She hadn't seen him in a while.

As he stood there with a tentative smile, Hazel felt a mixture of emotions. On one hand, Logan was familiar, her best friend of twenty-two years, and on the other hand, he was a complete stranger, like the distance she'd feel with an acquaintance or coworker. It was difficult to wrap her head around.

"Hey, what's going on?" she asked.

"I just thought I'd stop by and see how it's going."

Logan took a step back, unsure.

It broke her heart a little, even though she didn't want it to. He was unsure with *her*. *Her!*

"You can come in. I'm a little busy. I'm putting in a new showerhead." And failing. But she didn't say that part.

"You want some help?"

No.

"Sure."

Hazel nodded him inside and led him back to the bathroom.

Spike wandered over from the kitchen.

"Hey, Spike." Logan kneeled down and held out his hand for Spike to smell.

Cautiously walking over, Spike sniffed Logan's fingers a few times, gave him the tiniest of head-bumps, then ran like he was being chased.

"Endlessly entertaining as usual." Logan laughed. "At least I got a couple of sniffs."

"That's more than Cora got the other day."

"Spike's only ever really loved you."

And Ethan.

She shook the thought from her head, then focused on the abandoned showerhead in the tub.

"Did it pop off?" Logan asked with knowing smile.

It used to be cute, but now it was annoying, but she didn't lie. "Yeah. I need to put it on tighter."

Taking over, which was exactly the opposite of what Hazel wanted today, Logan grabbed the wrench. "I can help." He picked up the showerhead and twisted it onto the pipe, tightening it with the wrench.

Exactly what Hazel had done.

Turning on the water, Hazel inwardly cringed when it flowed out of the showerhead.

She knew she should be happy, but it annoyed her, it frustrated her, it made her feel like she couldn't do it on her own.

Hiss.

POP!

The showerhead flew off the pipe and smashed into the wall before it clunked back into the tub.

"Holy!" Hazel jumped from the shock of it.

Turning off the water, a surge of glee filled Hazel. Why did she suddenly have the urge to na, na, na, na, na, na Logan?

But instead of getting angry like he would have in the past, he actually laughed. "We really suck at this."

"Yeah," she admitted and laughed as well.

After a moment, Logan glanced at the showerhead. "Why didn't you call someone to do it?"

"I wanted to do it myself. I need to get used to that. I can't rely on you for things like this anymore."

"Hazel, when have I ever done anything like this myself? I'm the opposite of a handyman."

Hazel paused.

He was right. Logan never fixed anything around the house. He always hired someone else to do it.

She'd been so focused on doing it herself, she'd forgotten that Logan had always paid for help.

"You want me to call one of my guys?" Logan asked.

With a deep sigh, Hazel said, “Sure, thanks.” Her stomach wrenched, and she felt like she’d failed again. What was that? But she knew what it was. She was letting Logan have the power back, letting him make decisions, letting him take control. “Actually, Logan?”

“Yeah?”

“I’ll call someone myself.”

And from those simple words, a weight lifted off her. She didn’t need Logan to solve her problems. She could do it herself.

“Oh, okay. You sure?”

“Definitely.” She’d never been more sure in her life.

“All right, well, I really was just stopping in to say hi. Everything okay? Aside from the showerhead?”

“Yeah, everything’s good. It was nice seeing you.”

“You too.” An awkward moment. “Okay, I’m going to take off. Sorry about the showerhead.” Logan leaned down and hugged her.

She hugged him back. It was actually nice. “Bye, Logan.”

Without waiting to be walked to the door, Logan left, leaving Hazel staring at the mess that was her bathroom.

Spike showed up out of nowhere to rub his face against her leg. “Hey, buddy. Let’s clean up and get some treats.”

He happily meowed at that.

Hazel quickly got dressed, then went to the kitchen with a treat-promised Spike on her tail.

Laying a handful of treats on the floor for him,

Hazel sat on a barstool behind the island and slid over her laptop. Opening it up, she remembered why she'd closed it yesterday. She'd thought she'd set up her website using a drag-and-drop company and officially start her plant store.

But for some reason she couldn't motivate herself to do it last night, and today was no different.

Doubts flooded her brain to the point of paralysis.

And now she simply stared.

Hazel didn't even have a name yet, so how could she set up a website? She'd need to buy the domain first. But the domain of what?

Pet plants?

Plants for pets?

Safe plants?

All crap.

Thudding her head on the island, she regretted it immediately.

Ouch.

Growing plants was a hobby, not a business, right?

What had she been thinking?

I make no money.

Hazel was tired of being reliant on Logan's money. She knew logically it was "their" money since they'd been married twenty-two years, but it never felt that way to her.

How did I get here? she questioned. Hazel had been working since she was twelve, first as a babysitter, then at fifteen fast food, Home Depot at seventeen, and she'd never stopped until seven years ago.

Why didn't I get some kind of remote job? But what? Hazel had a horticulture degree, and she'd found that it hadn't helped her much in the job department.

Spike jumped up on the island and bumped his head on her cheek.

My lord, he was cute.

"Hey, buddy." Hazel scratched his head.

A wave of calm suddenly flowed through her.

Where did that come from?

Looking around as if somehow someone had pushed the emotion into her body, Hazel turned back to her computer.

"It's more than a hobby. Why do I always doubt myself?" Hazel said aloud, and another wave of calm hit her.

No, it wasn't calm. It was *faith*.

Faith that she could do this. That she needed to shove all her doubts and fears aside and try. Really try.

"You know what, Spike? I'm going to do it. I'm starting the store today. I've got seven mature plants here and ready to go. New beginnings. Like the tarot card said."

Spike thumped his nose under her chin in response.

"We just need a good name."

Flopping on his side, Spike reached out to Hazel with his paw.

"How are your paws so cute!" She began talking to him as if he were a baby. "You're the most perfect creature ever to exist. Yes, you are. Absolutely paw-fect." She laughed at her own dad joke.

Then she thought for a second.

"Spike. That's it! Paw-fect Plants!" Hazel quickly typed frantically into her computer to make sure it didn't already exist. It didn't! Quickly, she secured the domain name and linked it to the drag-and-drop website builder.

Pulling recent pictures of the plants off her phone and transferring them to the laptop, Hazel uploaded them to the site, using a fun template the builder provided. She added prices and some rough copy, but it was publishable. Not the greatest, definitely rudimentary, but publishable.

So hit publish.

Panicked adrenaline flowed through her.

"I'll make the banners later and make it look pretty. Yeah. The important thing is to open the shop."

So hit publish.

Swallowing hard, taking a deep breath, Hazel hovered the mouse over the publish button and clicked.

It was done.

Up.

Ready for sales.

Breathing in through her nose and out through her mouth, Hazel began to calm down. "Work in progress, right?"

Then she really looked at her new website.

There it was. Done. And it was kind of cute.

A smile grew not only on her face but from the inside as well. "We did it, Spike." She scratched his head.

She did it.

And it felt good.

A knock at the front door.

Perfect timing. Hazel needed to pry her eyes away from the website, or she'd be staring at it all day.

Opening the front door, she couldn't help the slight thrill she felt when she saw Ethan standing there.

"Ethan, hi."

Like clockwork, Spike immediately arrived at the door and stretched his arms on Ethan's leg.

"Hey, Spike."

Spike lowered himself and head-bumped Ethan's leg.

Shaking her head at the cuteness, Hazel said, "What's going on?"

"I was just coming back from ther . . . a meeting and wanted to say hi." Ethan gave a little awkward wave.

Which Hazel was trying to convince herself wasn't completely adorable. "Come on in. I can make us cookies. I can't promise they'll be as good as Grams's, but I am using her recipe." She needed to stop seeing him as adorable. Friend. He was a friend. Ethan was not interested in her in the least. They liked each other, they had their love of movies in common, and that was it.

"Um, yes, please."

They both walked to the kitchen, and Ethan sat on the stool Hazel had previously occupied while Hazel began gathering the ingredients and supplies for chocolate chip cookies.

"So how did it go with your dream guy?" Ethan asked, his voice unsure.

Hazel pulled out the flour and placed it on the island. She laughed and tried to form an expression that fully indicated how it went with Boone.

"Ooo, that good huh?" Ethan laughed.

"It was . . . well . . . not what I expected. He lives in a shipping container in the middle of Pacoima. And he's a conspiracy theorist that I'm pretty sure plans on assassinating all of the one percent. Oh, and he looks like Charles Manson now." That about covered it.

Laughing even harder, was that something else Hazel sensed? Relief?

Stop.

He doesn't see you that way.

"Charles Manson? Really?"

Dropping the measuring cups on the island, Hazel nodded emphatically.

"So no second date?" Ethan joked, and they both laughed.

"That wasn't even the first one. I let him down easy in a message, but I feel bad because I'm the one who initiated contact. Does that make me a horrible person?"

"Somehow I can't imagine a world where you're a horrible person," he said softly.

Hazel stopped measuring the flour to look at Ethan.

No.

He feels bad about how things went with the kiss, and he's just being nice.

Stop.

And besides, sometimes she really did *feel like a horrible person, or at least a very boring one.*

"I don't know," she began confessing. "Sometimes I think my ex came out as gay as an elaborate way to break up with me. So it would somehow hurt my feelings less."

She'd never admitted that to anyone, but there it was. One of her biggest fears laid out at this practical stranger's feet.

Ethan's smile was sincere as he made sure their eyes met. "Even if that were true, which I'm almost positive it isn't, it again shows that you're such a good person that he'd make something like that up just to hurt you less."

Stunned by Ethan's words, Hazel didn't know how to respond.

Luckily, Spike saved her by jumping up on the island and rubbing his head on Hazel's chest. Then he walked over to Ethan and did the same.

"I can't get over how much he likes you." She changed the subject.

"What's not to like? Don't answer that."

"I was going to say 'nothing,' but I'll keep it to myself." Hazel smiled at him.

Ethan smiled back.

Their eyes were not able to pull away.

Am I imagining this? Does Ethan possibly like me?

Looking away first, Ethan spotted her laptop. "You opened the store?" His face lifted happily.

"I did. I figured why not."

"Paw-fect Plants? That's paw-fect. If you want, I can offer my design skills to spruce it up?"

Hazel dropped the second cup of flour into the mixing bowl, and a flood of excitement raced through her. "You would do that?"

"Of course. Besides, this feels like a better payment

for the rattlesnake plant than Oreos." He looked back up at her.

His eyes!

She needed to break the tension because at this point, remembering how amazing that kiss was, she wanted to jump over the island and do it again. "I don't know, that *cocoa* was pretty good," she teased.

Laughing, Ethan said, "Okay, okay. But yes, I'd love to help."

Why couldn't Hazel stop staring at his eyes! Those beautiful brown eyes. Was he staring back or just wondering why she was staring?

But no, if ever eyes were to sparkle, his were like freaking stars.

Hazel wanted to kiss him.

Stop.

He said he wanted to be friends. Now get over it.

"Thank you," she said with gratitude.

"You're welcome." His voice was quiet and kind.

Kind was so sexy. Hazel was now glad she was on the other side of the island. She didn't know if she could control herself.

Ethan's expression shifted, like he'd suddenly swallowed something unpleasant.

"Are you okay?" Hazel hoped it wasn't her staring that put him off.

After swallowing hard, Ethan's voice cracked nervously when he said, "I have something to tell you."

Hazel never liked it when people started a conversation like that.

"You shared something personal with me, so I want to do the same." Was that a bead of sweat rolling down his forehead? And the crinkle of his eyebrows, and the anxiety reflected in his eyes. Hazel wanted to give him the biggest hug. Whatever he was about to tell her, she could see that it was difficult for him.

"If you're uncomfortable, you don't have to . . ." Hazel wanted to give him an out.

"No. I need to do this. I don't like to talk about myself. I get scared that people will run or judge me." Ethan let out a nervous laugh.

"Trust me, I would never do either."

Ethan's eyes bored into hers, and Hazel's heart skipped a beat.

"I don't have the greatest relationship with my family. Don't get me wrong, they're good people, they're just not very affectionate." Ethan paused, then continued, "I don't think I've ever heard my dad say he loves me. My mom has said it on special occasions, and my sister maybe three times? Four? Not a lot. So I don't say it. Even though I do love them." Ethan laughed nervously. "Too much information?"

Hazel went against her better judgment and moved around the island to embrace him on the stool. His arms wrapped tightly around her waist. So much emotion poured into that hug, only intensifying the longer they held each other.

After a long moment, Hazel pulled away. "I'm sorry you had to go through that, or are still going through that . . . or . . . I'm just sorry. I think a lot of people our parents' ages were taught that emotions made them weak or something horrible like that. But I guarantee they love you to pieces." Hazel wanted to say more, but she also wanted to respect the boundaries that he'd set. She suddenly understood why he'd pushed her away. It was too much too fast for him. But despite that, he'd put friendship on the table.

And Hazel would take that gladly.

"We definitely need these cookies now," Hazel joked as she slid back to the mixer, turning it on.

"Agreed." Ethan smiled. "I remember when there used to be a little round table where this island is."

"Oh, with the mismatched chairs! *Friends* was her favorite show in the nineties, so she had to recreate it in her kitchen." Hazel laughed at the memory.

Ethan laughed back. "Many a cookie was eaten at that table while Gladys gave me sound advice on life. I wish I'd followed it more."

"Tell me about it. She told me she wasn't sure about Logan and that if I changed my mind about him and decided to leave him, I could live here with her. That was a month after I met him, and we were already moving in together. I laughed it off, but dang, she just knew."

"Gladys had that Spidey sense for sure. I had a girlfriend once that I'm pretty sure wanted to murder me." Upon Hazel's open mouth, Ethan clarified, "I mean, I hope not, but one day when I was getting out of my car, Betty, her name was Betty, walked out of my house. I never gave her the key, by the way, she had it made by stealing mine, and she had this really serious expression on her face. She was holding a pair of gigantic scissors and kept walking toward me, like she had a purpose."

"Excuse me, what?" Hazel wasn't sure her eyes could open any wider.

"She's not even my worst girlfriend." Ethan shook his head, then continued, "As you can imagine, it was disturbing, but unlike Gladys, I have zero Spidey sense, so I kept asking Betty what was wrong as she moved closer and closer to me. She. Wouldn't. Answer. Just kept walking toward me."

"Ethan! This sounds like a horror movie!"

"Oh, it was, and Gladys was my Liam-Neeson-*Taken* hero, because she came out of nowhere, telling me I was late for our lunch date, and I shouldn't keep an old lady waiting. It was enough to distract Betty in time for Gladys to pull me into her house, sit me down at the table, give me a cookie, and then tell me she'd be right back. I could kind of hear them talking outside, then Betty's car started and drove away. To this day, I have no idea what Gladys said to Betty, but I never heard from her again. She even gave Gladys my key back. I can't tell you how many times your grandmother saved my butt, both metaphorically and physically. And there was always a cookie waiting for me and my horrible choices in life." Ethan laughed.

Hearing about her grandmother as such a fierce protector tightened Hazel's chest. She'd felt that mama-bear energy her entire life, but she had no idea Grams held it for anyone other than family. Knowing that she was a guardian angel to others only made Hazel miss her more.

The doorbell rang.

Hazel and Ethan both jumped at the noise. She hadn't realized she and Ethan had been in a little bubble until it popped with a ding-dong.

"I have some ideas I'll run past you," Ethan offered. "About the website."

Disappointed by the disruption, Hazel smiled reassuringly. "Great. Let me see who this is. It's probably a package."

Actually, come to think of it, the mail person was going to be a good cooldown for her overactive brain.

Arriving at the front door, Hazel opened it.

Oh god no.

Boone stood there with a large grin.

Boone!

Conspiracy theory, billionaire murderer Boone!

But, but, but, I messaged him.

And it had been as nice as she could possibly write it, making sure she apologized profusely for interrupting his life like that.

"Hello, beautiful," he said with a flirtatious smile.

Panic began to set in. She'd been *too* nice, that had to be it. Unfortunately, as a woman, it was always a balance between "too nice" or "too mean." Hazel always erred on the side of nice, but the older she got, the less she was starting to care. Because . . . yeah . . . Boone stood in front of her, completely ignoring her message.

"Boone. How did you know where I lived?"

Boone pushed his way inside. "It was easy with my contacts."

Gulp.

Cora was right, it was a huge mistake letting this stranger back into her life. He'd found her through his *contacts*? What the heck did that even mean?

He turned to her, trying to make his eyes sparkle, but he had nothing on Ethan. "I wasn't completely honest with you. I don't actually own that tiny home. My ex-roommate does, and he's kind of kicking me out. You think I could stay here for a while? It's such a big house, and we could rekindle what we might have had?"

Excuse me, what?

What in the freaking heck?

Hazel was too stunned to respond, so the only words that came out of her mouth were, "Uh, that's a lot."

Boone hugged her, but she didn't hug back. "I know," he cooed, "But it's gotta be destiny, right? You dream about me, find me, and now I need a place to stay? It was meant to be."

Hazel shoved him away. "Um, Boone . . ."

Words.

"My message . . ." was all that she could utter.

Boone brushed the air as if she had apologized. "I know you're scared like last time. I couldn't let you give up on our second chance. I had to fight for you."

Was that supposed to be sweet?

Hazel needed to respond right about now.

But she couldn't seem to form the right words.

Good old-fashioned fake dating

Okay. That guy sounded *crazy*. And Ethan knew a thing or two about *crazy*. Alice Panner came to mind. Ten years ago, he thought he was in a somewhat healthy relationship with her, for him anyway. But turned out she'd been living in his downstairs closet (unbeknownst to him) for a week. At the time, he had wondered how she arrived at his front door so quickly whenever they made plans. When he'd gone downstairs to get a sleeping bag for a camping trip, he found her, in said sleeping bag, reading a book about birds. It took calling the police to finally remove her from his house, and Ethan didn't want Hazel to have to do that with Boone.

Because he recognized that tone.

That guy was going to root in this house if he wasn't stopped.

Ethan knew Hazel could take care of herself, but he figured he'd help her out if this guy decided to be more aggressive.

Jumping up from the stool, Ethan yelled toward the front door. "Who is it, sweetheart?"

Fake dating.

Worked every time.

Or at least he hoped so.

Ethan wasn't exactly a fighter, but he could throw a punch if he had to.

Walking up to the front area, he almost jumped at the sight of Boone. Holy. He looked like a serial killer.

There was no way he was letting this guy anywhere near Hazel.

Hazel's eyes met his, and he could tell from his use of the word *sweetheart* she knew the plan and was completely down for it. But Ethan still wanted to respect her boundaries, so he kissed her on the cheek rather than planting a full-on kiss like he'd wanted to since he walked in the door.

Taking the lead, Hazel guided Ethan's arm around her waist, which sent a thrill through him. He couldn't think clearly for a moment as his hand rested on her waist. Ethan had never experienced this kind of chemistry with anyone before, and it surprised him.

Getting it together, Ethan looked down at Hazel affectionately. "Who's this, my little cocoa bean?"

Hazel snorted a laugh at their inside joke.

They already had an inside joke.

Why did that make him so happy!

Hazel leaned her head into Ethan's chest as she wrapped her arm around him as well. Ethan controlled the sense overload he felt from her touch.

"An old friend from work. Boone. Boone, this is Ethan." Hazel introduced the mountain man to Ethan.

Taking his free hand, Ethan shook Boone's.

Sweaty.

Ick.

But Boone was caught off guard. Ethan could tell from the way Boone's head reared back at the sight of him.

Boone directed his comment to Hazel. "I thought you said you were single."

Seriously, dude?

Ethan maneuvered Hazel so that he could wrap both his arms around her, holding her in front of him. She played along, gently tracing circles on Ethan's hands at her waist. He had to blink several times to steady his brain and fight the urge to start kissing her neck.

Swallowing down the intensity he felt in that moment, Ethan said with a grin, "We just made it official this morning. I'm moving in!"

Spike wandered in and rubbed his entire body on Ethan's leg. Of course Spike was brilliant enough to play along. Ethan smiled at the cat. "Hey, buddy." Then he turned his attention back to Boone. "One big happy family. You staying for lunch?"

Please say no.

Please say no.

But then again . . . if he said yes, then Ethan could

still pretend to be Hazel's boyfriend. And suddenly he found himself very conflicted over which way he wanted Boone's answer to go.

"Um, yeah, sure." Boone suddenly eyed Ethan suspiciously. This guy was going to be a problem.

But he had to hide his elation from Hazel. He should be upset that Boone wasn't leaving, but being able to pretend to be with Hazel was worth a little awkwardness. Ethan should just be honest with her and possibly make dating her a reality, but after this clown, Ethan didn't want to overwhelm her. That, and he was terrified. But definitely more the former.

"I can order us some pizza," Hazel offered as she wrapped her hand in Ethan's.

It took every bit of impulse control Ethan could muster not to kiss her. "That sounds perfect, cocoa bean." His stomach would hate him later from both gluten and cheese, but it would be worth every delicious bite.

"Pepperoni sound good?" Hazel asked as they all shuffled into the kitchen.

"Sounds amazing," Ethan agreed. Might as well go for the trifecta of heartburn.

"Sure, sounds great. Though a little unhealthy. I thought you ate better than that," Boone said in the judgy-est judging voice possible.

"I'm in the mood," Hazel replied with a smile. "Please, sit." She motioned with her free hand for Boone to sit on the stool behind the island, while Ethan and her stayed on the other side, hands still clasped.

"You making cookies?" Boone eyed the mixing bowl.

"Yeah, we were. You want some?" Ethan kissed Hazel's cheek and then unwrapped his hand from hers, only to wrap his arms around her from behind again, her head fitting perfectly under his chin. Was this heaven?

With Ethan's arms around her waist, Hazel began dropping piles of cookie dough onto a baking sheet.

"Nah, the pizza will be my one cheat item. I can't do cookies on top of that." Dang, this guy was something. What did Hazel ever see in him?

He immediately retracted that thought from his brain as he recalled every woman he'd ever dated. "Let me order the pizza on my phone." Before Hazel could argue about who would pay, Ethan quickly ordered two pizzas from his favorite local joint, one pepperoni and the other veggie. Somehow having a veggie option made him feel more healthy. It was a delusion he was willing to die for. "Done. Says it'll be here in thirty."

"Thanks for ordering." Hazel squeezed his hand affectionately, and it sent a blast to his brain.

"So how did you guys meet?" Boone asked sullenly. He was obviously upset by the situation, which only made Ethan happier.

"Funny you should ask," Ethan began. "You want to tell it, sweetie?"

Hazel tilted her head back to glance at Ethan, a small sparkle of amusement bouncing in her eyes. "No. You go ahead. You tell it better." With a grin, she turned back to the dough and cookie sheet.

Okay. I'll give you a story. Ethan smiled inwardly. "Well, Boone, I was a little like you. A man from Hazel's past. Well, not quite a man yet; we met in kindergarten. Isn't that right, cocoa bean?"

Hazel huffed a laugh. "Absolutely," she agreed as she took the baking sheet and pulled out of Ethan's embrace to place it in the oven.

"Kindergarten?" Boone's eyes rounded.

"It was love at first sight, for me anyway. And I asked her to marry me at recess. Do you remember what you said?" Ethan was having way too much fun with this.

Hazel closed the oven door, then swung her arm around Ethan's waist. "I said no." She smiled.

Ethan quickly wrapped his arm around her waist as well and withheld his laughter. She was making him work for this. "I was devastated. I went straight to her mother after school and asked her to put in a good word for me. But she sadly sided with her daughter."

"And then he moved away, and I didn't see him until junior high." Hazel grinned. "Sorry, you tell it."

Ethan was on it. "I had just moved back to town and wanted to meet other kids who liked the same things I did. The only things I was into at that time were *Star Wars* and *Indiana Jones*, so joining the George Lucas fan club was a no brainer. And my new school had an in-person meetup before school. How amazing is that? And when I walked in, there she was. President of the *Star Wars* division, and ready to start the meeting."

"But seeing him again. I was too shy to talk to him, and he thought I was being a snob." Hazel leaned into him.

"I still asked her out, though. There was a screening

of *Empire Strikes Back* at the dollar theater. I thought for sure she'd say yes."

"But I panicked and said no."

"Again." Ethan felt her hand tighten on his waist. Wait. Was she tying this back into him friend-zoning her?

"And we never spoke to each other again. And after high school, we never *saw* each other again," Hazel continued. "I actually contacted Ethan before I contacted you, but I hadn't heard from him, so that's why I went out to see you."

"I'm terrible with messages, so I honestly didn't see it. But here's the crazy part . . ."

Boone leaned forward, expectant. He was getting into this. Even Hazel's eyes were peeled toward him.

Ethan continued, "I was with my friends at Geeky Teas. You ever been there?"

Boone shook his head.

"It's this great store where you can rent out tables in the back to play Dungeons & Dragons, or any game really, but my friends and I were on our fifth campaign for D&D, and I was about to fight Asmodeus—and if you've ever played D&D, he's a big one—when Hazel walked in with a couple of her friends and a Risk 2210 box in her hands. That's also a great game, by the way."

"Always go for the moon territories first," Hazel added.

Ethan swung his gaze to Hazel, his heart leaping into his throat. She actually *knew* the game. This story may have been fake, but it only proved how much they belonged together. "This is why she always wins, am I right?"

Their eyes stayed locked, and they both couldn't quit grinning.

After a moment, Boone shifted out of his seat.

Ethan and Hazel turned to him. Was that actual happiness in Boone's face?

"You know what? You two are meant for each other. That story is incredible." Boone saluted. "I'm going to take off."

"You don't want to stay for the pizza?" Hazel asked, but Ethan could hear the relief in her voice.

"Nah. It would just give me heartburn."

Pretty much.

"Oh, well, okay. It was nice meeting you, then." Ethan pretended to act slightly disappointed.

Boone held out his hand, which Ethan shook with his free hand, his left arm still wrapped around Hazel.

Boone's eyes briefly met Hazel's. "Uh, it was nice catching up."

"You too, Boone. Thanks for stopping by." Hazel lifted her hand to wave at him.

With one last smile at the two of them, Boone opened the front door and shut it behind him.

They both waited a good minute to hear Boone's car pull out of the driveway before Ethan finally pulled his arm away. An ache sat in his chest as she disentangled herself from him, but she turned to him with that dazzling smile of hers. "Holy . . . thank you," she said.

"You were right. He totally looks like Charles Manson."

"Right?" Hazel shook her head. "But that story was

magnificent. I almost started to believe it myself."

"I can't believe you've played 2210." Ethan was still surprised by that.

"Best Risk variation ever. You should see the fill-in cards my friends and I made. They're hysterical," Hazel said.

She was referring to the game's option to make up your own destruction cards. They could be pretty epic. Ethan made one that nuked anyone who attacked him. He'd only been able to use it once.

"We'll have to get a group together and play sometime," he said quietly.

"I'd like that." Hazel smiled.

A long moment passed between them, the waft of baking cookies growing stronger.

"So you were into Boone back in the day?" Ethan decided to tease her a bit.

"He didn't used to be a conspiracy theory mooch back then. Or maybe he was, and I didn't notice," she confessed thoughtfully. "But he actually seemed really happy for us. It reminded me of why I did like him back then. He could be really sweet."

"He definitely calmed down there at the end." But Ethan kind of wished he'd stayed for lunch. He wanted to keep fake-dating Hazel.

Spike wandered up, stretching his arms on Hazel's legs, and she picked him up. "You did such a good job, Spike."

Ethan reached over and scratched Spike's ears, to his delight, while Hazel held him in her arms. His hand touched her arm, and they looked at each other.

He wanted to kiss her so badly.

"You still want pizza and cookies?" she asked shyly.

Ethan continued to scratch Spike's head, but his eyes never left Hazel's.

If he didn't leave that instant, he'd kiss her.

And what was wrong with that?

Nothing?

Panic.

"I should probably go," Ethan said as a drip of sweat moved down his neck.

Spike was fully loving the attention he was getting.

Ethan and Hazel continued to stare at each other.

Now was the moment.

Spike wouldn't mind.

"I'll save some of both for you, then, *cocoa bean*," she teased.

Right. Time to leave. He did say that didn't he?

"I have some ideas for your shop. I'll come back this week to show you?" Good. Make plans to see her again. It may be for work, but he'd take it.

"That would be awesome, thank you." Hazel smiled.

Ethan finally pulled his hand away from Spike, but heart-wrenchingly away from Hazel as well. "Okay, well. See you later."

Kiss her!

"See you." She blushed.

Oh-my-god-I-can't-even-see-straight!

He needed to get out of there to gain some kind of self-control back. Opening the door, he stepped out but turned to Hazel before he shut it. "Maybe tomorrow I can come by and work on the site with you?" Screw a generalized "next week." He needed to spend time with her as soon as possible.

Please say yes.

"I'd love that."

She'd love that.

His heart soared.

"It's a date," he said.

Hazel raised an eyebrow. "A date?"

Ethan's eyes widened, and a drop of sweat immediately dripped down his forehead. This was what he wanted, so why was his body sabotaging him?

Before he could say yes, Hazel shook her head with a smile. "I'll see you tomorrow."

She shut the door.

For the third time, Ethan stood staring at Hazel's closed door.

He should be committed.

Chapter 14
Ethan

Invites and possibilities

"All I had to say was 'yes, a date.' What is wrong with me?" Ethan grumbled as he walked into his house. Sometimes talking aloud helped him to fully realize what a moron he could be. Yup. Total idiot.

"Let me count the ways."

Ethan yelped and jumped back three feet.

"Mateo! What the heck?" Ethan was grateful he didn't have a heart condition. Though he was male and in his late forties, so maybe he did.

Standing from the couch, Mateo laughed. "Sorry. I let myself in. But I have a gig for you, and it pays *a lot*."

Perking up at *a lot*, Ethan motioned Mateo to follow him into the kitchen. He needed sugar, stat.

Going straight for the fridge, Ethan opened the door and searched inside.

There it was.

Leftover cheesecake from The Cheesecake Factory. Peanut butter cup fudge ripple, three whole slices left. It was his favorite and would help mask his feelings well. Grabbing two forks, he placed the plate on the kitchen island, where Mateo now sat on a stool.

"Welcome to a night of heartburn, my friend, with a possible side of the runs." Ethan had no illusions about eating this much sugar, but his soul needed it, so he was willing to take all the risk. Getting old was a Russian roulette of a good time.

"That alone should deter me," Mateo groaned, but took the fork anyway.

The first bite was glorious, and Ethan fully took it in before asking, "Tell me about this high-paying job? How high paying are we talking about?"

"Enough to cover you for a few months. Catch is, the event is this Friday, so the invite has to be done in two days. And by two days I mean I need it Wednesday Morning." Mateo scrunched his face as if waiting for Ethan's utter rejection of the terms.

"Today is Monday," Ethan said, mouth slackening.

"Did I mention it's a lot of money?" Mateo smiled haphazardly.

"Due Wednesday morning, I'm assuming they go out Wednesday afternoon. Will anyone show up to this thing?"

"Technically, the actual *lame* e-vite was sent out months ago by the previous person in charge, but I took over today, and I want something magnificent. It'll be a reminder invite, but I have the budget, and there's no one else I know who can do it justice. Or at least capture what's in my head." Mateo ate another bite of cheesecake.

"All right, you're killing me here. What is it?"

Mateo's eyebrows lifted in excitement. "The charity through the studio is going to throw a costume ball downtown at The Majestic."

Something different than the same old social media posts he'd been making for the last year instantly intrigued Ethan. "Print or e-vite?"

Smiling, Mateo tilted his head to the side happily. "Both."

Ethan slapped his hands together with excitement. He realized he did that a lot. Clapping. He made a mental note to talk to Jane about it. But he was excited all the same. "Oooo, I haven't done print in a minute. I'm in."

"I haven't even told you the best part." Mateo scooted forward in his stool. "It's theme is characters from the eighties."

"Ooo, the wheels are turning." Ethan ate another bite of deliciousness. The eighties were his decade. Trying to narrow down which characters to put on the invite would be the real challenge, though. There were so many iconic ones to choose from.

"I'm thinking Victorian eighties. *Dynasty* meets *Time Bandits*."

"Of course you are, but yeah, that sounds awesome." Ethan knew his friend too well.

"So, is it doable?" Mateo crossed his fingers.

Ethan finished off his slice of cheesecake with a roll of the eyes in appreciation. "You know it is," he said with his mouth full.

Mateo sat back, and the side of his mouth slid up in a sly smile. "You think you might invite the neighbor?"

"Hazel? Maybe. I screwed up again, so I'm not sure if she'll ever take me seriously. We're meeting up tomorrow, though," Ethan admitted, the cheesecake no longer doing its job.

"A date?" Mateo's tone sounded hopeful.

Inwardly, Ethan groaned, not wanting to relive his freeze up. "That's exactly what she asked."

"And you answered . . ." He still sounded hopeful.

"I didn't. I just dripped in sweat like an animal, and she shut the door. Again." He really did that, didn't he? Why!

Mateo shook his head, obviously trying not to laugh. "Therapy isn't helping?"

"No. It is. I would have told her no if I hadn't had a session." Ethan knew this was true.

"Progress." Mateo's eyebrow lifted in appreciation.

"Tomorrow. I'm not going to blow it. That old flame was a bust, so I have a window of opportunity here," Ethan said out loud, trying to motivate himself.

Mateo nodded, encouraging. "Okay. I like this attitude. Tomorrow it is. Just don't dump her if you find out she doesn't like chocolate like Alice."

"Seriously, who doesn't like chocolate? None of it, not milk, not dark, not mint? That's insane. Acceptable deal-breaker for me." Even as he said it, Ethan knew that was an excuse. He'd broken up with Alice because he'd been scared. But not this time. Not with Hazel. But he did have to reply defensively, "And I already know Hazel likes chocolate from our first date . . . or encounter . . . or whatever you'd call that magical night we met."

Mateo clutched his hand to his chest. "Awwww. Well, if you find out she doesn't like pizza . . ."

"Ha! Too late, she just ordered it and is probably eating it as we speak." Ethan felt weirdly triumphant.

"All right. All right. She's perfect." Mateo laughed.

Ethan ate the last of Mateo's slice.

Yes. She was.

Tomorrow.

He had a good feeling about this.

Looking at the time, Ethan groaned. "I've got my weekly parent Zoom in twenty minutes."

"Are you going to tell them about therapy?" Mateo asked, a curious gleam in his eyes.

"No, but my therapist gave me homework. She wants me to pretend that they have a phobia of emotions so I don't take it so personally. She also wants me to express my feelings to them." Now that he said it out loud, it sounded like a terrible idea.

"Oooo, can I stay? This sounds way more entertaining than what we've got scheduled to shoot tonight."

"No, you can't stay. And you and Austin working a night shoot?"

"As the executive producer I don't have to stay the whole time, but Austin is on set until three a.m., if we're lucky, so I'm going to stick around for moral support."

"You should nap." Naps were also a thing for getting older.

Mateo sighed in defeat. "Yeah. Good plan." He looked down at his empty plate. "God, I'm going to regret that."

With a loud gurgle of his stomach, Ethan replied, "I already am."

"I'm not far behind you," Mateo said as he stood up and headed for the door. "Good luck with the invites. I can't wait to see what you come up with."

Ethan walked him to the door and waved as Mateo got into his car and backed out of the driveway. Even after he had driven away, Ethan still stood in the doorway, dreading the video chat with his parents. At least his sister wouldn't be there. The trio had a tendency to gang up on him and tell him how he was doing everything wrong in his life.

Stalling long enough, Ethan sauntered back into the house and to his office. The walls were adorned with some of his favorite movie prints, from the German version of *Adventures of Baron Munchausen* to the original *Aliens* print to *Raiders of the Lost Ark,* but also some classics as well, Magritte's *The Son of Man*, Van Gogh's *The Starry Night* (with a flying TARDIS in the top corner, of course; talk about a *Doctor Who* episode that made him sob), and his other nerdy find of a spoof of Magritte's *This Is Not a Pipe*, with the Mario Bros. green pipe. He made his office his happy place, surrounded by his favorite inspirational pieces.

With a quick pat on the head to his *Escape to Ashdonia* Nikolas Dragontine Pop doll, he flipped on his monitor and clicked on the Zoom link his mother sent him yesterday.

Right on time.

Within moments, his parents were on screen, sitting next to each other in front of their computer camera, arms barely touching.

"Hi, Ethan," his mother said with a smile. She was in her seventies but looked a lot younger. Never one for makeup, but she did have her hair cut short and dyed brown. She wore a blue button-up blouse with a brown cardigan.

"Hey, Mom; hey, Dad," Ethan replied.

His dad shifted in his seat, then nodded. "How is everything?" A little older than his mother, Ethan's dad was going to turn eighty next year. He was almost completely bald with a few white whisps at the side of his head, clean-shaven, and he wore a light-yellow button-up shirt with only the top button loose. He kind of looked like a potato if Ethan was being honest.

"Good. I just got a new gig I'm excited about."

"Gig? What kind of word is that?" his father grumbled. "You can't even call your work a job now?"

"Because it's not a steady job, Roger. Remember, it's *freelance*." His mother said the word like it was a curse.

Forty-nine years old, never had any kind of financial crisis, and still they didn't think what he did was "real."

And to make matters worse, his sister, Cordelia, popped onto the screen. "Am I late?" she asked.

"You're a doctor; you're never late—your work matters." His father's pride for his sister and disdain for him all in one sentence.

Okay. Here was the time. He needed to express his feelings.

"Yeah, you're late, although I didn't even know you were coming. But I need to tell all three of you that . . . that you're all kind of mean."

Was that his feelings? Or name calling? He'd have to ask Jane later.

"Mean?" His mother reared back in shock.

"I feel like anytime we talk about what I'm up to, you always have to insult me and my work. I own my own house. I pay my own bills. I have savings. I'm a success to anyone else in the world except you guys." *I said the word* feel, *so that should count.* But it physically felt good to be honest with his family. And he found that he didn't really care what their response would be. Telling them those things were for him, not them.

"We obviously measure success very differently." His father crossed his arms.

Um, what? "Okay, Dad, then how would *you* measure success?" Ethan crossed his own arms.

His father had no answer, but his face was growing four shades of red darker.

Noticing this, his mom turned to the camera. "You're going to give your father a heart attack. And we're not mean. You're too sensitive, and you always have been."

Cordelia rolled her eyes. "Ethan, don't be a baby. You design websites. You're not saving the world."

Phobia. Phobia. They're scared of emotions.

Nope. Didn't help.

He wanted to strangle his sister.

Ethan gulped in a deep breath instead. "How's it going with you guys, since talking about me seems to upset everyone, including me."

As if a magic blanket had covered his family, their entire body language relaxed and their faces were relieved.

"Good." His mother rolled over the "ickiness" of Ethan's previous comments. "We went to see the new exhibit at the Contemporary Art Museum."

"Oh, I've been meaning to go there," Cordelia chimed in.

And the conversation went to mundane, surface-level small talk.

At least they weren't being mean.

After about thirty minutes (that was about all any of them could take), Ethan said, "I need to get back to work." Then he decided to be crazy and said, "Love you, guys."

All three of their faces went white and froze.

And Ethan could see . . .

It really was fear.

They looked petrified.

His heart softened a little.

Maybe small talk was all they were capable of giving and that was okay. Ethan wanted more, but he couldn't force them. Open, honest, and loving. That was what he truly wanted in life. Before they were forced to mumble something or downright attack him for being "sensitive," Ethan hit the Leave Meeting button.

Staring at the blank screen of his monitor, a warmth filled him. That had been a little rocky, but he was proud of himself.

And he wasn't making it up, he needed to get to work on the invite.

Before he got started, his phone vibrated.

A text.

He opened his phone, and he froze.

It was a text from his mom: *We love you too.*

His eyes welled up as he swallowed a lump in his throat.

Well, what do you know?

It felt like the beginning of something. Something good. Something healthy.

Calmness filled him.

And with a smile, he opened up Photoshop, starting a new file.

The blank page.

Sometimes it could be the most exciting, and sometimes it could be the most terrifying. But Ethan's head was filled with ideas for the invite, so in this case, he went with exciting.

He worked with the design aspects first rather than collecting all the eighties movie and television character images he'd be bookmarking for later.

Black and gold (hoping that Mateo had the budget to gold-foil the text and accents).

Framing the front of the invite with an art nouveau

edging, simple lines, weaving at the corners, with the perfect swirls and decorative arrows pointing to the blank middle.

This alone was enough to spark his excitement. Part of him wanted to create a gold emblem in the middle, with detailed eighties references inside like Easter eggs, but he knew Mateo would want more "eighties" than that. The nouveau frame would have to suffice for his "Victorian," which he knew for a fact Mateo had no idea what that meant. Mateo was right. Hiring Ethan would give him what he wanted. Because if he'd hired another graphic designer and the only notes he gave were "Victorian eighties," Ethan didn't want to think about what that would equate to. Mateo could have gotten lucky, but with this short time frame, he needed someone he could trust.

Time to narrow down which eighties characters he planned on silhouetting on the cover, gold foil as the shading. He'd need to find images where the contrast was high enough to cast enough light on one side of the person in order for him to pull out enough of the character for people to recognize.

It was a long and tedious process, so there was no time like the present.

Once he started, he put his mind on autopilot. His eyes knew what to look for as he scrolled through pages and pages of images with the simple search of popular characters from the eighties. As his brain often did with these types of tasks, it wandered.

Into thinking of Hazel.

Pretending to date her had felt so real. They just fit.

Ethan wanted to know everything about her, and weirdly (for him anyway), he wanted to share back. Mateo and Austin were the only two people he'd truly opened up to in his adult life.

Shaking his head at his own inner thoughts, he found a couple images that would work and placed them in a file.

Obviously, thinking about Hazel brought up a lot of his emotions.

He knew he had to wait a week for therapy, but maybe Jane would see him sooner.

Ethan grabbed his phone to text her.

Seriously, are you blind?

Hazel pulled out the last pan of chocolate chip cookies, breathing in the blissful aroma. Just like Grams used to make. Placing it on top of the oven, Hazel couldn't resist and spatula'd a piping hot cookie into her hands. Bouncing it back and forth between her hands from the hot lava melting chocolate, eventually it cooled enough for her to eat. The buttery brown sugar base and semisweet chocolate melted into her mouth, and she closed her eyes from total euphoria.

After enjoying the rest of the cookie thoroughly, Hazel turned to the island and grabbed the two pizza boxes and what was left of the pizza and stuffed it in the fridge.

Spike immediately replaced them, staring at Hazel, waiting patiently for either treats or scratchies. Hazel attempted the scratchies first, which seemed to satisfy him.

Glancing over at her laptop, Hazel sighed, trying not to think about the fact that Ethan volunteering to help her had affected her in a way that made her already feel her mind wanting to fantasize and overanalyze everything. If their kiss hadn't been so mind-blowing, she probably wouldn't be fighting herself so much. But it had been. It had been so powerful that she could almost feel every detail of it as if it had happened seconds ago.

"What the heck, Spike? Why isn't he interested?" Hazel didn't want to go there. She was trying to stick to positive self-talk, since her go-to for most of her life would have been an entire list of why he wasn't interested.

No.

Hazel needed to be nicer to herself.

Her therapist would always remind her that Hazel would never treat one of her friends the way she treated herself.

Thinking on Ethan more, she slowly started to relax. "I can't force it. I definitely don't want to do that again. Friends. Accept it. And he's going to help me with my store. How amazing is that?" She scratched Spike's cheeks for emphasis. "Now let's get away from these cookies before we eat them all."

Scooping Spike into her arms, Hazel headed toward the bedroom.

It was far too early for sleep, but plopping Spike down on the bed, Hazel steeled her determination and began tackling the rest of the boxes. It was time to fully move into this place. Over the last week, she'd unpacked every other room. She'd hung up all her movie posters throughout the house, and she'd finally decided to make the second bedroom a craft room with a living wall. Five long racks with five-inch-diameter metal pots hanging from the rungs, about six per rack. She'd already planted every kind of lettuce she could get seeds for, and tons of herbs like rosemary, dill, thyme, oregano, and basil. The little sprouts had already started to grow, and she could tell it was going to be a beautiful wall. She didn't know exactly what she would "craft," but she'd bought a couple of tables on Amazon and placed them against the wall for future projects.

But the master bedroom she just couldn't bring herself to unpack.

When she ran in place for a few seconds to pump herself up, Spike jumped and backed up a few feet from being startled.

"Sorry, boo boo." With a few apologizing scratches, Spike was fine again. She tossed him a toy mouse, and he eagerly bit down on its head and back-kicked the living heck out of it.

Hours later, every box had been emptied, broken down, and made ready for recycling. But more importantly, all her clothes, knickknacks, and everything else she wanted in her bedroom were put in place. Exhausted but elated to finally be finished unpacking, Hazel pried off her jeans and slid into bed. Her shirt would have to work as pajamas tonight. Let's face it, pretty much whatever top she wore for the day ended up being her pajamas *every* night.

Reaching over to her nightstand, Hazel clicked off the lamp, then cozied up in her blankets. It didn't take long for Spike to snuggle in close, ready to fall asleep with his human.

Before closing her eyes, Hazel stared up at her ceiling. "All right, Grams, good first effort with Boone. There's no way we could have known that he'd changed so much. But let me see my Dream Guy's face this time. Please? If you can un-blur him for me? Okay. Thanks. Love you. Good night."

Here's to hoping.

Hazel closed her eyes.

***

In the white room again, Hazel pulled her arm in with a closed fist in a moment of triumph. She couldn't remember a time when she'd had this many lucid dreams so close together. *Thank you, Grams.*

Dream Guy appeared in front of her like a mirage coming to life.

But still a blurred face.

Come on, Grams!

"You're actually here," Hazel said.

"Yeah, you made it pretty clear with Gladys that you wanted to see me," he answered with a slight laugh.

"I also made it clear that I wanted to see who you are." Maybe? Please? A little peek?

"You'll find out when it's time," he answered like he was the master of the universe or something.

"This is just annoying," Hazel grumbled impatiently.

As she said it, the white room began to swirl with

colors, shifting into a new location like last time, until Hazel stood in the middle of a crowded quad full of college students.

"This is my college," she said aloud, recognizing the campus.

Standing alone, Hazel couldn't seem to move as more and more students walked by her.

Arms wrapped around her waist from behind. "Guess who?"

Hazel knew that voice.

She whirled around in his arms, her whole being lighting up. "Theo!"

Her college crush and best friend, my god he was beautiful.

Leaning down, Theo kissed her until she thought her head would explode.

***

Hazel woke up to Spike licking her cheek. "Spike. What the heck? That was a good dream," Hazel scolded groggily.

Grabbing her phone, she checked the time: 8:00 a.m. "Fine. I'll get up."

Throwing on an outfit she hadn't worn in weeks (due to it being in a box) felt satisfying in a way that made her wish she'd unpacked sooner, floral princess-sleeved T-shirt and black jeans.

She made her way to the kitchen and grabbed a cookie off the tray. "Breakfast of champions." Biting into the chocolate goodness, it was worth every calorie.

Pulling out a plate, Hazel transferred all the cookies

over and covered the top with plastic wrap.

The doorbell rang.

That seemed to be happening a lot lately.

A twist of dread hit her stomach at the thought it might be Boone again, so she slowly made her way to the front door, looking through the peephole.

Ethan.

Hazel couldn't control the race of her heart at seeing him through the peephole.

They'd never discussed a time when he was going to come over, so she guessed he was an early bird.

Like her.

Opening the door, Hazel smiled at him. And though she knew she shouldn't care, she was doubly glad she'd unpacked and wore a cute outfit.

Stop it, Hazel!

Ethan had two large duffel bags perched over each shoulder, while holding black metal stands in each hand. "Too early?" There was a tint of worry in his expression.

"Not at all. Come on in. What is all that?" Hazel asked as the two made their way to the kitchen. She knew it must be some kind of equipment, but she wasn't sure for what.

Once in the kitchen, Ethan dropped the bags on the floor and placed the stands gently on the island. "Lights, backdrops, mats. Everything we need to make the best photos for your site. But since your main selling point is that the plants are safe for pets, I figure Mr. Spike could pose for a few shots." His smile reached his eyes in the most adorable way.

Stop.

Remember the dream last night with Theo. Yes, Theo. Grams sent you Theo. Hazel vowed to look him up as soon as Ethan left.

No more projecting her own feelings onto Ethan.

Breathe.

Good.

Now enjoy yourself with your new friend.

"If you can get Spike to cooperate." As sweet as Spike was, getting him to stand still for a photo wasn't exactly easy.

"Me and Spike have an understanding," Ethan said with confidence.

"Oh, really?" Hazel laughed.

"Yeah. I'm pretty sure he's my soulmate, if you hadn't noticed." Ethan nodded as if this answer was obvious.

Hazel laughed and then nearly snorted as Spike, on cue, ran up to Ethan and head-bumped his leg.

"Oh my god." Ethan couldn't seem to believe the timing himself. Then his eyes found the plate of cookies. "Can I . . . ?"

"Help yourself." Hazel brought over the plate, and Ethan immediately inhaled it.

"Just like Gladys's."

Hearing Ethan say her grandmother's name filled her with happiness.

Stop.

"You lead and I'll help." Hazel motioned to the back door.

Ethan gave a mock salute, and the two of them headed

to the greenhouse out back.

Time flew to the point where Hazel had no idea how long they'd been working. Ethan had been right, Spike acted like a supermodel with every shot, posing, rolling on his back showing his belly, playing with the leaves of a plant, basically being an adorable cat model.

A true pro, Ethan maneuvered the lights, placed background drops in the perfect positions, laid the plants on textured mats. He was putting his all into this photo shoot, and Hazel couldn't be more grateful.

Only once did Spike have a diva moment and demand treats, but as soon as his belly was full, he was back to giving Ethan his best poses.

And laughing.

The best part.

Hazel and Ethan laughed and joked and ate cookies until Hazel started to feel that I've-only-eaten-sugar-today nausea sensation in her belly.

"We should probably have lunch and not just cookies," she said, massaging her stomach.

"Good call." Ethan laughed, then showed her the viewfinder of his camera with the latest picture of Spike sniffing a plant.

"That looks amazing." Their arms touched as she leaned in to see the photo.

Ethan leaned a bit of his weight into her, and Hazel's stomach fluttered, and not from the sugar.

"Thanks," he said. "I think we've got some good ones."

"You really should let me pay you something," Hazel

offered. She stayed where she was, wanting to be even closer to him.

"Your company is payment enough." Ethan's voice was husky.

Hazel!

How was this man single?

Forcing herself to step away, Hazel decided she'd ask. "So what about you, Ethan? Why are you single?"

They were still inches from each other, though, and Hazel had to remind herself to breathe.

"I think the way I acted after our kiss should be answer enough." His eyes were full of . . . regret?

Hope flooded Hazel's brain, but she tamped it back by laughing. "You really shut that down fast."

Why did he bring up the kiss?

Was she imagining what she thought she saw in his eyes? Did he regret it? Could he possibly . . .

Ethan lifted his camera and took a picture of Hazel and the plants behind her. Sweeping his eyes around the room for another angle, he observed with awe, "This place really is like a fantasyland. I feel like I've walked into Hobbiton or something."

Chest swelling at his words, Hazel answered, "I used to call this place Ashdonia when Grams was still around."

"It really is like we're in that world." He took another picture.

"Not yet, but that's the goal. I want it to feel like I've found the door to Ashdonia when I step inside." Hazel could see her vision so clearly, and it was close, but not there yet.

Ethan stared at her, his eyes smiling.

Her stomach fluttered like she was on a sugar high, which to be fair, she probably was.

But all she could do was stare back and imagine him kissing her again.

Placing the camera down, he stepped closer.

Was this going to happen?

"Hazel? You in the greenhouse?" Cora's voice came from the house.

Hazel took a step back, breaking the tension between her and Ethan.

"Yeah, we're back here," Hazel called out to her friend.

"We?" Cora exited the kitchen door.

"I'm Ethan." Ethan stepped forward, giving his free hand to Cora to shake.

Pulling her hand away, Cora's eyebrow rose in appreciation. "Cora. You're the neighbor?"

"My reputation precedes me." Ethan smiled.

Cora nodded in approval and added, "Oreo date. Nice touch."

Ethan lifted his camera slightly, turning to Hazel. "I'm going to upload these pics to my laptop. We can pick which ones you like, and I'll make them pretty."

"Thank you again." Hazel didn't feel like she could convey enough how much she appreciated his help.

Smiling shyly, Ethan said, "Of course." Then he turned and walked back into the house.

Cora's eyes bored into her best friend as she whispered, "He's totally into you!"

Her whisper wasn't quiet enough for Hazel. "Shhh. And no he isn't. He made that clear after our kiss, remember?"

A good reminder for Hazel as well.

Because . . . gah!

"That could mean anything. The kiss could have scared him," Cora rationalized.

"Cora. Just don't. I can't get all worked up about a guy that isn't interested. After everything with Logan. I can't." And that was the truth of it. The pain would be too much.

Instantly, Hazel deflated.

She'd already been reading into her time with Ethan whether she planned to or not.

And it needed to stop.

Ethan called from the kitchen, "There's some great ones here with Spike. Come see."

"Coming," Hazel answered, then gave Cora the I'm-serious look. "Now don't do anything to embarrass me or force us to flirt or any of that nonsense."

"Fine," Cora groaned.

Hazel wrapped her pinkie around Cora's, to Cora's obvious displeasure, then dropped it.

When Hazel walked inside, Ethan sat on a stool behind the island, laptop open. He was smiling as he scrolled through the pics, Spike already in a curled ball by his laptop.

Cora's eyes widened at the sight, then she looked at Hazel, and they had another voiceless conversation:

Cora: *Are you seeing this with Spike?*

Hazel: *Stop!*

Cora: *Okay, but I'm telling you. Spike only likes* you.

Hazel: *Cora!*

Hazel ignored Cora and walked behind Ethan to view the photos.

The most perfect picture of Spike playing with a plant.

"What? Cora, look at this." Hazel wanted to squee at the cuteness.

Cora hurried over, and her mouth dropped. "That is ridiculous. And you're going to help her put all this on the online store?"

"Yes, ma'am." Ethan looked like he immediately regretted saying the word *ma'am* but also didn't want to make it worse, so he went back to looking at his laptop.

Cora gave Hazel another look of approval, and they began another conversation:

Cora: *Are you kidding me? He's adorable!*

Hazel: *He's not into me. Let it go.*

Cora: *You are so stubborn.*

Ethan tweaked the photo of Spike in an editing program until it looked like it came out of a magazine.

Impulsively, Hazel hugged him from behind, but immediately regretted it. Stupid Cora getting in her head. But Ethan placed his hand on her forearm, returning the hug.

"I can take these home and do some more editing. I took the liberty of getting all the image size info from your store, so everything will fit perfectly," Ethan said as Hazel pulled out of the hug.

"Thank you so much." She felt like a broken record.

Ethan pulled a flash drive out of his laptop, handing it to Hazel. "I'm going to pick some of my favorites, but look through them all and let me know which ones are yours."

Hazel handed him another cookie, which he took with a smile. "Deal," she agreed.

Ethan took a bite of the cookie. "How are these so good? Gladys was a genius."

Cora's eyebrows practically disappeared into her hairline. "You knew Gladys?"

"Greatest neighbor of all time, present company excluded."

Cora: *Are you seriously kidding me right now?*

Hazel ignored her. "I used her recipe, but I can never get it totally perfect."

Ethan's eyes sparkled. "No, you did."

Cora mouthed, "Oh my god!"

Thankfully, Ethan wasn't paying attention.

But Hazel was.

And her heart tugged in response.

Hazel! Let it go!

Chapter 16
Ethan

Oh, come on! Another one?

Ethan packed up his laptop, elated at how the day had gone. He'd even almost kind of told Hazel he liked her. Not really, but he still felt as if he made progress. Bringing up their kiss was a good start. Right?

Maybe if you'd actually expressed some verbal regret about friend-zoning her, it might have, but you just stood there, staring at her.

He was already second-guessing himself, and he hadn't even left her house yet. Usually, the second-guessing and berating of every word that he said the entire day wouldn't happen until he got home.

But he *really* liked her, so his neurosis must have been pushed up a notch.

Cora sighed, as if what she was about to say wasn't her idea. "I did come over here with a purpose."

"Do tell." Hazel sat down on the stool next to him.

Being this close to her drove him insane.

Cora eyed Ethan as if she didn't want to continue.

Uh-oh.

"Your dramatic effect is palpable," he joked.

"*Palpable?*" Hazel shoved her shoulder against his with a laugh.

"Leave me alone." He laughed back. *But don't really. Could you just shove me again? Please?*

Finally, Cora shook her head in what appeared to be frustration as she eyed the two of them. Why would they frustrate her? Cora had seemed like she liked Ethan for Hazel. Or at least, that's what it felt like.

"I ran into Theo, and he asked about you," Cora spit out.

Theo? Who is Theo?

Don't panic.

But the way Hazel's head lifted up to Cora's, eyes wide and . . . excited? Thrilled? Definitely happy. "Theo Johnson?"

I already hate the guy.

"Yup. And he looks great. He really wants to meet up with you." Cora's eyes flashed at Ethan, almost daring him to say something.

Gah! Should I say something?

Ethan could literally feel Hazel slipping through his fingers as he sat there on a barstool, doing *nothing*.

Hazel jumped off her stool and stood in front of Cora, eyes still wild and open. "Cora. I had a dream about him *last* night. It's been twenty-four years since I've seen him, and I had a dream about him, *and* you happen to meet up with him today? *And* he mentioned me? *And* he wants to meet up?" Her voice pitched higher with each sentence.

Well, damn. That's as rom-com-y as they come.

Ethan's whole chest felt like it caved in, his stomach twisting in agony.

I think I just lost her.

I had a chance today. A real chance. And I blew it.

"The odds are astronomical!" Hazel was obviously on cloud nine with this news.

Ethan had to agree. The odds *were* astronomical.

Cora kind of groaned, though, as if she wasn't convinced. "We have lived in the same city our entire lives, so it makes sense we'd bump into people in our favorite places." Cora's eyes glanced at Ethan, almost like she was trying to make him feel better.

But he didn't.

Not when Hazel's whole being was lit up from the inside.

Whoever this Theo was, she'd obviously liked him. Loved him even.

"It's destiny." Hazel's words hit Ethan square in the heart.

Not the D-word.

"Is it, though?" Cora kept giving Ethan some kind of visual cue that he couldn't decipher.

He figured he should say something at this point. "Ex-boyfriend?"

Hazel shook her head. "I wanted him to be, but no. He was one of my best friends in college. It never went beyond that, but I always wanted it to."

Ethan wanted to go home and crawl into his bed and never leave again. "Well, this sounds like a sign. Or destiny, or whatever. You're going to call him, right?"

Please say no.

Wait. He thought he was starting to understand "Cora language," because he very distinctly felt like her widened eyes and lifted eyebrows were saying: *Do you really mean that?*

But no. Ethan was seeing what he wanted. Cora didn't know him. Why would she care what Ethan thought of some guy Hazel used to like. "I'm going to clean up these pics, and I'll show them to you later?"

At your wedding to Theo.

Hazel seemed surprised at Ethan's abruptness. "Oh yes, thank you, Ethan. I really appreciate it."

Lifting his laptop into his arms like a security blanket, Ethan wanted out of there. "Do you mind if I pick up the rest of my equipment tomorrow?"

"Of course." She was positively buzzing, then she smiled conspiratorially at him. "Maybe I'll have some news about Theo."

Ethan's stomach twisted again. He grabbed his camera and probably looked silly clutching both the camera and laptop, but he forced a smile. "Can't wait."

And he pretty much ran.

Okay maybe not *ran*, but definitely a brisk walk.

So far, every time he left Hazel's house, he had failed in life in epic proportions.

There had been a perfect opportunity to apologize for

friend-zoning her, but her beautiful, sparkling eyes made him freeze.

To be fair, he'd only had one therapy session. Jane still hadn't texted him back from yesterday. Maybe he should call?

Yes.

Call therapist.

Fix self.

Easy.

But first?

Crawl into bed and GrubHub In and Out.

It's a date

Hazel's mind raced. Theo? She literally had been having the most amazing dream about him last night until Spike had woken her up from it. And Cora ran into him? After twenty-something years?

Thank you, Grams!

"Cora, give me Theo's number." Hazel wanted to get started immediately.

Cora pulled out her phone, definitely not as enthusiastic as Hazel would expect her to be, but she couldn't think about that. Cora was always more of a realist, so she was just looking out for her. As she pulled up Theo's info to text to Hazel, Cora mumbled something. Hazel swore she heard the word *clueless* in there somewhere.

"What was that?" she asked her friend.

"Nothing," Cora sighed.

Ignoring Cora's strange mood at this sudden turn of events, Hazel opened Theo's number on her phone.

All she had to do was hit Call.

Holding her hand to her chest, Hazel took a deep breath. "Oh my god, I'm so nervous."

Cora's face softened at Hazel's obvious nerves. "He was one of your best friends. Try to put yourself back when it was normal to call him."

But that dream kiss?

It was hard to not think about as she readied herself to call.

And he was so pretty. That intimidated her back then, let alone now. "Is he still pretty?" Hazel was kind of hoping for a "not as much" to help with her nerves.

"He's very much still pretty. Now, you got this. Hit Call," Cora encouraged.

Gulp.

I'm going to do it.

Okay, I'm doing it.

Why aren't I doing it?

Hazel hit Call as she fanned herself frantically with her hand. "It's ringing!" she said a little louder than she expected.

"Phones often do that." Cora smiled.

"Shut it."

Then his voice came through the speaker of her phone, the very voice from her dream of him last night.

Theo.

"Hello?" Deep and rich with a little hint of gentle

and sweet, just like she remembered.

Everything about this man was beautiful.

"Theo? It's Hazel." Did she croak that out? If Cora's face was any indication, she definitely did.

"Hazel!" The energy in Theo's voice went up three notches. "I didn't think you'd call. I mean, I hoped you'd call, but I wasn't sure after how we left things."

Um, what?

Racking her brain, Hazel came up with nothing. All she remembered was graduating and drifting apart.

She turned to Cora for help, mouthing, "How did we leave things?"

But Cora's face was as blank as hers. She even added an obligatory shrug. "I don't remember," she whispered.

At a loss, Hazel scrunched her face, trying to think of something to say that didn't imply she had no idea what he was talking about. "Yeah. Twenty-four years makes that all fade away, though. I can barely even remember."

Cora snorted a laugh, and Hazel waved her to be quiet.

"I just figured . . ." he began. *Figured what? What did he figure? Think, Hazel, think!* "Never mind. I'm happy you called. Listen, Cora told me you were starting your own plant store. I went into horticulture myself, and there's this amazing expo that's happening tomorrow if you'd like to go with me?"

"Like a comic-con for plants?" A buzz of excitement coursed through Hazel. Not only did an expo sound amazing, but Theo was also into horticulture? The coincidences were becoming overwhelming. No. Not coincidences. Fate. Although she did remember him being really into gardening back when she knew him, it was actually what caused them to meet, and her grandmother taught him a few tricks as well, but still. Fate.

Theo laughed. "Only you would put it that way, but you definitely could call it that. You in?"

Was she blushing? "Yeah. I'm in."

"Great. I'll text you the address and where to meet." There was a pause on Theo's end, and Hazel could have sworn he was smiling and blushing as well. "See you then," he finally said.

"Can't wait."

Hazel ended the call and rushed to Cora, hugging her, not able to contain her excitement.

Pulling away, Hazel took a moment to reflect on the phone call. "How the heck did I leave it with Theo?"

"We should pull a card," Cora suggested.

"Ooo yes, let me get one of my decks." Hazel walked over to the bookshelf in the living room and pulled out a standard tarot deck. She'd had some luck with it in the past, and it would do in a pinch. Like now.

Bringing the deck over to the island, Hazel shuffled thoroughly, then she spread the entire array of cards covering the area in front of her. Swirling them all around, closing her eyes, she finally picked one.

Turning it over, her eyes widened.

The Lovers.

"Cora!" Hazel squeaked in excited shock.

Cora raised an eyebrow at the card. "Okay, but

remember, The Lovers means that love is coming into your life, but it also warns that it may be between *two* temptations."

Hazel knew where Cora's head was at, and suddenly her lack of enthusiasm for Theo made perfect sense. "Would you stop with Ethan? He's not interested."

"Isn't he, though?" Cora didn't look convinced in the least. "Because the guy that was just here was very into you."

Hazel couldn't control the butterflies flapping around like monsters in her stomach at hearing that. No. She *wouldn't* go there. "Stop. We kissed. He friend-zoned me. End of story. I have to take it at face value. I'm not doing the reading-into-everything game."

"But you said it was the best kiss you ever had."

"Cora!" Hazel needed to shut her down before her words would bore their way into the tiny cracks she'd already made for herself in regards to Ethan.

"Fine. Enjoy your plant comic-con with some guy you haven't seen in twenty-four years." Cora crossed her arms.

"I will. Thanks," Hazel claimed defiantly and held up the tarot card in emphasis. "Now help me figure out what to wear."

Chapter 18
Ethan
A magical discovery

"How did you feel when you got that text?" Jane asked, her smile unable to hide how thrilled she was at Ethan's news of his Zoom call with his family.

"I actually teared up, but then . . . just happy. Like they *heard* me," Ethan admitted.

"That's amazing, Ethan."

"And with only one session." Ethan wanted to give Jane all the credit. Without her, he never would have said he loved his parents to their faces on a weekly Zoom call. Which, thinking that made him realize how messed up that was.

"I'm only steering you. You've done so much work on your own before you stepped in here. But I'm happy that your parents responded."

"It feels like a good beginning." Ethan smiled.

"Now what about Hazel? Have you told her how you feel?" Jane's tone was thoughtful.

"No. I freeze. And now she's going to meet up with another one of her past guys again," Ethan grumbled.

"Another one?" Even Jane seemed surprised.

"Right?" Ethan lifted his hands in emphasis. "Some guy she went to college with. Apparently, he's really into plants like she is, and I kill them, so . . ." Ethan slunk into his chair.

"No negative self-talk, remember?"

"I was going to tell her I like her. I swear I was going to, but then I didn't, and then her friend Cora said she ran into the guy, and she'd dreamt about him, and . . . yeah." Ethan had nothing more to say about it.

"Hazel can't consider you a viable option until you tell her you're a viable option." Jane breathed in deep. "What are you afraid will happen if you tell her?"

"That she'll reject me."

"But you rejected her, and she's still your friend. You don't think you could do the same?"

Ethan stopped his anxiety-ridden brain for a moment. "I'd still want to be friends. I don't want her ever to be out of my life."

"Then you have nothing to lose."

"And if she does reject me, can I call you immediately?" Ethan was already feeling the panic.

"You can *email* me, and we'll set up a time to meet, yes." Jane set the boundaries.

Relief flooded through him.

He could do this.

Maybe he could do this.

Most probably he could do this.

"That's our time, but you should feel very accomplished. You did great." Jane smiled.

Ethan's chest swelled with pride, but more than that, a sense that he was moving in the right direction. It was a foreign feeling, but he found that he really liked it.

With a thank-you and a quick calendar setup for their next meeting, Ethan exited Jane's building feeling centered.

Pretty soon, he'd be able to confess his feelings to Hazel. He knew they'd only spent a few times together, but Ethan really liked her. A lot. Too much maybe? And now she was probably off seeing some new guy from her past while he was groaning about it in therapy.

Theo.

What kind of name was Theo?

And Boone.

What? Did she only like guys that sounded like characters from a romance novel? Would the next one be Tristan? Or Connor? Or Chase?

Breathe.

Jane told him to breathe when he got worked up, and he was officially worked up.

After the third breath, he was dizzy but a little calmer. Maybe he should slow it down next time instead of gulping air like he was drowning.

He turned the corner of the building to walk to his vehicle when he spotted Mateo and Austin leaning up against Mateo's Toyota parked next to his car.

Mateo observed him carefully as Ethan approached. "Whoa, you look beat. I'm glad to see you're taking therapy seriously." He nodded his approval.

Austin smiled in appreciation as well. "Good on you, Ethan."

"What are you guys doing here?" It came out a little more abruptly than he'd intended, but he didn't feel like hearing them pat him on the back for spilling his guts.

Mateo grinned. "We thought we'd take you to your favorite cafe for lunch and celebrate your insane turnaround on those invites you gave me the files for this morning. I have a box of them here if you want to see your handiwork?"

Beaming on the inside, Ethan hurried the last five feet to their sides.

Austin handed him the invite with an impressed smile.

Ethan carefully took it into his hands, examining every detail. The black textured card stock and gold inlay border turned out beautifully. And the gold silhouetted artwork carved into the paper itself, of the classic eighties characters he picked, ranging from Sloth from *The Goonies* to Princess Leia from *Star Wars.* It definitely belonged in an eighties fairytale.

"The gold turned out so well." Ethan traced the decorative border with his finger.

"And along with your hefty paycheck, you get a plus-one." Mateo's expression was pointed.

"I'm seriously invited to this?" Ethan asked. Mateo had hinted at it before, but usually the graphic designer wasn't a consideration when it came to invites, especially ones that made "reminder" invites and not even the original e-vite.

Austin crossed his arms with a satisfied smile. "It's a pretty exclusive list too. We're going to drop these off at headquarters after lunch. They are to be messengered to each person who RSVP'd."

"Ooo, messengered. That is fancy."

"What about your neighbor woman? You could take her?" Austin eyed him hopefully.

Handing the invite back to Austin, Ethan shook his head. "Nah. She's already moved on to some guy she knew in college."

"I thought you said an ex-coworker?" Mateo asked.

"That one didn't work out. This is a new one." Ethan didn't really want to talk about it.

But Mateo and Austin wouldn't let it go.

Austin observed, "So nothing serious?"

"I really don't know, guys." Ethan tried to act like he was over it, like he didn't care, but he was never any good at hiding things from Mateo. Or at least, Mateo knew him so well he could read him better than anyone.

"I've never seen you like this about anyone before. Especially someone that appears healthy and non-toxic," Mateo said thoughtfully.

Under his breath, Austin added, "Although she is trying to reconnect with all her exes. Not sure how healthy *that* is."

"I heard that," Ethan grumbled. "But honestly, you guys were right. Therapy is helping me. It just might be too late for me with Hazel."

Austin patted Ethan on the back supportively. "Don't give up. She really does sound great. But even if she ends up with college guy, you'll find someone."

Nodding, Ethan gave them both a reassuring smile he didn't feel. "How about that lunch?"

Mateo and Austin side-hugged Ethan.

"We'll take my car. Get in." Mateo motioned to the back door.

The café was only a mile away, so it didn't take long to get there. It was called Nookish Corner and was also a used bookstore, which always felt like the perfect combo to Ethan, plus they had an amazing chicken, brie, and green apple sandwich with arugula that he needed in his belly.

But as they walked into the café, he caught something out of the corner of his eye on the bookstore side of things.

"Hang on, guys. I have to check something out." When he arrived at the table in front of the store, an old copy of *Escape to Ashdonia* was displayed.

Hazel's favorite book.

She'd mentioned that she wanted the greenhouse to become her Ashdonia.

Mateo arrived at his side, looking back and forth between the book and Ethan. "Austin is ordering for us and getting a table. You going to buy that?"

"It's Hazel's favorite book." Ethan was rooted in place.

"And you don't know if you should get it for her? She probably already has a copy," Mateo's said softly.

The store owner, Brady, walked over. "But this is an original."

Brady said that about every book, trying to get a little extra money out of the deal.

"All right, Brady, how much?" Ethan asked.

"For you, Ethan? Twenty bucks. Look, it's even signed." Brady peeled the card stock cover back to reveal a signature that was definitely not Freya Fairweather. It looked like . . . John Larry? With an inscription of "I miss you" above it. And Ethan was also pretty sure that an original copy of *Escape to Ashdonia* would at least be a thousand bucks.

But he liked Brady, so he acted surprised. "That's amazing, Brady, thank you."

Puffing his chest, Brady led Ethan and Mateo to the counter, ringing up the book.

Mateo looked at his friend thoughtfully. "You really buying this book for Hazel?"

"I don't know if I'll have the guts to ever give it to her, but yeah. It's a first printing, after all."

Mateo laughed.

Placing the book in a bag, Brady handed it over after Ethan paid.

A bubble of joy swelled up in Ethan's chest at the thought of giving Hazel the book. He knew she probably already had a copy, but one signed by John Larry?

Now that was a prize.

Oh, Theo

Deep breath.

Hazel sat in her car in the parking lot of a high school where the plant expo was being held. Not intending to, she'd arrived an hour early. She was amazed her car made it. The gurgling sounds had lasted at least ten minutes. She definitely should get that looked at. Just not today.

The expo was in such an odd location that she'd been afraid she'd get lost, so she left an hour and a half before their set meeting time. Turned out, it only took a half hour to get there.

Through the fencing, Hazel saw peeks of green, enticing her to exit her car, but she was going to wait until it was five minutes before they were scheduled to meet.

Her phone rang.

"Hey, Mom. How's Spain?" Hazel asked, thrilled to have her mother help stall for time.

"Amazing. It's so beautiful. I just wanted to check in with you. You haven't called in a few days."

"I'm good. I'm actually meeting up with Theo from college. Do you remember him?"

"Of course! I think he spent more time with your grandmother than you. He loved to garden."

Okay, maybe the "astronomical odds" that he was also into plants wasn't so astronomical.

Trying to make simple things into "signs" like you did with Logan.

"Yeah, actually, we're meeting at a plant expo, in fact."

"Are you sitting in the parking lot?"

"Yeah."

"How early did you get there?"

"An hour."

Her mother chuckled, and Hazel could hear her dad laugh as well.

"Hi, Dad."

"Hey, kiddo."

"I won't keep you, but don't put all your eggs into one basket." Her mother's tone was light, but Hazel developed a Cora-sized itch at the back of her neck.

"Did Cora talk to you?"

A pause.

"Well, yes, and she told us about your neighbor . . . Hazel, he sounds . . ."

Hazel interrupted her, "Mom. Stop."

To her credit, her mother did.

"I'm going to go see Theo now and have an amazing day, okay?"

A sigh. "Okay, sweetie. Tell him we said hello."

"I will."

Hazel ended the call. She had to take in a few deep, calming breaths. The last thing she wanted to think about before her date with Theo was *Ethan*.

Deep breath.

Glancing at the clock on her phone, it was time.

Leaving her vehicle, Hazel walked toward the front entrance, her stomach roiling.

"Calm down. Breathe. You got this. No big deal," she repeated under her breath.

As her feet hit the cobblestones of the entrance, she couldn't resist taking a better gander past the gates. Her heart sang at the sight of booth after booth of every color imaginable. "Whoa," she said in appreciation.

"My thoughts exactly," Theo's familiar voice came from behind her.

Whirling around, Hazel came face-to-face with Theo. Looking exactly like her dream, only a bit grayer and with more wear around the eyes. Simply beautiful. Even his clothes made him look like a model, fitted T-shirt where you could just see the outline of his six-pack abs, jeans that fit him perfectly, and Doc Martens.

Hazel froze for a moment as she took a mental picture of him, then shook herself out of it. "Theo. It's so good to see you."

"You too," he said as he reached down (my god she forgot how tall he was) and hugged her.

It was a good hug.

A hug for the ages in fact.

But it was going on a little long.

Should she pull away?

Should she wait for him to pull away?

They were still hugging.

Finally, Hazel pulled away with a shy smile (or she hoped it was endearingly shy and not awkward).

But Theo didn't seem to notice as he waved two tickets triumphantly. "I got us passes." He held his arm out for her to take.

Immediately, Hazel remembered Ethan doing the same right before their kiss, and her stomach turned at the memory.

Theo, she reminded herself. She was on a sort-of date with Theo.

Stupid Mom for putting Ethan in my head.

Stupid Cora for putting Ethan in my mom's head.

Stupid me for letting it work!

"Shall we?" Theo asked, still smiling.

"We shall." Hazel looped her arm in his and pushed all thoughts of Ethan aside.

Giving the person at the entrance their tickets, Theo led Hazel into paradise.

Long aisles that seemed endless, with booths filled with every plant imaginable. There had to be at least twenty rows if Hazel were to count. She'd never seen this many plants in one place before, and it sent her heart reeling. Everywhere her head turned was a cornucopia of green mixed with splashes of bright-colored flowers. For a moment, it overwhelmed her, but then her excitement took over and she was ready to shop.

Arm still wrapped in Theo's as they walked down the main aisle, Hazel couldn't open her eyes wide enough to take it all in.

"If this expo had existed back in college, I would have taken you and your grandma. She taught me so much. You know she was the reason I went into horticulture?"

"I didn't know that. She would have loved that."

"Loved?" Theo's forehead crinkled. At Hazel's nod, he shook his head. "I'm so sorry. She was quite a lady. I still use her weight trick for watering."

"Same," Hazel responded with another stab to her gut. The very trick she'd taught Ethan.

Why was he ruining this date?

But Hazel's attention was soon veered to a nearby booth. She pulled away from Theo, hurrying to the booth. "This Boston fern is gorgeous." She admired it. The entire booth was draped with every type of fern imaginable.

Theo picked up another fern that looked more like octopus legs. "What about the asparagus fern? It's got a Cthulhu vibe to it. Good for stores."

Shaking her head, Hazel checked the long strands of leaves on the Boston. "Asparagus ferns are poisonous to pets. My whole store is pet-friendly plants."

"Oh, I love that. Then yes, let's get rid of this one." He placed the asparagus fern down, then searched the vast variety of ferns in the booth, finally picking up a smaller one with branches that reached upward. "The *Nephrolepis obliterata* or Kimberly Queen fern. Completely safe for animals." He held it out for her to examine.

Hazel put down the Boston to touch the tiny thin leaves of the Kimberly, and their hands touched.

Not the electric tingle that Ethan gave her, but she definitely didn't want to pull away either.

Stop comparing him to Ethan! I'm not even comparing him to Logan! What the heck is wrong with me?

"It's perfect." Hazel kept her hand touching Theo's.

His eyes pierced into her. "My thoughts exactly."

Heat reached her cheeks, and she looked away, motioning the vendor. "I'll take the Boston and the Kimberly."

"Good choice," the vendor said kindly, taking both ferns and placing them in a box. "That'll be an even twenty for both."

Handing him the twenty, Theo picked up the box. "We should probably get a cart. I'm going to get some plants too."

Spotting an area up ahead with a row of flatbed dollies, Hazel nodded toward them.

As they both walked toward the flatbeds, Hazel began to feel comfortable with Theo, more like how they used to be. Before she could chicken out, Hazel said, "So Theo, I have to be honest with you. I don't remember how we left things. I thought everything was good between us."

Rearing his head back in surprise, Theo almost dropped the box. "You seriously don't remember?"

She really didn't.

"Graduation? Sandra?" Theo prodded.

Oh god.

It all flooded back into her brain. Every painful moment of it.

It had been graduation day, and Hazel and Theo were sitting next to each other in a sea of empty fold-out chairs. Early as usual. Most of the students were milling about chatting, not many wanting to sit down yet.

Hazel had wanted to warn Theo about his girlfriend. Not because she was jealous but because she genuinely didn't like her. And maybe a little because she was jealous. She'd given him the whole spiel: Sandra wasn't what she seemed, she was different around his friends, she was just . . . mean. Hazel actually told him that she didn't think Sandra should be his girlfriend.

She couldn't believe she'd forgotten his face. It had been a cross between sadness and anger, and then he said the kicker. That Hazel was too late, he'd proposed that morning.

Aaaannnd Sandra was right behind her. She'd heard every defaming word Hazel had said.

Okay, it made sense why she blocked it out.

"Yup. I remember now." Hazel tried to give Theo a look that was as apologetic as possible. "How is Sandra these days?"

Crap. Was Theo married?

"I honestly don't know. You were right. She was mean."

Phew. And duh.

They arrived at the cart section, and Theo placed the box on one of their surfaces.

"I'm really sorry," Hazel said.

Theo pushed the cart forward as they continued to walk down the main aisle of the expo. "Are you, though?" He smiled.

Hazel laughed. "Not really. And now I can give you a twenty-four-year-old 'I told you so.'"

Theo smiled and shook his head. "And what about you? Cora said you got married but are recently divorced. And she said other things as well." He scrunched his face, obviously not sure how much Hazel wanted to talk about Logan.

"Yeah, let's not ruin the date," Hazel answered.

Theo replied, "Oh, this is a date?"

Hazel stopped in her tracks with panic. Why did she say that? Him even asking implied that he didn't think it was a date. *Breathe, Hazel. Breathe.* The humiliation threatened to knock her out.

But Theo stopped with her, gently taking her hand. "It's a date. It's a date. As long as you want it to be?" Now he looked like the shy one.

"I would," she answered, instantly relaxing because they were both on the same page.

"After we finish shopping, let's go for dinner?" he asked with a smile.

"I'd love that," Hazel answered, her stomach doing excited somersaults.

Theo's eyes sparkled at that, and the two of them continued down the aisle.

Chapter 20
Ethan

Daydreaming and wishes

Ethan sat down at his desk ready to make progress on client work that was due next week. He'd already figured out what he wanted to design, so he knew it wouldn't take long.

But as he directed the mouse to the appropriate folder, he *accidentally* signed into Instagram.

He'd started following Hazel yesterday, and she'd quickly followed back, but he'd somehow managed to restrain himself from total online stalking until now. He'd already looked up to see that the plant expo *lover boy* wanted to take her to was today, so he needed to know if she was there.

With him.

Bad idea?

Oh, definitely.

He clicked on her page, then promptly closed his eyes, not wanting to see.

This was helping no one, so he opened one eyelid and did a quick scan of her pics.

Heart sinking, both eyes open now, Ethan stared at a selfie with Hazel and *Theolicious44*.

Ew.

Theolicious?

How?

How is she interested in him?

Then he really looked at the photo.

That guy was way too good-looking for his own good.

Definitely a *dream guy*.

This is unhealthy.

Ethan closed out Instagram and redirected the mouse to his current work folder, but he saw another folder right next to it labeled "Hazel_store."

It wouldn't hurt to work on her website first. Maybe it would be the perfect surprise for her when she got home from her plant date with what's-his-name.

Plants, seriously?

His stomach sank.

Why would she pick Ethan, plant-killer extraordinaire, over a guy who shared her passion?

She wouldn't, moron. That's why she's on a date with him and not you.

Nope.

No negative self-talk.

Jane had shut that down in their last session today when Ethan had spiraled about his perceived unworthiness. He had a lot of work to do to build up his self-esteem, but he was already feeling lighter.

Clicking on the folder, he opened the photos in his editing program.

The first picture that popped up was of Hazel.

Oh, and the plants.

But Hazel.

Her eyes looking into the camera. He wondered what she'd been thinking in that moment. It was the last photo he took, right after they skirted around him shutting down any romantic connection after their kiss. What kept stopping him from telling her how much he regretted that? It was so ingrained into his DNA, he wondered if he'd ever be able to open up, even with therapy.

Man, his family had really done a number on him.

Ethan knew to his core he wanted to be a verbally affectionate person as well as physical, but when it had been trained out of him his entire childhood, then suddenly set free at eighteen, he shut down. It was easier that way.

Kelly had been the only one he'd let in.

And look what happened there.

But Hazel was worth it.

Worth risking it all.

He just needed to destroy decades of toxic behavior.

No big deal.

Ethan groaned.

Viewing more of the photos, he knew he had some good ones, and he began playing around with different settings to find the perfect mood for Hazel's site. Some of the pictures with Spike were like the cat was a dang cat model. Man, he loved that feline.

A few hours had passed before he knew it, and he was ready to publish the new updates. He could swap out whatever she wanted, or scrap the whole thing, but he wanted anyone that may stumble across her site to see that it was professional. Not that what she'd done was horrible, but to a graphic designer, it was pretty horrible.

Now it had a vibe. Warm tones, rack-focused photos featuring Spike and the plants, and a few candids of Hazel amongst her Ashdonia.

Sitting back with a satisfied smile, he almost wanted to text her to show it off.

But he knew she was on her date.

Her photos on Instagram didn't lie.

She didn't know he knew that she was on a date, though.

Was he making sense?

How did young people date these days with built-in apps that allow you to track the people you like at all times?

Back when Ethan was in high school and even through his twenties, no one had cell phones, they had landlines. The only way someone could get a hold of you was through calling them at home or at work. That was it.

He quietly longed for that simpler time.

But also, he wanted to track both Hazel's and Theo's posts.

Sorry, *Theolicious44*.

Why?

Scrapping that particular toxic urge was harder than he expected, but he managed to stop himself.

Sighing in triumph, Ethan stared at a candid of Hazel on her newly minted website.

She was so beautiful.

Thump.

Ethan yelped from surprise at Spike jumping onto his lap.

"Spike! You scared the crap out of me. How the heck did you get in here?"

Spike answered by giving a few biscuits on Ethan's thigh, then promptly curling into a ball on his legs.

True bliss filled every cell in his body.

My god, he loved this cat.

Oh, ew, oh seriously, no, gross

The day sped by as both Hazel and Theo ended up stacking up two flatbed carts instead of one. His expertise was invaluable, and Hazel knew she had some amazing plants for her store. Ethan could come over and take more pictures.

Dang it.

No Ethan talk!

But she reminded herself that they were friends, and that he'd volunteered to help her.

But still.

No Ethan talk.

By the time they left the expo, it was already after six, and they were starving. Since they'd both driven to the expo, they had to drive separately, but she gave him directions to Nookish Corner, and they met there. Afterward, they'd wandered around the bookstore, and Hazel had felt a pang of disappointment when the paperback of *Escape to Ashdonia* that had been displayed on the front table for weeks had sold. Why hadn't she bought it when she had the chance? Since she had half of Ashdonia in her car at the moment, she'd thought it would be a good omen to buy it. Oh well, it wasn't meant to be. She quietly said a little prayer to the book gods that it found a good home.

Theo offered to help her move the plants to the greenhouse, so they both pulled into her driveway to park.

"It's in back," Hazel said as they exited their cars.

"I remember." Theo smiled.

The two of them lugged all twenty of Hazel's new plants into the greenhouse, went inside to wash their hands, and walked out to the front.

And now it was time.

Time to end the date.

Standing at her front door, Hazel and Theo were inches from each other.

"I had an amazing day." Theo gently brushed Hazel's cheek with his hand.

"Me too," Hazel said, though she was disappointed that his touch hadn't caused any romantic flutters.

But if his kiss was anything like her dream . . . she knew it would be good.

"Can I call you again?" Theo asked, though his eyes told her that he already knew the answer.

"You better," Hazel flirted.

Hazel's chest filled with anticipation.

Here it came.

Theo leaned in.

His lips met hers and . . .

Oh god.

No.

Theo's mouth opened so wide, Hazel was afraid he would swallow her entire jaw.

Oh.

Ew.

This was awful.

Was that his tongue?

Incoming.

Incoming.

Incoming.

He shoved his tongue so far into her mouth she choked the kiss to an end.

Nope.

Bad kisser.

Terrible kisser.

Deal-breaker.

Logan had been terrible too, and it took years for her to teach him how to kiss her how she liked.

But no chemistry. Awful kiss.

Sorry, Theo.

Her heart ached as yet another dream guy wasn't what she thought they'd be.

"Wow," Theo sighed happily.

Apparently, he thought differently of the kiss.

Oh god, did Ethan feel the way Hazel felt now after they had kissed?

She couldn't take that.

"Yeah, wow," was all Hazel could say.

Was she a horrible kisser too? It was all a matter of perspective, right?

Her ribs grew tight at the thought.

Theo nodded to five large bags of fertilizer resting against Hazel's house that she hadn't even noticed. "You need help bringing those into the greenhouse? I could stay a bit longer."

"No. I got it. Thanks. Good night, Theo."

Theo tipped an imaginary hat with a smile. "Call you tomorrow."

"Theo, wait." Hazel couldn't let him leave without being honest. He deserved that much. They might not have physical chemistry, but he was still a wonderful guy.

His eyes lit up, hopeful.

And it crushed Hazel. "I'm so sorry, Theo, but I think we should just be friends." The mirroring of Ethan saying almost the same thing to her cut her deeply, but she had to do it.

Theo's face fell. "Was it the kiss?"

She couldn't hurt his ego with the truth, so she said, "It's just, I had such a wonderful day with you today, and I realized when we kissed that I really love our friendship. I feel like if we'd been into each other romantically, we would have explored that in college. Does that make sense?"

After a moment, he nodded. "I get that. We always were best buds. I really missed you."

"I missed you too."

Theo smiled. "I'll call you when the next gardening event is happening. I think there's an underground tomato fest in Silverlake next week."

Hazel smiled. "I'm in."

Theo closed the distance between them and gave her a hug. A nice, Theo-style, warm, fuzzy hug.

"Good night," he said.

"Good night, Theo."

He walked to his car and slid inside, starting the engine. Watching Theo drive away, Hazel couldn't help but feel like she'd failed at life in some way.

What's wrong with me?

Who knew manure would be the highlight of my night?

As soon as Theo's car was completely out of view (so as not to offend him), Hazel wiped all of his spit off her face.

She loved the guy, but that kiss was like being mauled by a golden retriever (though *that* she would have at least enjoyed). "Ew. Ew. Ew." She needed a shower or at least a good face scrub. Looking up at the sky, she shook her head. "Why?"

"How was the date?"

Was that?

Ethan.

He walked the rest of the way across the street, Spike in his arms. "Apparently, Spike didn't want to be alone tonight. I have no idea how he got in my house, but when I was working, he curled in a ball on my lap."

Hazel laughed. "Spike," she gently scolded, giving

him a little scratch on the cheek while he was still in Ethan's arms. Looking up at him, she confessed, "The date was perfect, better than perfect, dream worthy." Her heart still grumbled at how she had zero chemistry with Theo.

Ethan's eyes darted to Spike, and he wasn't smiling.

Was he . . . ?

He definitely seemed disappointed.

Maybe Cora was right . . .

No. Stop. I'm shifting focus to Ethan because he's literally the best kisser I've ever kissed. He probably thinks your kiss was a sloppy mess.

"Well, hey, that's great," Ethan managed to say.

And did Spike just head-butt his chin to comfort him?

Did he need comfort?

Time for the horrendous reveal.

"But the good-night kiss? It was quite possibly the worst kiss I've ever experienced. I can still feel his spit on my cheek. The guy was like a vacuum-cleaner-fish-monster." It felt good to rant.

Ethan laughed. "So not your dream guy?"

"I guess not." Hazel scratched Spike's cheeks with both hands to his delight while Ethan held him. Then she went for it. "Well, if *you* hadn't rejected me . . ."

She searched his eyes to gauge his reaction.

His smile was kind but serious as well.

It almost seemed like he wanted to kiss her.

Even Spike looked up at Ethan from his arms, anticipating.

But Ethan talked instead. "You know I decided to go to therapy after that kiss."

Oh, man.

It must have been pretty bad if it made him go to therapy! Her stomach twisted. "That bad, huh?"

Ethan made sure their eyes met when he said, "That *good*."

I can't breathe.

Can I breathe?

Okay, I can breathe.

Her entire body vibrated with energy.

The kiss wasn't terrible.

He went to therapy because it was so good.

Wait. What?

But it looked like he was going to kiss her now, and after that horrible fish-mouth kiss, Hazel was ready.

The tension built between them as neither of them spoke.

Is he going to?

Should I maybe?

After a long moment, Hazel decided not to push. When she reached to take Spike into her own arms, Spike decided to jump out of Ethan's grasp and walk to the side of the house where the five bags of fertilizer were propped.

"I forgot about those," Hazel groaned.

Ethan seemed to see the fertilizer for the first time. "That's a lot of fertilizer. You're not building bombs and your plant store is a front? Because it won't take them long to track down my designs. I'll be an accomplice. But if it's the right target, I got your back."

Hazel laughed as she walked up to the first bag and grabbed the top corners. "I thought I ordered five-pound bags, not fifty pounds."

Ethan took hold of the bottom corners, and the two began to walk toward the backyard. "Fifty and five are an easy mistake."

"It's a sign I need to grow my business," Hazel joked.

"It's a sign you should get your money back," he teased.

Arriving at the greenhouse, they plopped the heavy bag on the ground just inside the door.

"So any more exes you plan on hunting down?" Ethan asked quietly.

Hazel wiped her brow, thinking. "Maybe Dennis?" She suddenly thought of the hot toxic boy she dated in her early twenties.

Ethan cracked his back. "We're way too old for labor."

Stretching her arms, Hazel nodded. "Tell me about it."

"Who's Dennis?" Ethan attempted to ask nonchalantly.

Hazel came clean. "My toxic twenties relationship."

"Twenties? I'm still in those," Ethan admitted.

Hazel laughed. "What if he's better now, though?"

"I'm thinking you'll have better luck with dating apps at this point."

"No. Those were terrible. The connections I've been pursuing were genuine, but I shoved them aside so I could marry a guy that wasn't even attracted to me." Her chest squeezed. She hadn't expected to say something like that out loud, but there it was. The reality she'd been fighting since Logan came out. She'd been in a twenty-two-year relationship with someone who never wanted her in that way.

Ethan stepped closer to her. "Don't say that." He lifted his hand as if he wanted to touch her, but then lowered it quickly.

"But it's true. Two decades of hiding, of believing a lie about myself. That I wasn't pretty enough, thinking my self-esteem was so low because I could tell he didn't look at me like he wanted me. There's truly nothing like the feeling of being desired. That's why I was so hopeful today. I could feel it from Theo. And it felt good." Why was she telling him all this? She hadn't even told Cora any of these thoughts.

Ethan's stare intensified, and Hazel's heart thudded in her chest.

More than anything she wanted him to kiss her.

Was it one-sided?

He said the kiss was good.

"But then he almost swallowed your face," Ethan said, his voice husky, one side of his lips turned in a roguish smile.

"On full suction."

They both laughed at that.

"But you and your ex, you were together what? Twenty years?"

Hazel sat on the edge of the table.

Ethan sat next to her, their legs touching.

A shiver raced down her spine at his touch.

Dang it.

Why doesn't he like me?

Or if he does, why doesn't he like me enough?

"Twenty-two, yeah."

"And it was good? Most of it anyway?"

Hazel leaned her head against the wall of the greenhouse. "Yeah. That's what makes it so hard."

Turning his body to face her, Ethan's eyes bored into hers. "He loved you and you loved him. That's more than most people get in a lifetime."

She'd never thought of it that way. "I guess," Hazel admitted.

Ethan's hand brushed next to her leg, and another thrill raced through her.

"I *know*. Look at me?" Ethan's smile was sad. "We're the same age, and I've never had a love like that. Trust me, you're still in the lucky category."

Back to staring.

It took everything in Hazel's power not to grab him and pull him into her. But she didn't think she could take the rejection. After everything she'd confessed, it would be too painful.

After another long moment of silence, Ethan finally said, "It smells like manure."

Hazel and Ethan laughed again.

"Yeah." Hazel appreciated Ethan's way of making her laugh in any situation.

But his brows furrowed, becoming serious once more. "I'd never gone to therapy before, and it's helping me work through all . . . all my stuff . . . like . . ." He stopped, hands suddenly fidgeting.

Hazel leaned forward and placed her hand over his.

Electricity shot through every one of her fingers at touching him. "Like after our kiss?"

Ethan nodded, hand now gently holding hers back, eyes still searching for words. "I regret that."

Hazel's heart dropped.

He *did* regret kissing her. "The kiss?" She had to know for sure.

But Ethan shook his head. "No. The metaphorical running away part."

Oh boy.

If she didn't stop herself, she was going to jump him right on the table, plants be damned.

She stood up abruptly. "I should head in. I'll bring the rest of the bags in tomorrow. Thank you so much for all your help."

Ethan stood, forehead crinkling. "I'm sorry. Did I mess up again?" His voice was small.

His vulnerability broke her. But she couldn't let him reject her again. She *couldn't*. No matter how much it seemed he wanted to possibly try things again with her.

Hazel reached up and kissed him on the cheek. "No. I'm just really tired. Vacuum kiss and all."

Ethan smiled, but his expression hadn't changed. "Okay. Well, good night."

"Good night, Ethan."

Ethan stayed a beat, then started to walk away.

"Ethan?" Hazel fought internally about letting him go.

His head turned.

She didn't know what to say.

Finally, the words came to her. "I'm glad you're going to therapy. It sounds like it's helping you."

"Thanks." Ethan gave her a small, heartbreaking smile, then turned and left.

Hazel watched him go.

If ever she needed a dream for clarity, it was now!

One last try

Hazel sat on the floor of the greenhouse wondering how she got there. She'd been known to sleepwalk over the course of her life, but she never left the house entirely.

When she stood up, her eyes instantly watered as she truly took in her surroundings.

Early morning light filtered in through the windows, creating a beautiful golden glow on the plants around her. And there were thousands of them.

When did this happen?

Every inch of shelf, counter, and table was overflowing with green, healthy leaves from all the thriving flora.

An old-fashioned wrought-iron bench stood in the corner.

Ashdonia.

It was the symbol in *Escape to Ashdonia* that would let

the characters know they'd made it from their world into Ashdonia.

"Hello, dear."

Whirling around, Hazel was face to face with her grandmother. Without hesitation, she hugged her tightly.

Finally, pulling away, Hazel said, "I'm dreaming?"

But it felt so real.

Her Grams reached up and touched Hazel's cheek lovingly. "The only way I can see you."

Tears fell down Hazel's cheek. "Grams, I keep messing up. You keep sending me these dreams, and I think I'm just doing something . . . wrong."

Before taking her hand away, her grandmother wiped the wetness from Hazel's face. "You could never do anything wrong when you're simply finding out what you want. No regrets, right?"

Her words impacted Hazel more than she expected, but they rang true. "No regrets," she repeated.

Grams waved her hands, displaying all the plants. "You're almost there. I see even the bench arrived."

"My greenhouse isn't anywhere close to this one," Hazel said in awe.

"You're closer than you think." Grams smiled. "But not quite yet."

Grams clapped her hands together in one short burst.

Clap!

The greenhouse was gone.

Back to the white room.

Standing before her was her Dream Guy, in his blurred-face glory.

"Hey," she greeted. Part of her wanted to scream and try to find her grandmother again, but the larger part of her knew that Grams had sent Hazel here for a reason. Maybe she could finally figure out who this guy was.

"Hey," he said back.

"You're a hard man to track down."

"Am I?" he asked, genuine confusion in his voice.

"Yeah," Hazel answered, appalled.

He scratched his head aggressively. "Sorry. Seriously, this wig though."

As Hazel opened her mouth to respond, the dreamscape changed into . . .

Her old apartment from the nineties, when she lived in Van Nuys.

Clothes strewn on the floor, square TV, carpet, dingy couch, lots of teal and pink, yup, definitely her old apartment.

My lord she was a slob.

"Why am I here?"

Out of the bedroom walked Hazel in her twenties and Dennis, also in his twenties, and pretty much represented the grungy, slightly unwashed hair, hot guy of the time.

As Hazel grew older, so did her desire for both a clean house and a clean partner. Apparently the younger version of herself could care less.

Dennis and young Hazel stared at each other as if the world was about to end.

"So dramatic," she scoffed at the memory.

Pulling young Hazel into his face (because yeah, it

was like a full-on head smash), Dennis's lips met her younger self's.

That boy could kiss.

Hazel could almost feel the memory happening directly to her, but watching it gave her a pang of envy. Even though it was something that had happened to *her*, watching it play out in front of her made her realize that she'd never had that kind of passion with Logan, and she missed it.

Only Ethan had roused any of those old types of feelings.

So why wasn't she dreaming of him?

Where was Ethan if he was so perfect?

Grams had just visited her and brought her to the greenhouse of her dreams. Wouldn't she have said it was Ethan then? But she'd sent Hazel straight to the blurred-face version, giving Hazel time with the man himself. So, if Grams or the universe wanted her to be with Ethan, she would have dreamt about him already. Right?

Maybe dreaming about the men of her past was Grams's way of warning her not to get hurt again.

And Ethan could potentially *really* hurt her.

His rejection after their kiss already had crushed her more than she could admit to herself.

Hazel moved aside as the passionate couple of her past fumbled by her to the couch.

At this point, the dream was getting awkward. Hazel stared up at the ceiling trying to give them some . . . what? Privacy? This was ridiculous. The twenty-year-old on the couch was *her*.

"Is this some sort of message? Grams?" she asked aloud.

Dennis and young Hazel started to rip their clothes off.

Quite dramatically actually.

"Whoa. I know I'm watching me, but this is incredibly uncomfortable." Asking the ceiling again, she said, "Are you saying *Dennis* was my dream guy? You do remember how toxic he was, right?"

***

Hazel woke up with a start, only to find Spike on her chest making biscuits.

"Spike, buddy. You gotta stop waking me up like that," she scolded groggily. But she didn't mean it. He was ridiculously cute right now, making those biscuits. He rubbed his head under her chin. "Good morning to you, too."

Leaning over to her bedside table, she picked up her charging phone. 10:00 a.m.

"All right, I'm getting up. The master needs his treats obviously." Ten o'clock was late for Hazel. She must have needed the sleep.

Spike meowed in response.

"I said the T-word. My mistake."

He pranced around the bed, looking up at her with eyes that begged her to go to the kitchen and give him his num-nums.

"Okay, okay. Geez."

Getting out of bed, she quickly got dressed right as

the doorbell rang.

"I swear, who the heck?" But her heart suddenly raced at the thought that it might be Ethan.

Stop.

Tying her hair back in a ponytail (just in case) she hurried to the front door and opened it.

Cora stood there.

"Cora, hey." Hazel's voice cracked from still waking up.

"You were still in bed? It's ten a.m.!" Cora reared back as if she were affronted.

But not as affronted as Spike. The detour to the front door was not in his plans. He meowed quite aggressively to let her know.

"Yes, Spike, we're going to get your treats." Hazel nodded for Cora to come in, and they walked toward the kitchen.

"I'm assuming getting up late means your day with Theo went well?" Cora asked as she sat down on a barstool.

Hazel pulled down the bag of treats while Spike weaved through her legs as if he'd never been fed before in his life, and she could see his entirely full bowl of kibble in her line of sight. Laying down a small pile for him, he chowed down while purring loudly.

Standing up, Hazel scrunched her nose. "Vacuum-fish kisser."

Cora's head reared back. "Oh ew, no. Never again. Not after the years of training Logan you had to do."

"Right?" Hazel nodded. Cora knew her so well. "Grams visited my dreams again last night. She said I was closer than I think, and then I dreamt about Dennis."

"Oh no. We're not going into hot toxic boys of the past mode." Cora shook her head *and* waved her finger. She meant business. "Gladys would *not* approve."

"Maybe he's changed?" Hazel formed it as a question to soften the blow of Cora's potential reaction.

Cora sighed heavily, obviously exasperated. "Hazel."

"I know, I know. Dennis *was* toxic. It was because of him I went for healthy and safe . . . and gay apparently. But it's been almost thirty years. It *is* possible he's changed. Look at Ethan. He's our age and going to therapy for the first time," Hazel rationalized.

"Wait. Back up. Ethan is going to therapy?" Cora tilted her head.

Hazel grabbed a cookie off the plate and took a bite. "Yeah, last night he said after he friend-zoned me because of our kiss, he started going to therapy."

Saying it out loud gave it more impact.

And Hazel stunned herself mid-bite.

Cora's eyes widened, impressed. "Hazel."

"Cora."

"Not even Logan went to therapy for you, and you really tried to get him to go. He went *after* you two separated."

Barely able to swallow her lump of cookie, Hazel looked at her friend, not willing to fully accept the implications.

"Give me your laptop," Cora ordered.

"Why?"

"Just give it to me." Waving her hand, Cora awaited the laptop.

Hazel picked up her computer from the counter, then

slid it over to Cora on the island.

Flipping it open, Cora began to type. "Okay, just to shut your brain up, let's look up the old Dennis man."

Hurrying around the island, Hazel stood behind Cora. She knew she shouldn't care, but her curiosity was too powerful.

Typing in Dennis's name, his Facebook profile popped up, and Cora clicked on it.

A profile picture of a very handsome, fifty-year-old Dennis.

"He still looks good," Hazel observed.

Rolling her eyes, Cora clicked on his photos.

A wall of beautiful images of Dennis with his wife and two kids, truly happy. One after the other, years of familial bliss.

Hazel slumped her shoulders. "He looks really happy."

"And you're sad about it? Hazel. Okay. Now, let me show you this. I checked it this morning." Cora typed in Hazel's website.

It was stunning.

Pictures of Spike and the plants, even some of Hazel touching a leaf or smelling a flower. Every photo a glimpse into how Ethan saw her.

Cora shook her head in awe. "The boy really likes you. He's going to therapy for you, for goodness' sake." She turned to her friend, clasping Hazel's hands in hers. "Hazel."

Looking into her friend's eyes, she felt it. "Cora."

Tears came to both their eyes.

She needed to see Ethan.

They both knew it.

"Would you go already?" Cora smiled.

Hazel wiped her tears and hugged her best friend.

With a kiss to Cora's cheek, Hazel raced to the front door.

The time for fear was over.

Ethan could still reject her.

But she had to try.

She felt it in every fiber of her soul.

Dream Guy or not, Ethan was her guy.

Running across the street, she knocked on his front door.

Chapter 24
Ethan

I can't get any luckier

Ethan closed his laptop when he heard the doorbell ring and started walking over. He'd finished another pass of Hazel's website, and he couldn't wait to show her. Even though he wasn't sure how they left things last night, he still felt hopeful.

As he opened the door, his heart jumped in his throat when he saw Hazel.

And with one look, he knew he'd be happy as long as she was in his life, even if she never gave him another chance. Just to be near her was enough.

Before he could utter a hello, Hazel grabbed his T-shirt and pulled him in for a kiss.

Ethan's mind went blank from the shock of it.

Was he dreaming?

He was dreaming.

This couldn't be reality.

But feeling her lips pressed against his, his brain went from blank to goo, instinct and passion taking over. The more they kissed, the more he never wanted it to stop. Never in his life had anything ever felt so good, so right.

Hazel pulled away, and his chest ached for more.

"Whoa," they both said at the same time.

Her smile sent a thrill through his entire body, and he found himself smiling back.

"You want to hang?" she asked, and he could tell there was a bit of fear there.

Fear of him rejecting her again, no doubt.

"Of course. Come on in." Ethan waved for her to enter.

Hazel eyed the fold-out table Ethan had set up behind his couch. Its surface was currently a chaotic mess of cut-out pieces of construction paper, paints, pencils, and at least three pairs of scissors. Because you could never have too many pairs of scissors. They were like socks; they'd disappear, never to be found again.

"What's all this?" She motioned to the mess.

Ethan shrugged, amused. "My therapist says I need to reconnect with my inner child. I really didn't know what she meant so I reverted to kindergarten crafts. But as you can see, I got nothing." He'd tried for exactly an hour before he jumped back on his computer.

Raising her eyebrow, Hazel admired a red construction paper circle with a glued square in the middle. Then suddenly her eyes widened in excitement.

"I have an idea. Go get every blanket and sheet you own, and I'll be right back."

And she was gone. Out the door and back to her house.

He had an inkling of what she was planning, but frankly, he needed to sit down. Still reeling from the kiss, Ethan's insides fluttered with giddiness. He didn't want to jinx it, but he knew he was falling in love.

And it didn't scare him. Not in the way he always thought it would. Talking about how he'd felt about Kelly Churlington, her cheating hurt him. So deeply he'd never given anyone a real shot after that. But he'd never loved Kelly. It was the betrayal that held him back, not a broken heart.

Hazel was different from any woman . . . no . . . any *person* he'd ever met. And they fit.

The kiss was a mind-blowing, amazing, written-in-the-stars kiss.

He wasn't sure if he could hold himself back when she returned.

Oh, wait. She gave me a mission.

Good. I need a distraction, or my head is going to burst.

Ethan raided each closet he knew to hold any kind of blanket, sheet, or comforter. Turned out Ethan had a lot more than he'd expected, more than enough to do what he suspected Hazel wanted to do.

As he dropped the large pile of materials on the couch, Hazel opened his door with a couple of turquoise nylon bags and a few blankets of her own.

Following at her feet was Spike.

Of course.

He meowed a hello, and Ethan fought the urge to pick him up and kiss him too. He didn't know what that said about him, that he wanted to kiss both a beautiful woman and a cat, but here they were.

"Hey, Spike, coming to join the fun?" he cooed.

Spike hurried his steps to rub his head against Ethan's legs.

"I think I know where you're going with this." Ethan helped her with everything she carried, bringing it to the fold-out table.

"Blanket fort?" Hazel smiled mischievously.

"Blanket fort," he confirmed his guess.

Hazel untied the knot on top of one of the teal bags. "Grams always had to take it up a notch. I found these in the attic." She dumped the contents of the bag onto the table's surface.

Twelve-inch teal tubes with hard plastic purple balls with holes all around it. Demonstrating to Ethan that the tubes went into the holes to create a structure caused Ethan's neck to sweat. It was a little too visually close to how he was feeling about Hazel right now. "What's in the other bag?" he asked, needing to get his mind out of the gutter.

Not missing a beat, Hazel emptied the second bag, this one filled with fairy lights, battery-operated pillar candles ranging from three inches tall to twelve inches tall.

Okay, now it was getting romantic. He could get into that.

Ethan whistled in appreciation. "This is next level. Gladys may have been the world's perfect grandma." And she had the world's perfect granddaughter.

Hazel's smile was instant, but then he noticed tears welling in her eyes. "Whoa, what just happened."

Before Ethan could contemplate further on what he'd said, Hazel's lips were on his.

His stomach flip-flopped as he kissed her deeper, losing control of his senses.

Pulling away with a shy smile (which was ridiculously cute and only made him want to kiss her again), Hazel said, "They're good tears. Grams was the best, and she'd be thrilled that we're about to make the most epic blanket fort ever."

Ethan grinned at that. "Damn straight we are."

Spike rubbed against Ethan's leg in agreement.

Taking the parts, Ethan and Hazel began to build a frame for the fort.

"How's therapy going?" Hazel asked.

"Pretty good. Working through some old baggage."

"I need to make an appointment with my therapist to talk out why the heck I went on a journey of past boyfriends. I'm kind of glad I did it, though. Now I'll never have to wonder." Hazel connected a fourth pole and stood it up. "Tall enough? Or one more level?"

"I'd say that's good. Not tall enough to stand, but not short enough that we have to crawl," Ethan suggested.

"The science of blanket forts as adults." Hazel laughed.

"If we knew then what we know now." Ethan

finished his fourth pole, then reached over to Hazel's to connect them.

Their hands touched, and he couldn't help but smile at her, as simply touching her electrified him.

"So what have you learned so far?" she asked, still keeping her hand on his.

Ethan was ready to crush the frame and kiss her again, but he answered, "I'm learning I'm a big chicken when it comes to relationships. I run from the good ones and run to the bad ones. But my therapist has helped me see what I'm missing out on." He squeezed Hazel's hand.

Hazel ducked her head down and concentrated on the framework. "You don't think you'll run this time?"

Fear. He heard the fear in her voice, and all he wanted to do was hold her in his arms. Holding her hand firmly, he leaned his head down until she made eye contact with him again. "I'm not going anywhere."

A long moment passed between them.

"And not just because this is my house," he joked.

Hazel laughed.

And it was the best sound he'd ever heard.

"Good," she said, "because I kind of like you."

Ethan's heart pounded. "I kind of like you too."

After a moment of more building, Hazel asked, "Okay, what was the dumbest reason you broke up with 'one of the good ones.'"

"Ooooo, that's tough. There were a lot of them." He laughed. He thought about it, then said, "I broke up with Ally Bendington because I had gone to a fair and got my very first tarot card reading. The psychic pulled the Empress and the Death cards. I convinced myself that Ally was going to kill me because she was obviously the Empress and that hooded guy on the card was her minion."

"Obviously." Hazel laughed.

But did she look a little nervous? Cautious? Was he freaking her out admitting this?

"You know, if she did represent the Empress, the Death card means a major change in your life. That actually sounded like a positive reading." Hazel finished another row of framing.

"I'd get in my head about it. That's why therapy is helping." Ethan wanted Hazel to know he was trying to be a better man than that.

Hazel nodded, then smiled up at him. "Well, you haven't run yet, and we are making a blanket fort in your living room, so I'd say it's definitely helping."

A surge of pride and warmth flowed through him. And the truth was, he wouldn't want to be anywhere else.

Each of them had a wall of framing that needed to be connected. As they created a corner, their fingers touched again, and Ethan didn't want to let go. Staring at each other, the corner not quite secure yet, neither of them pulled their hands away.

Ethan pulled Hazel into him, fort structure be damned, and their lips came together in an explosive kiss. Hazel's hands grabbed his back, pulling him in closer, and he unconsciously moaned in response. He tightened his grip on her waist, needing to be closer to her as their lips moved in perfect synchronization, his head swimming with the intensity.

Hazel pushed herself away first, gasping for air. “Wow.”

Truer words were never spoken. “I’ll say.” Ethan found he was out of breath too.

Fanning her face as if to cool herself down, Hazel’s cheeks blushed, and all he wanted to do was cup those beautiful cheeks and kiss her again.

“Wooh.” She seemed to be pulling herself together, something he wasn’t sure he’d be able to do. “Let’s get this corner connected.”

Ethan laughed. “Good plan.”

Taking in deep breaths, Ethan and Hazel pieced together each connection until they had two walls in a ninety-degree corner. “Only two more walls to go,” she said happily, still giving herself the occasional hand fan.

Linking the rods together, they both began building the last two walls.

“Okay, since we obviously have great taste in films and were at the same showings, tell me the coolest thing you ever did in Los Angeles?” Hazel asked.

“One of the coolest things I ever did in LA? Hmmm, let me think.” Ethan took a moment, then remembered. “Back in my twenties, there was a pop-up Chris Isaak concert in a parking lot in Westwood. It was pretty incredible having a private concert like that.”

“You’re not serious.” Hazel clutched her chest.

“I am. Wait a minute . . . did you?” Ethan began.

“Yes! Cora’s husband, Jack, called us from a pay phone and told us to hurry. We lived in Studio City and raced there. We got there right when he started. It wasn’t that big of an audience either. I can't believe we were both there too."

"We could've been standing next to each other."

"I swear, Ethan." Hazel shook her head, awed.

"Your turn." Ethan grinned. "What was the coolest thing you ever did here?"

"I mean, the Chris Isaak parking lot concert is definitely up there." Hazel finished another row. "But I'd have to say, when Cora used to get us into movie premieres by lying and saying we were on the list."

"What?" Ethan laughed. "And it worked? My video store coworker tried that once, and he was almost arrested."

"You met Cora. Imagine telling her she wasn't on the list. She used fear." Hazel laughed.

"'Fear is the path to the dark side.'" Ethan did his best Yoda impression but failed miserably, which made them both crack up.

"Cora could utilize the dark side pretty well back in the day." Hazel's eyes sparkled when she talked of Cora, the love of her friend oozing off her. "But my favorite? I'd have to say *Rumble in the Bronx* at the Chinese." She stopped and eyed Ethan seriously. "You didn't . . . ?"

Ethan chuckled. "No, I was not there."

"Just making sure, since apparently, you and I spent our twenties together and didn't know it." The impact of that statement was not lost on Ethan, but she continued before he could dwell on it further. "It was the first Jackie Chan film to come to the States, and Cora's husband, Jack, was his biggest fan. He had every Jackie Chan film he could get his hands on, from pirated VHS tapes to buying the original laser discs on Ebay, he was obsessed, so of course, Cora had to get us in. This was '95, so I was working at Plants & Things, and they were lowly production assistants at the time, but dang, if Cora didn't sell herself as a studio exec. I was with her, and *I* was scared of her. She walked up to that table with all the confidence in the world and waited as they scanned the clipboard for her name. When it wasn't there, she started dropping names left and right and how she was going to fire her assistant."

Hazel smiled at the memory. "But they were all apologies and let us in, then gave us invites to the after party. I remember standing inside the building next to the El Capitan across the street from the Chinese at the after party and seeing Jackie Chan walk in surrounded by bodyguards, and like an idiot, I said, 'Hello, you were amazing,' and he was seriously the kindest person. His smile was so huge. His eyes were so sparkling and sweet. He said 'Thank you so much,' and he bowed a couple of times, then whoosh, he was gone. No one really knew who he was in America back then, but he was a giant movie star everywhere else in the world. He was so humble. It always stuck with me." She finished the last rung on her wall. "Meanwhile, Steven Seagal stood against the wall, arms folded, waiting for people to approach him and shower him with compliments, which they did, but ick."

"That's crazy." Ethan couldn't stop staring at Hazel as she began attaching the third wall to their finished corner. "I never did anything like that, but I miss doing things. I feel like I don't do anything anymore."

Ethan attached his last rung of the fourth wall.

Hazel took a deep breath and nodded thoughtfully. "Same." Then her eyes met his. "We'll just have to start doing things together."

"Deal." He found his whole insides were smiling.

Ethan dragged over his wall, and the two of them attached it to the three finished ones, making a rectangle frame. "Let's try to move this in front of the couch."

Very carefully, they transferred the light plastic frame around the couch, then placed it up against it.

After another half hour of laughing, sharing, and decorating the interior of the fort, Ethan leaned against a pillow propped on the base of the couch. He sat on a bed of more pillows and blankets, while Hazel finished tucking a sheet into the top of the frame, to cover it completely on the inside.

It was beautiful. Out of a magazine. Fairy lights, flickering candles (he couldn't believe how real they looked), blankets on the floor and walls. A true childlike fairy tale.

Spike curled up into a ball on the pillow next to Ethan.

"This is the best blanket fort I've ever been a part of," Ethan admired.

Hazel sat on a pillow on the other side of Ethan so as not to disturb Spike. She leaned against the couch base as well. "I really needed this."

Ethan watched her and wanted to pinch himself, feeling grateful she was spending time with him.

"What?" she asked, cheeks blushing.

"You're beautiful."

Hazel turned away slightly from the compliment.

Then Ethan remembered. "Hey, I got something for you."

Ethan reached under the blanket behind them to the couch, then searched with his hand for *Escape to Ashdonia*. Grabbing hold of the paperback, he pulled it through, handing it to her.

Her eyes grew wide, and her mouth opened. "Did you get this at Nookish Corner?"

"You've been there?" he asked in shock.

"It's my favorite place to eat," she exclaimed.

"Me too!" Ethan shook his head in awe. "I did buy it there. The owner said it was a first printing, but he also said that Freya Fairweather signed it, but you can clearly see the signature says . . ."

"John Larry," they said in unison.

"And who did he miss?" she wondered aloud.

"Right?"

"I've been wanting to buy this for weeks, but I kept talking myself out of it." Hazel looked at the book like it was a prized jewel. "I can't believe you got this for me." She looked at him with genuine surprise and affection. "Thank you. This is . . . this is just so thoughtful."

Ethan's chest filled with a joy he couldn't contain. "You're creating your own Ashdonia in your greenhouse, and we pretty much just made one here. Anyway, I saw it and thought of you."

Hazel leaned in and kissed him with an intensity

that made his head swim. Their lips parted, and their kiss became even deeper and more mind-blowing than any of their previous kisses. Ethan could kiss her forever, and his life would be complete.

Finally, Hazel pulled away and handed him the book. "Read it to me?"

Nodding, Ethan held his breath as Hazel snuggled her back into his chest as he wrapped his arms around her, holding the book in front of them both to read.

Was this heaven?

Ethan was pretty sure he'd died and gone to heaven.

Spike woke up, stretched, then plopped down on Hazel's lap.

Yup, heaven.

"Chapter one: Olivia Fry was a peculiar young woman . . ." Ethan began.

And Ethan read to her. He'd never been happier in his entire life than sitting inside that blanket fort and reading to the woman he was falling for.

After about an hour, or maybe two, of reading, he heard a little snore out of Hazel.

Chuckling to himself, he whispered, "You asleep?"

Hazel shook herself awake. "Your voice is so soothing. I'm sorry."

"Don't be sorry. This has quite possibly been one of the best days I've had in a really long time." The best day. Of my life.

"Me too," she said with a yawn and a stretch.

"Oh, I just remembered." Ethan handed the book back to Hazel, then shifted his other hand back up the blanket, to the couch. After another patting down of the cushion, he found what he was looking for and pulled it down. The invitation he designed for the ball.

"How much stuff do you have stored on your couch?" Hazel teased, but then she focused on the invite when he handed it to her. "Wait a minute."

"What is it?"

"Cora has been trying to get me to go to this ball for weeks! She's been fitting half of Hollywood for this thing." She laughed.

"Really?" Ethan reared his head back with a smile. "That's crazy. I just found out about it on Monday when I designed this invite."

Examining it more carefully, Hazel said, "It's beautiful."

"Thank you," he said. "You want to go with me?" he asked nervously.

Hazel turned to face him, causing Spike to lazily crawl off her lap with an annoyed stretch. "I've honestly wanted to go ever since Cora told me about it, but I didn't think I'd be up for it. But with you? And an eighties costume ball to boot? Um, yeah."

Relief hit him like a wave, only to be replaced by a flood of excitement. "What should we dress as? It's tomorrow, so we might be screwed on our costumes."

"Cora is a costume designer and has access to some insane costumes. Leave it to me." Hazel bit her lower lip, obviously thinking of the possibilities.

"As long as I'm not a pirate, we'll be fine. I have very bad memories of being a pirate."

Hazel laughed. "Oh really? When was this?"

"Halloween 2005. Champagne, cork, almost lost an eye. That stupid eye patch saved me." Ethan remembered with a shudder.

"So that's actually a good memory. Being a pirate saved your eye."

Laughing, Ethan conceded, "True. But I can still hear and feel the thud of the cork on that plastic patch. It's very traumatic."

"Okay, deal. No pirates. I can't think of an eighties pirate anyway."

"*Ice Pirates*," Ethan reminded her.

"Ooooo, I loved that movie as a kid." Hazel grinned with excitement.

"I see that look. You're already thinking of the costumes." Why did he mention *Ice Pirates*? Because it was a darn good movie. No. No pirates.

Laughing even harder, Hazel put her hands up. "I promise. Not even *Ice Pirates*."

Spontaneously, she kissed him again, but this one was far too short, but her giant smile was worth it.

"So it's a date?" She raised her eyebrows.

And this time, Ethan was ready for his answer. "It's a date."

Wait. You know each other?

Maisie wrapped her arm in Hazel's. "We going to find you the most amazing costume ever?" she asked with a grin.

"I'm so glad you're back." Hazel pulled Maisie in for an arm-entangled side-hug.

"Are you kidding? Mom would have killed Dad if he didn't show up to this thing tonight. She's dressed half the people going." Maisie laughed.

"I'm right here," Cora butted in. "I wouldn't have killed anyone, but it would be nice for my family to be there."

"I can't believe it took a guy to convince you to go and not Mom," Maisie teased.

"I agree with my daughter." Cora laughed.

"Ha-ha. I just hope I can find us something fun."

"*Us.*" Maisie squealed with delight.

"Okay, okay, no jinxing." Hazel felt as confident as she could about Ethan, but she had to admit, there was an intrusive voice that kept reminding her of how he ran away after their first kiss. Would he do it again?

They reached the entrance to a giant warehouse at the back of the studio lot that Cora had access to. She swung open the metal door and held it for Maisie and Hazel to walk through.

After entering, Maisie disentangled herself from Hazel and rushed to Prince's iconic costume from *Purple Rain*. "Mom, can I?"

"But what about what we planned with your father?"

"Mom, do your really expect me to be your third wheel?" Maisie crossed her arms.

"Fine. You know where the dressing room is. Come out here once it's on so I can fit it for you." Cora nodded toward the back of the room, where a row of doors to the dressing rooms stood.

"Thanks, Mom." With another squeal, Maisie yanked the costume off the rack and headed toward the doors.

"Should I even ask?" Hazel eyed her friend.

"We wanted her to match our costumes," Cora confessed.

Hazel laughed. "Cora! She's way too old for that."

"I know, I know." Cora stared after her daugher, then sighed. "They grow up so fast."

Hazel gently squeezed Cora's arm in affectionate support.

Cora waved to the room with a smile.

Taking it in, Hazel inhaled an awed breath.

She stood in quite possibly the most magical room she'd ever stepped inside. Racks of costumes from every movie and TV show imaginable in at least twenty long lines filled the entire space and each wall as well.

Though stunning, it was also overwhelming.

Not just too many to choose from, but too many to even look at.

But examining the closest dress to her, a period piece somewhere in the Jane Austen era, Hazel had to know. "Are these the originals?"

Cora threw back a laugh. "God, no. They're all replicas. Anything we get here is on loan, though. Try not to spill anything on whatever you pick."

"That's a big ask coming from me. Are you sure I should do this?" Hazel swallowed hard at the thought of bright red punch drenching whatever she picked. Maybe she could find something red and save herself the worry.

"The ball is tonight, and I'm not letting you wear some Party Shop costume on your first real date with a guy you actually like." Cora crossed her arms for emphasis.

A very handsome man who looked to be their age walked in. "Cora?" His eyes rounded with delight.

"Mateo!" Cora exclaimed and took the man into a giant hug.

Pulling away, Cora waved to Hazel. "Mateo, Hazel. Hazel, Mateo." Then to Hazel, she said, "Mateo and I go way back, worked on a few projects together. He's an EP for Mad Era Studios."

Mateo paused, his eyes squinted in what looked like

disbelief. "Your name is Hazel?"

"Yes?" Hazel had no idea where this was going.

"Was your grandmother named Gladys, by any chance?" Mateo watched Hazel, waiting for the answer as if he were waiting for the reveal of some kind of surprise.

"She was. Yes, Gladys was my grandmother. Did you know her? There are a lot of Hazels. Why would you pinpoint her? She died three years ago." Hazel's mind flew a mile a minute.

"I'm Ethan's best friend." Mateo's head bobbed from Hazel to Cora like he couldn't believe what was happening.

"No way." Cora's eyes were now widened to their max.

"Way," Mateo confirmed.

"Wait." Hazel still couldn't wrap her head around what was happening. "You're saying you're my neighbor Ethan's best friend? The man I'm going to this ball with tonight? And you and Cora know each other?"

"Yup." Mateo nodded, his expression showing he could barely believe it as well.

"Whoa," was all Hazel could say.

"Sounds like destiny to me." Maisie walked up with a huge grin, the *Purple Rain* costume fitting her like a glove.

"Maisie!" Mateo reached down to hug her.

"Hey, Mateo, how's Austin?"

"He's good." Mateo pulled out of the embrace and took in Maisie's look. "You better be wearing this to the ball."

"Oh, I am." Maisie twirled.

Cora examined her with a sewist's eye. "Only a couple

alterations, but it fits you well."

"You look stunning," Hazel beamed. "Purple is definitely your color."

"Thanks, Aunt Hazel." Maisie leaned her head on Hazel's shoulder.

A deep welling of rightness filled Hazel, from being there with Maisie and Cora to meeting Ethan's best friend. "I still can't believe the small-worldness of it all."

"Believe it." Mateo laughed. "And I'm assuming you're here to pick out the costumes for tonight?"

"This is insane." Hazel's sense of reassurance at coincidentally running into Ethan's best friend blew her mind. Plus, the fact that *her* best friend had known Mateo for years?

Fate.

"Well, come on, guys, go explore and have at it." Cora waved to the sea of costumes before them. "Maisie, let me pin you up."

"You don't have to tell me twice." And Mateo was off, exploring the racks of clothes, shaking his head as if still contemplating their new discovery.

Taking off, herself, Hazel wandered each aisle trying to find the perfect costumes. There were so many good choices, *Spaceballs, Back to the Future, Breakfast Club*. She'd stopped dead in her tracks when she saw Buttercup's red dress from *Princess Bride*, but dang it, Westley was a pirate, so that one was out, and she continued her search.

Mateo yelped in excitement a few racks over. "Oh, I think I found mine and Austin's."

"I wanna see." Maisie craned her neck to get a peek at Mateo's location.

Hazel was excited to meet Austin as well. As she walked down the next aisle, her heart stopped. "Cora! Maisie!" she yelled.

Cora dropped her pins, and she and Maisie hurried to Hazel's side.

Taking a deep, calming breath (because internally she was squealing like her thirteen-year-old self), Hazel pulled out the golden gown that the character Olivia Fry wore in the movie version of *Escape to Ashdonia.* Full skirt bottom with metallic chiffon layers, golden-beaded corseted top with giant, over-the-top eighties puff sleeves. Next to it was the character Nikolas Dragontine's masterpiece of a costume, gold velvet jacket, flowy ruffled shirt, tight black leather pants, that Richard Grinthal pulled off so well. Hazel didn't know a single friend of hers that didn't have a crush on Nikolas in junior high.

"Cora! It's Olivia!" Hazel exclaimed.

Cora hugged her tightly, knowing how much Olivia and *Escape to Ashdonia* meant to her. "Hazel, it's perfect."

Pulling out of the hug, she asked Mateo from afar. "Ethan said he loved the movie and the character Nikolas, but do you think he'd be up for wearing this?"

Mateo walked over holding what looked like normal eighties attire, one plaid button-up shirt, one purple long-sleeve T-shirt, a pair of jeans, and a pair of khakis. It wasn't until Hazel saw the pair of Ray-Ban sunglasses that she knew.

"*They Live*?" she asked.

“Heck yeah.” Mateo grinned. “Good catch.”

“One of my favorites,” Hazel approved.

“Dad made me watch that movie. That’s the one with the creepy faces when they can only see with the sunglasses, right?” Maisie asked.

“Frank and Nada, our favorite bromance. Maybe we’ll even re-create the fight scene.” Mateo actually looked like he was considering it.

John Carpenter’s *They Live*, a classic eighties movie with wrestler Roddy Piper and Keith David and one of the most epic fight scenes in cinematic history. It lasted six minutes. Hazel had been to a screening at the Egyptian Theater with a Q&A afterward, and when someone asked why the fight scene was so long, Carpenter simply said, “I cast a wrestler.” Hazel swore he’d added a “duh” under his breath, but Jack and Cora claimed they didn’t hear it.

Mateo lifted the sleeve of the Nikolas jacket. “Who wouldn’t want to be Richard Grinthal for a night?” he said as if that closed the argument.

“True,” Cora agreed.

“Plus, he has a Pop doll of Nikolas in his office. He’ll be more than down,” Mateo elaborated.

Hazel held the dress up to her and could tell it would fit perfectly. It was a dream come true.

Mateo turned to Cora. “Who are you and Jack going to go as?”

Maisie giggled, and Mateo’s eyes lit up. “Oh, you have to tell now to get a laugh like that out of Maisie.”

Even Hazel didn’t know. “Yeah, spill.”

Cora shook her head. “It’s going to be a surprise.”

"Well, now it has to be epic for a buildup like that." Mateo grinned.

"Not as epic as Hazel and Ethan are going to be. I mean really, who can top Olivia and Nikolas?" Cora winked at Hazel.

"Cora! You're deflecting." She knew her friend's tactics well, but Hazel's phone rang, so Cora was saved from interrogation. Placing the dress back on the rack, she pulled her phone out of her pocket. "It's Ethan. He must have sensed we picked out his costume." She answered the phone. "Hey, you're on speaker with Cora, Maisie, and *Mateo*?"

"What?" Ethan's voice sounded as shocked as all of them had felt.

"Turns out your girl's best friend and her family have been my friends for half a decade." Mateo laughed.

"What?" Ethan repeated.

"I think we broke him," Mateo joked.

"I'm just. Wow. That's . . . I mean . . . wow."

"We really did break him." Cora laughed.

Hazel knew how he felt, but she also had a moment of panic at the fact that *Ethan* sounded a little panicked. She decided to change the subject. "So. What do you think about going as Olivia and Nikolas from *Escape to Ashdonia*? The ballroom scene?" Hazel asked.

"Are you serious?" The awe in Ethan's voice was palpable.

Maisie nudged Hazel affectionately with her shoulder.

"I'm staring at the costumes now." Hazel's grin was officially plastered to her face.

"Um, do I even have to answer? Definitely, with the intensity of a million suns," Ethan said.

They all laughed.

"Look, I'm going to have to meet you there. I have an errand to run. Is that cool?" Ethan asked.

Oh no. Was this him freaking out?

Stop.

No fear, remember?

"Of course." Hazel hid the disappointment from her voice.

"Great. Just give the costume to . . . Mateo . . . so crazy . . . and he'll get it to me." Ethan now sounded like he was chuckling at the turn of events.

"Oh, I will? Of course I will. I'll text you when I leave," Mateo responded.

"Great. See you at eight." Ethan hung up without saying goodbye. He sounded distracted at the end.

Hazel exchanged an awkward look with Mateo.

"Everything's cool with Ethan, right? You know him better than anyone," Hazel asked, realizing she now had an inside track to Ethan besides her neurotic brain.

Mateo sighed like he wasn't sure, but his smile was supportive. "Don't worry. I'll make sure he doesn't freak out."

"You think he's freaking out?" Hazel didn't want to say it out loud, but she felt compelled to.

"The boy freaks out about everything. He once broke up with someone because she asked for his Netflix password. But you're the first person I've ever seen him make this much effort for. You're fine. He's fine." Mateo placed a hand on Hazel's shoulder and squeezed.

She appreciated it.

Pulling his hand away, he carefully took the Nikolas costume off the rack. "I'm going to drop this off to him now. I'll text you later, Cora."

"Thanks, Mateo." Cora hugged him followed by Maisie.

And Mateo hugged Hazel as well. He was a good hugger.

"See you there," Mateo said and saluted as he left.

Hazel placed the dress up to her frame again, trying to clear her head of paranoia.

"We'll need to take it in a bit. Let's go get Doris—she's a wizard—for both of you." Cora eyed the two of them.

"You think everything is going to be okay?" Hazel needed her best friend's reassurance.

Cora nodded. "And if it isn't, I'll kill him."

"Me too," Maisie added.

Chapter 26
Hazel

The ball of all balls, and he really has some balls

Hazel walked up to the red carpet of The Majestic in downtown Los Angeles. It took her a moment to fully take in the scenery before her since she'd been so preoccupied by trying to find a parking spot that wasn't a mile away. She'd found one a block over, but walking in heels for a block was close to torture.

A Hummer stretch limo was parked in front of the theater and let out a handful of costumed guests, then moved forward for the next limo to do the same. The line of limos went back all the way to the parking garage. Hazel was glad she hadn't taken Mateo up on his offer to ride with them in the limo he rented. Cora and fam, on the other hand, had jumped at the chance.

Thinking on it now, Hazel realized she might have made a mistake. Now both her and Ethan would have cars. She was skipping ahead, but still. She was excited.

As she walked in, there were press taking pictures like an old movie premiere of all the outrageous eighties characters. It took her a moment to realize that when the press were yelling for "Olivia" to turn for the cameras, they were actually talking to her. It wasn't until one of them called her "*Ashdonia* girl" that it dawned on her. Never one to like a lot of attention, Hazel turned and waved a bit for the cameras, then hightailed it inside the building.

The lobby stunned her with its intricately carved accents on every wall, the ceiling, even the baseboards. They weren't kidding around back in the old Hollywood glamour days. A giant chandelier draped from the center of the ceiling, dripping with crystals in a circular tier ending with one giant crystal for its peak.

Staircases on either end of the lobby seemed to be where party goers were headed.

Hazel couldn't imagine what this theater had been used for, as there didn't appear to be an actual theater in sight, but she followed the herd, and in particular a pretty fabulous Indiana Jones and Marion couple, as they chose the left staircase. Once up the main set of steps, it split into a V with two more staircases, but from the wooden railing above, Hazel could tell they both led to the same place. For a moment it felt as if she were in the movie *Labyrinth* with all the staircases. Just as long as none of them went upside down, she'd be fine.

When she finally reached the top, two giant ten-foot carved mahogany doors stood open, letting people into the main ball area.

Out of breath, and lucky she didn't trip on her heels, Hazel was grateful to have two feet on the landing.

She didn't feel as bad for being out of shape when a Flash Gordon was practically panting by the time he made it up himself.

She really needed to exercise more.

By the time she reached the entrance, Hazel was back to normal but stopped in her tracks when she took in the scenery before her. The architecture itself would have been something to gawk at with its art deco design and detail in almost every inch of every wall and ceiling.

But the decorations?

It was like Hazel stepped into the *Sixteen Candles* gymnasium crossed with *Time Bandits/Brazil* Terry Gilliam machinery decor. Not to mention the corners dedicated to photo opportunities, with backdrops of the bigger eighties movies like *Star Wars, Indiana Jones, The Goonies, Die Hard, The Breakfast Club, Terminator*, and oh! *Escape to Ashdonia*! They'd definitely have to get some pics there.

Hazel hadn't been this excited for a long time. It was nice to simply enjoy the moment and dive into the fantasy of it all.

Searching for Cora, Jack, and Maisie amongst the crowded room of characters, Hazel spotted Maisie in her *Purple Rain* costume by the food table.

With a quick wave, Hazel walked toward her.

Then she realized that Cora and Jack stood beside her.

Oh. My. God.

Hazel laughed as she approached the most adorable eighties couple in the entire ball.

Ripley and Hicks from *Aliens*.

Yesssssss.

Jack in space marine armor, camouflage pants, and army boots. He was a pretty handsome guy, no Michael Biehn, but handsome.

But Cora.

Cora looked like a badass in Ripley's outfit from the end of the film, white T-shirt, gun-belt suspenders, and blue cargo pants, and in true Cora fashion, her bag was a mini clutch in the shape of a xenomorph alien head. Even her brown curly wig was perfection. But the bag! It was insane.

"You made that, didn't you?" Hazel shook her head in amazement.

"It only took a month, but yes. I need to fix the zipper, though." Just like Cora to find imaginary flaws in her flawless work. "We tried to get Maisie to be Newt, but she looks glorious as Prince."

Jack grumbled, "She does look amazing, but it would have been so cute."

"Let it go, Dad." Maisie rolled her eyes, then her smile widened. "Hazel, you are stunning."

As Maisie said this, Hazel started to notice a lot of eyes on her and her elaborate costume. Some even clapped in appreciation.

"Ethan is going to flip out." Cora fluffed up Hazel's sleeves.

Hazel had never felt more beautiful.

Completing the group, Mateo and his boyfriend, Austin, arrived.

Mateo's mouth dropped. "Wow."

"Right?" Cora agreed with Mateo.

Hazel blushed at the compliments, not really sure what to say, since she was literally the worst at receiving them. But she managed a small, "Thanks, guys."

Focusing back on Mateo, she laughed. He'd chosen Keith David's character Frank, and his boyfriend was Roddy Piper's character Nada. Hazel knew his name was Austin, but she hadn't been properly introduced yet.

"Hazel, this is Austin," Mateo said.

Hazel shook Austin's hand while Mateo hugged Cora's fam.

Austin smiled warmly. "You look incredible." Then he said under his breath to Mateo, "That boy better not flake."

"Shut it." Cora elbowed him in the stomach.

"It's nice to meet you," Hazel said, though his words about Ethan set her teeth on edge.

Cora motioned to the food table. "We look a bit conspicuous at the snack table."

Austin shook his head. "We look glorious. And I hired the caterer. Trust me, you're going to want to eat all of this."

As if seeing the food for the first time, Hazel had to agree, it all looked delectable.

But she wasn't hungry. Not only was the bodice tight, but her nerves were flipping circles in her tummy.

Cora hugged her as if sensing her worry. "He's coming. Don't panic."

"Ethan will be here," Mateo agreed. "He said he might

be a little late because he had to pick something up."

That gave Hazel some comfort, but then she saw the clock on the wall. "It's already twenty past eight, though." Taking a deep breath, she said, "Yeah, I'm not going to stress. He'll be here."

Mateo's smile was reassuring. "Absolutely."

Austin's nostrils flared slightly. "He better."

Another jab to his side, this time by Mateo.

Her eyes flew to Austin's, and real fear crept into her chest.

Maisie nudged Hazel with her arm. "Maybe he texted you?"

"Right. Phone." Pulling out her cell phone from her pocket. Yes. The dress had pockets. Best costume ever.

No missed calls. No texts.

"Nothing from him on my phone." Hazel showed the others as if she had to prove it.

Mateo and Austin checked their phones as well. Even Cora did. But it all added up to a resounding shake of their heads.

"He's probably already outside. Let's give him some time. There's a long line of limos, and parking is horrible," Mateo reassured her.

"True." Parking had been terrible.

Positive.

Think positive.

Reaching inside herself, she put aside her worry. "I'm actually starving. Let me get at that." Corset and nerves be damned, she was going to eat.

Displayed in multiple tiered, silver trays was an array

of beautifully designed hors d'oeuvres she'd ever seen. One plate looked like pigs in a blanket, but a fancy version with tiny sausages and flaking crust. She immediately ate four, and the pastry melted in her mouth. Hazel had no idea what was in the sausage, but she wanted to eat five more.

And she did.

Maisie motioned her farther down the table. "Oh, Aunt Hazel, try this one."

It was a crispy rice round base with spicy tuna and a slice of a jalapeño pepper on top. Hazel's eyes rolled back in her head from the pleasure. "That's the best thing I've ever tasted."

Cora laughed and nodded to the full dance floor as "True" by Spandau Ballet played on the speakers. "We're going to go dance. You two okay?"

Maisie handed Hazel a small plate of mini-flatbreads with roasted tomatoes, basil, and mozzarella. "We're good. You guys have fun."

Hazel took down three of the flatbreads. Her corset was busting, but it tasted too good.

Cora and Jack traveled to the dance floor followed by Mateo and Austin.

Watching them as she ate, she sighed, perfect couples.

"No sighing." Maisie put a stuffed olive in her mouth. "He's coming."

"Yeah."

"Oh no." Maisie's eyes widened.

"What? Are you going to puke? Did you eat too much?" Hazel was feeling queasy herself.

"No. Oh, Aunt Hazel, I'm so sorry." Maisie's whole face crinkled as if she were about to break out in tears.

"Sorry for what? Maisie, what is it?" Hazel couldn't imagine what caused the shift in Maisie's mood.

"It's Uncle Logan . . . I mean Logan . . . I mean jerk-face. Whatever you want me to call him, I'll call him." Maisie puffed up, stepping in front of Hazel protectively, just like Cora would.

Hazel's heart dropped.

Logan? Here?

She didn't want to look.

But she kind of wanted to look.

She looked.

There, across the dance floor, walked in her ex-husband of twenty-two years, with a beautiful man on his arm. The man from the Instagram photo she'd seen a few weeks ago. And Logan was dressed as Jareth, David Bowie's character from *Labyrinth*, and his boyfriend was David Bowie from the *Blue Jean* video, turban and contour makeup on point. They looked stunning.

Time stopped.

Hazel forgot to breathe.

But then . . .

She did breathe.

And she was . . . fine?

Was she really fine?

Staring at Logan and his man, she knew . . . yes, she really was fine.

It hurt a little, but just a little.

That went away too when she saw the two of them

glance at each other.

Love.

"Are we going to beat him up?" Maisie asked, probably worried that Hazel hadn't spoken yet.

Hazel wrapped her arm through Maisie's. "No, we're not going to beat him up. And you can call him whatever you want to, but I suggest Uncle Logan or Logan."

"You're not mad?" Maisie's eyes were full of worry.

"No. I'm not mad. He looks really happy, don't you think?"

Maisie watched Logan from afar, then nodded. "Yeah, he does."

"Then I'm happy. I'd be happier if Ethan was here, but . . ."

"So we can beat *him* up if he doesn't show?" Maisie side-hugged Hazel.

"Most definitely." Hazel hugged her back.

Before she and Maisie could go back to the dessert side of the food table, Logan stood before her. "Hazel . . . I didn't know you'd be here. You look amazing."

"Thanks, you guys look pretty amazing too."

"This is Mark. Mark, this is Hazel."

Hazel shook Mark's hand. "Nice to meet you."

"You too. Logan has nothing but good things to say about you," Mark said politely.

"Oh, that's nice. Thank you." What? What were the words that were coming out of her mouth?

Logan laughed. Because he knew her. And he knew she was nervous. He whispered something to Mark, and Mark nodded, heading toward the bar.

Holding out his hand, Logan asked, "You want to dance?"

A quick glance at Maisie, giving her the I'm-okay smile, then she followed Logan out onto the dance floor.

"Time After Time" by Cyndi Lauper started to play.

Great, a slow dance.

But Hazel was surprised that she felt nothing but friendship. No chemistry. No shaky hands, or nerves, or tingles, like she had with Ethan. Simply two friends dancing.

"You seem happy," Logan observed.

"I am." Or was she?

"Did I say something wrong?"

"No. I'm just waiting on my date, and I'm starting to worry he isn't going to show." She hated admitting that to Logan, but he'd been her best friend for the last two decades, so sharing came naturally.

Cora and Jack were suddenly next to them, Cora's face asking, *Is everything okay?*

Hazel nodded and gave her the I'm-fine-I'm-good expression.

"Hey, Logan," she addressed him.

"Hi, Cora. Hi, Jack," Logan said politely. "I love your costumes."

"Yours too. Where's your date?" Jack asked innocently, but got a kick in the shins from Cora. "Ow."

Hazel and Logan laughed.

"He's at the bar getting us some drinks." Logan nodded toward Mark.

"I'm okay," Hazel mouthed to Cora.

With an audible sigh and a disapproving glance toward Logan, Cora led Jack away from them.

"Still as protective as ever," Logan observed.

"Till the day we die."

The song was coming to an end.

Logan touched one of her puffed sleeves, then waved his hand at his *Labyrinth* costume. "You know you want to say it. You've always wanted to say it, and now I'm literally wearing Jareth's costume."

"Sarah didn't say it at the ball, though." But he was right, Hazel wanted to say her favorite line from *Labyrinth.*

And it *would* be so fitting with Logan.

"Say it. I can take it." He smiled warmly at her.

Taking a deep breath, she said, "You have no power over me."

And like in the movie, it felt as if time cracked, and the words vibrated into the core of her being.

Because he didn't.

Hazel had truly moved on.

The song ended, and Logan kissed the top of her head. "Goodbye, Hazel."

"Goodbye, Logan."

Logan walked off the dance floor toward the bar.

"Safety Dance" by Men Without Hats began to play.

Hazel stood alone in the middle of the dance floor, couples all around her.

Before she could fully panic, Cora and Jack were by her side, dancing.

"Still no call?" Cora asked over the music.

Hazel checked her phone.

"Nothing. I hope he's okay." What if something happened to him? He might *not* have run.

But he ran from their first kiss.

And he had a pattern of running from women he liked.

It *was* in his nature.

Mateo and Austin danced over to them, waving their phones.

"Sorry," Austin confirmed he hadn't received a message.

Mateo sighed heavily, showing no messages on his phone either. "He's over an hour late. I'm so sorry, Hazel."

Hazel's heart dropped.

He wasn't coming.

Fighting tears, Hazel moved toward the exit. "I'm gonna go."

They all stopped dancing.

Before she could leave, Mateo pulled her in for a hug. "Don't go. I can talk some sense into him. He probably panicked."

Wiping away tears, Hazel pulled out of the hug. "I can't be here."

"I'll go with you." Maisie came up from behind.

"No, Maisie, you stay. I'm really okay. I just can't be here."

"I can drive you home in your car?" Cora touched her arm.

"No. You guys have fun."

Cora, Jack, and Maisie hugged her, then Mateo and Austin joined in.

A giant group hug.

It felt nice.

But she needed air.

"Thanks, guys. I'll call you in the morning." Hazel didn't specify who she was talking to, but she didn't care.

Air.

Air would be good.

Reaching the exit, she dialed Ethan's number for the tenth time. It went to voicemail like it had the first nine times. "Hey, Ethan. I hope you're okay. I'm pretty sure you freaked out, though, and decided not to come. I wish you would have just told me." Tears choked her voice, but she continued, "I'm all dressed up." *Breathe. Breathe. Calm down.* "I . . . don't call me for a while . . . I . . . just don't call." Ending the call, she dropped the phone in her pocket.

Pushing her way through the crowd and making her way down the stairs in an emotional panic, Hazel really did feel like Sarah in *Labyrinth*. And each man she passed, their face blurred, like the Dream Guy in her dreams. What was happening? Hazel was losing it. Her obsession with finding the Dream Guy was finally taking its toll.

She'd let herself be vulnerable with Ethan.

She'd trusted him.

Stupid.

A man with a blurred face stopped her. "How long is it going to take for you to find me?"

Hazel shoved past him and down the stairs.

Another blurred man stepped in her way. "It's been years. Are you sure I even exist?"

This was all in her head.

Hazel was breaking.

A third blurred man stepped in her way. "This wig is itchy."

"Oh please!" Hazel groaned and pushed past him, down the last stair, across the lobby, and into the open air.

Running down the sidewalk in her heels was a struggle, but nothing compared to what was happening internally.

"Hazel!" Ethan's voice rang in her ears.

More delusions.

She needed to get home.

But when he blocked her way, Hazel realized it wasn't a hallucination. Ethan stood before her, the cab he'd taken driving away.

He wore the entire Nikolas Dragontine costume, makeup included, but no wig, just his normal hair.

So definitely not Dream Guy.

Not that *he* existed.

Ethan's head tipped back. "You look amazing."

Hazel couldn't.

She couldn't hear his excuses. How he freaked but then came to his senses.

It was too late.

"I gotta go." Hazel walked past him.

Ethan caught up to her quickly, gently touching her arm, stopping her. "Whoa, whoa, whoa, didn't you get my message?"

Oh, no. He wasn't going to pull the whole *didn't you*

get my message excuse. The oldest one in the cell phone era book.

Hazel pulled out her phone, showing him zero calls, zero texts.

"No. I didn't get any messages," Hazel said coldly.

"I sent texts to Mateo and Austin too. They should have told you," Ethan said frantically.

"They didn't get any messages either. Look, Ethan, I get it. You're not ready. You panicked, and now you decided to come anyway. But you don't have to use the 'didn't you get my message' bit." Hazel figured she'd call him out.

His face fell.

He obviously regretted it.

But she couldn't do this again.

She couldn't go through the yo-yo effect of Ethan running every time things got real.

"It's not a bit. I really did send you all messages. I was running late because I had to pick something up, and then my car broke down on Laurel Canyon. I guess there wasn't enough reception for them to go through? I don't know. But they towed my car. That's why I had to take the cab." His eyes were sincere.

He was telling the truth.

Hazel knew it, but it didn't matter.

"I promise you, I'm not panicking." He held both her arms with his hands, eyes frantic.

Too much.

Hazel's chest squeezed.

It was too much.

She believed him.

But she'd also believed he'd run.

Everything was too vivid, too heightened.

Her lungs tightened, and she had to breathe in deep to gain any semblance of calm. "I believe you, but my mind went fully the other way. I dared to believe again with you. I let my heart be vulnerable, and even though I understand logically that you did nothing wrong, now my brain can only hear 'run,'" she choked out.

"It's your fear. Trust me, I know that voice well," Ethan pleaded.

"I know you're right, and what we have could have been great. But all of this made me realize that I'm not ready." Hazel's admission shocked her as much as she could see it shocked Ethan.

His hands dropped to his side, his head as well.

She couldn't leave him like this.

But she also knew what she'd said was right.

She wasn't ready.

Reaching up gently, Hazel kissed Ethan one last time. "I'm sorry, Ethan."

And she ran.

Chapter 27
Ethan
Aftermath

"This is all my fault." Mateo ran his hand through his hair.

"No. I gave her every reason to think I'd panic." Ethan didn't want his friend to blame himself, though Ethan kind of did. A bit. Just a bit. No. Ethan *had* given Hazel plenty of red flags. He didn't blame her for running.

The two stood in Ethan's kitchen sharing a plate of Oreos.

Mateo made a face as he took a bite. "These taste like chemicals."

"You don't have to eat them." Ethan had already had ten. His depression was hitting him hard.

But Mateo finished the cookie. "It's my fault. I put all that doubt in her head. How was I to know therapy was working that quickly?"

"Because I told you it had." Ethan sighed deeply.

"You're not giving up on her, are you?" Mateo asked, sadness behind his eyes.

"Never. I'll be like Rory from *Doctor Who*, 'the boy who waited.' But I do need to get away for a while. Knowing she's across the street and I can't see her kills me. Maybe some distance will help." His heart ached at the thought of possibly never kissing Hazel again, never building another couch fort, never holding her in his arms while he read her favorite book.

But he meant it.

He'd wait for her.

Because when you found your person, no one else could compare.

Mateo dropped his head at seeing whatever expression was on Ethan's face. "I'm the worst friend on the planet."

"Seriously, Mateo, it's not your fault. But you understand why I need to clear my head?" Ethan couldn't argue with him all day; he needed to get out of there.

Slowly nodding, Mateo swallowed hard. "Yeah. Maybe Cora and I can fix this . . ."

"Don't. Just don't."

It was too painful.

"If or when Hazel wants to talk to me, she knows how to reach me." But Ethan wasn't holding his breath for anytime soon. The look in her eyes told him everything.

She was done.

Hopefully not forever, but for now, she needed space.

Him being late and her ex showing up with the new boyfriend had probably overloaded her senses.

He understood.

But he'd never give up.

Sighing, Mateo handed over his car keys. "Take as long as you need. I've got Austin's car, and we'll pick up your car from the mechanic when it's ready."

Ethan took the keys and forced a smile he didn't feel. "Thanks. I'll call you when I get there." Wherever *there* was. He hadn't decided yet.

And with that, Ethan walked out the front door and into Mateo's car.

It took everything in him to hold it together.

Pulling out of the driveway, he gave one last pathetic wave to Hazel's house.

Ethan drove away.

I'm an idiot

Hazel stood, leaning over the kitchen island, drinking a cup of coffee and staring at nothing. She didn't bother to look in the mirror, knowing full well her "Olivia" hairdo had turned her day-after hair into a tangled mess of hairspray and rat's nests.

She made the right decision.

Right?

Then why did her chest ache like there was an anvil pressing down on it?

Spike jumped up on the island and batted around the copy of *Escape to Ashdonia* that Ethan had given her.

Her heart squeezed at the sight. "Oh, Spike. Am I an idiot?"

Spike stopped playing with the book and stood on his back legs to head-bump her chin. "I love you, bud."

He head-bumped her again. “So is that a yes?”

The front door jiggled, and Cora walked into the kitchen. “You okay?”

Hazel had called Cora later last night to tell her what had happened, but Ethan had filled them in already.

“Not really. But I will be.” Would she, though?

“You don’t believe him?” Cora asked.

Hazel knew her friend so well she could tell Cora believed Ethan.

So did Hazel.

“I just. I don’t know. I’m obviously the one running now.”

Cora nodded, and there was a heavy pause between them.

“I don’t know if it means anything,” Cora began, “but I truly believe he’s *the one*. Your Dream Guy.”

Like a bullet to the chest, Hazel almost stumbled backward at that.

Her lungs started to seize up again, and she pulled in air quickly.

Spike climbed on Hazel’s chest, sensing her emotion, then licked her cheek.

“I think Spike agrees with me. Seriously, Hazel, who has Spike ever liked besides you?”

“No one,” Hazel answered.

It only made it hurt worse.

She wanted to cry, but she was also frozen in her own mixed feelings.

Cora gently took Hazel’s hand in hers. “I think you’ve been so obsessed with what’s happening in your dreams, thinking your grandma was helping you out being in this house, but if you recall, you found Spike right after she died. You literally named him Spike because of the memories you had with her watching *Buffy*. Maybe you should have been paying more attention to him?"

Spike purred, meowed, and head-bumped her chin again.

A small seed of hope sprang inside Hazel's chest.

Before she could think on it further, Spike jumped off the counter and scratched at the back door.

Both Hazel and Cora eyed Spike in confused curiosity.

Cora nodded to the closed door. "Well, go on. Spike obviously wants to show you something."

Hazel opened the door.

The greenhouse at this point was a stunning array of green through the windows.

There was a large, four-foot-tall, five-foot-wide package in front of it.

"What is this?" Hazel asked as if Cora could answer her.

Spike rubbed his face on the box as Hazel pulled an envelope off of it, opening it.

There was a card inside.

"Read it out loud," Cora said.

"The final touch. Ethan."

Electricity raced through Hazel.

What could this be?

"Open it!" Cora had less patience than her.

Hazel popped the box open, and in front of her was an old-fashioned wrought-iron bench, just like the one on the cover of *Escape to Ashdonia* and the one in the movie.

"Holy," was all Cora could say.

Holy was right.

"Cora." Hazel turned to her best friend.

Cora nodded, knowing exactly what Hazel felt.

Ethan was the one.

There was no doubt about it.

And she loved him.

"Hazel."

Hazel's phone beeped, causing her to jump. It was a voicemail from Ethan, dated twelve hours ago.

"It's from Ethan. From last night." Hazel's hands shook.

"Put it on speaker," Cora demanded (as only a bestie could).

Hazel hit play, and Ethan's voice came through the phone: "I'm almost there. I left something in your backyard. It's not creepy or anything. I hope you like it, but on my way back, my car broke down. It's being towed to the nearest car shop. I'm sure I'll be paying a fortune. Anyway, I'll be there soon. I love you . . . I mean . . . actually, yeah, I mean I love you. Okay. I'm sweating now. This wig is itchy."

Both Hazel's and Cora's mouths dropped at Ethan saying the exact words of Hazel's Dream Guy.

"Go! Now!" Cora yelled in excitement.

Hazel's entire being filled with such an intensity of love that she thought she would burst. Adrenaline kicked in next, and she was running.

Racing across the street, she rang the doorbell and pounded on the door.

Mateo and Austin answered.

She tried not to show her utter disappointment at not being able to grab Ethan and pull him into the kiss of lifetime.

"Hazel. Hi. We were just leaving. Austin came to pick me up," Mateo said gently.

"Is Ethan here?" That came out a little more panicked than she'd wanted.

Mateo shook his head. "He left. I gave him my car. He said he needed to get away for a while."

Austin rubbed Mateo's arm supportively. "Mateo's been blaming himself for this mess."

"That's because it is my fault. I put doubt in your head, Hazel. In all our heads." Mateo was beside himself.

"I helped with my snide comments." Austin was obviously trying to make Mateo feel better. "And to be fair, the boy has always run when things get serious. Always."

Not helping.

"Do you know where he went?" Desperation threatened to close her lungs again.

Mateo examined Hazel more carefully, then his eyes popped open. "Is this a rom-com moment? Are you going after him?" His eyes were hopeful and beaming, awaiting her answer.

"Heck yes," she confirmed with confidence.

Mateo and Austin both let out a yelp of happiness.

Austin handed Hazel his phone. "Take my phone. I

have Ethan on my Find My app. Follow that map!"

Hazel squealed.

The three hugged. "Thank you!"

Hazel raced across the street and jumped in her car. Connecting Austin's phone to her car's CarPlay, she activated the Find My app, clicking on Ethan's name.

There he was.

A little red dot on her GPS map.

Heart racing, Hazel peeled out of her driveway and flew down the road.

Using her own phone, she called Ethan.

It rang and rang and rang and rang . . .

"Ethan, answer." Hazel's palms began to sweat.

She had to catch him.

Ethan's dot headed onto the 5 toward Santa Clarita. "Where are you going?"

After an hour of driving (and speeding), Hazel was getting closer and closer to Ethan's dot. She had no idea what she'd do when she caught up with him. Honk her horn? Wave her hands? Cut him off? She'd worry about that when she saw his car . . . correction . . . Mateo's car. Wait. What did Mateo's car look like? Shaking her head, she realized she didn't need to know. She just needed to see Ethan driving, and then she'd figure out what to do.

At this point, there was nothing but hills and brush the farther north she drove. But his dot was strong. Was he going to Sacramento? What the heck?

Glancing back and forth between the map and the road in front of her, Hazel nearly slammed on her brakes when the dot suddenly disappeared.

“What?” Hazel tried to open Austin’s phone while driving but realized it was too dangerous, so she dropped the phone on the passenger seat. “Come on. Not when I’m this close. Keep driving, Hazel. He wasn’t that far from you.”

Hazel hit the gas.

She flew down the highway.

Luckily, there weren’t that many cars, which would make it easier to spot him when she caught up with him.

A little faster.

And then her car gurgled like it had never gurgled before.

“No. No. No. No. No.” Hazel grabbed onto the steering wheel with all her might as her whole steering froze, and the engine began to rattle. She managed to drive the car to the shoulder and park.

As she turned off the car, smoke poured out of the engine block.

“Please, no.”

I guess I should have taken it in earlier.

Hurrying out of the car, Hazel looked up at the sky. “Seriously, universe?”

Hazel pulled out her own phone to call for help, trying to hold back tears. “It’s okay. Everything will be okay. He’ll get his messages, and he’ll understand. It’s not over yet.”

A car pulled off to the side, parking behind her.

Oh. Maybe someone who can help! Hazel’s chest lightened.

Ethan stepped out of the car.

Hazel froze. Was she hallucinating again? Was he a mirage?

As he walked closer, she saw that it was absolutely Ethan.

"Ethan?" she said in disbelief.

"Hazel?" Ethan's mouth dropped.

And then something happened to Hazel in that moment.

An overwhelming force of emotion took over her, and she was filled with a happiness beyond description.

And she ran.

But this time, she ran to Ethan rather than away.

Hazel embraced him full force.

From the shocked expression on his face, Hazel was obviously the last person he expected to see stranded on the highway, but his arms wrapped around her so tightly Hazel never wanted him to let go.

Finally they pulled away but still stayed in each other's arms.

"How . . ." Ethan began.

"Austin gave me his phone. He has you on Find My."

Ethan smiled from ear to ear. "What's happening?"

"I got your message, and I got the universe's message. You're it. You. We've been circling each other our entire adult lives, just missing each other, or possibly sitting right next to each other." A knot formed in her throat from emotion. "And after thirty years, we finally met. In my grandmother's backyard with the most perfect cat who knew better than the both of us that we belong together." Hazel reached up and touched Ethan's cheek.

"I love you, Ethan Rhodes. I'm sorry I ran from you last night." Everything spilled out of Hazel in a rush.

"Of all people, I get it. I've always run from relationships. Making up excuses. Some of them legit. But I didn't want to do that with you. For the first time in my life, I finally feel like I got this. *We* got this." Ethan beamed.

Hazel didn't think his eyes could sparkle more, and she was willing to bet hers were doing the same. "We got this."

Ethan kissed her then, the kiss to end all kisses.

Completely lost in his lips moving in perfect harmony with hers, Hazel would be content to live on the side of the highway the rest of her life if it meant staying in Ethan's arms.

When they finally pulled away for air, Ethan nodded to Hazel's destroyed car. "Can I walk you home?"

They both laughed.

"Let's drive."

Epilogue
Hazel
Happily Ever After

"Are we really doing this?" Hazel asked as they pulled into a gravel parking lot overlooking a small lake.

A bridge stood in its center, spanning across the narrowest part of the body of water. It had metal mesh fencing for its sides and a cement-and-metal walkway about ten feet above the lake's surface.

From the car, she could see that sections of the fencing were covered in tiny bright-colored objects, like giant intertwined polka dots.

"Is that it?" Hazel eyed the bridge.

"That's it. The Geek Love Bridge." Ethan smiled.

They both wore their full *Escape to Ashdonia* costumes, but this time Ethan donned the brown fluffy mullet wig, scratching it momentarily. "Sorry. Seriously, this wig, though."

As if Hazel needed any more signs . . .

Her smile grew wider. "I might need a wig later. I feel like my hair is going to fall out with the amount of hairspray I have in it."

Ethan stared at Hazel with an intensity that made her stomach flutter. "You look beautiful."

"So do you," she answered.

Ethan laughed. "I'm pretty sure only Richard Grinthal can pull this look off."

"No. It's definitely working for you." And it definitely was.

"Oh, really?" Ethan raised an eyebrow.

"Really," Hazel confirmed.

Hazel and Ethan leaned across the parking brake and kissed. As they broke away, Ethan's eyes lingered on Hazel's.

"We still going to go out there dressed like this?" Hazel asked.

It was the middle of the day, and though there weren't that many people in the parking lot or on the bridge, she did feel a little self-conscious in a giant eighties ball gown.

"Um, yeah, we are." Ethan's grin was contagious.

To be fair, he was far more conspicuous.

But this was the Geek Love Bridge, after all, and the people here were *their* people, and they'd love it.

"Gah, let's do it."

"You got the bench?"

"Got it," Hazel confirmed.

Pulling it out of the pocket of her dress, Hazel stared at it in awe. Ethan had commissioned a mini Ashdonia wrought-iron bench, with a top that snapped shut like a padlock, their names carved into the metal.

When they exited the car, a couple near them saw their costumes and clapped. The woman said, "You two look spectacular."

"Thank you," Hazel responded with a large grin.

Ethan placed his arm out for Hazel to take, which she did happily.

The closer they moved toward the bridge, the better Hazel could see the colorful items attached to the sides.

The Geek Love Bridge was like any other love bridge, but as it was created by nerds and geeks, there were many more options to show one's love other than plain padlocks. From eighties McDonald toys to quite a few Thanos's gloves to Link's sword to Mario Bros. brick boxes, too many fandoms to name. It was a cacophony of what it was to be a geek.

As they arrived on the bridge, several more heads turned, a few excited gasps, a couple of laughs, and a round of applause.

"I wish you two could keep those. I could pretend they got lost." Cora walked up from behind, Jack by her side.

The foursome exchanged hugs.

"Oh, Roberta Coolidge brought up Paw-fect Plants at a luncheon today, so expect more orders," Cora beamed.

Hazel's plant business blew up the day after the ball while she was chasing Ethan down with her car. Cora had sent Roberta the link to the site and, true to her word, she told all of her friends about Hazel's store. At this rate,

Hazel would have to expand to a bigger nursery soon. It was more than she'd ever dreamed.

"Let me see." Cora nodded toward the bench.

Hazel handed it to her.

Jack whistled low. "That's amazing work. Where did you get that made?"

"A shop downtown that makes movie props. Making miniatures for doll houses is their side hustle. I just asked them to add the locky part on top," Ethan answered.

"Locky top? Is that the technical term?" Hazel teased.

"It is actually." Ethan smiled.

"Actually, it is," Jack confirmed with a grin.

Cora handed the bench back to Hazel. "We want to watch."

Hazel and Ethan laughed, then walked to the center of the bridge. "Right or left side?" Ethan asked.

"Left. For Short Round." Hazel mock saluted.

"For Short Round. He told Indie to take the left tunnel, and he just didn't listen." Ethan saluted back.

The four laughed.

Hazel and Ethan took the Ashdonia bench and snapped it shut onto a chain link of fence.

"I love you," Hazel said.

"I love you," Ethan answered.

Cupping her face with his hands, Ethan leaned down, and his lips pressed into hers, moving in perfect synchronicity. Per usual, Hazel's mind dissolved into goo from his kiss and touch.

Cora and Jack clapped like they were watching a show.

"Cora." Hazel rolled her eyes, smiling as they pulled out of their kiss.

Looking back at the bench, Ethan said, "We should sign John Larry's name on it. Our little inside joke."

"Why is that a joke?" Cora asked curiously.

Hazel snorted. "Some guy named John Larry signed a copy of *Escape from Ashdonia* and wrote, 'I miss you.' It was sweet. It's that copy I always ogled at the café bookstore, and then Ethan bought it for me."

Jack reared his head back, amused. "Some guy?"

Hazel and Ethan exchanged confused glances. "You guys know who he is?"

Cora shook her head. "I swear, no one ever knows the name of screenwriters. John Larry is the author Freya Fairweather's grandson, and he wrote the script for the movie."

Hazel was floored. "What?"

Ethan's eyes widened. "That's kind of amazing."

Jack nodded. "Yeah, you have quite a collector's item."

Hazel turned to Ethan. "That's insanely magical, I'm not going to lie."

"*You're* insanely magical." Ethan laughed. "That didn't sound right."

"It sounded perfect."

Ethan leaned down, and their lips parted into a magical kiss.

And standing on the Geek Love Bridge, kissing the man she loved, Hazel knew she'd found the one.

Her Dream Guy.

www.ingramcontent.com/pod-product-compliance
Lightning Source LLC
Chambersburg PA
CBHW020336310726
48979CB00015B/2394/J

* 9 7 8 1 9 4 9 8 7 7 6 5 6 *